ALSO BY CLARE BELL

Ratha's Creature
Clan Ground

(Margaret K. McElderry Books)

TOMORROW'S SPHINX

TOMORROW'S
SPHINX
CLARE BELL

Margaret K. McElderry Books
New York

Copyright © 1986 by Clare Bell

All rights reserved. No part of this book may be reproduced or transmitted in any form or by any means, electronic or mechanical, including photocopying, recording, or by any information storage retrieval system, without permission in writing from the Publisher.

Margaret K. McElderry Books
Macmillan Publishing Company
866 Third Avenue, New York, N.Y. 10022
Collier Macmillan Canada, Inc.

Composition by Maryland Linotype Composition Company
Baltimore, Maryland
Printed and bound by R. R. Donnelley & Sons Company
Harrisonburg, Virginia
Designed by Christine Kettner

10 9 8 7 6 5 4 3 2 1

Library of Congress Cataloging-in-Publication Data
Bell, Clare.
  Tomorrow's sphinx.
  "A Margaret K. McElderry book."
  Summary: Two unusual black cheetahs share a mental
link, one cat coming from the past to reveal scenes
from his life with the young pharaoh Tutankhamen,
and one struggling to survive in a future world
ravaged by ecological disaster.
  1. Tutankhamen, King of Egypt—Juvenile fiction.
[1. Cheetahs—Fiction. 2. Tutankhamen, King of Egypt—
Fiction. 3. Egypt—Civilization—To 332 B.C.—Fiction.
4. Science fiction] I. Title.
PZ7.B3889153To 1986   [Fic]   86-8479
ISBN 0-689-50402-0
First Edition

This novel is a work of fiction. Any references to
historical events; to real people, living or dead; or
to real locales are intended only to give the fiction a
setting in historical reality.

To:

ARTHUR,
of Marine World/Africa USA,
a cheetah and a gentlemanly representative of his kind.

All the dedicated people there and elsewhere
who are working to understand
and protect the cheetah (Acinonyx jubatus).

TOMORROW'S SPHINX

ONE

The sun's light shone through the tawny haze rolling above the land. Kenket balanced on her long legs at the crest of a ridge, swinging her tail and feeling grit between her paw pads. She narrowed her eyes and raised her whiskers, squinting along the black tearlines on either side of her short muzzle.

The sun sat on the distant hills as though crouched to stalk the moon, the white gazelle, her eternal prey. It was just before dusk, a good time to hunt. Kenket gazed into the pale gold disk, trying to see the sun-cheetah's markings. It was said among those elders who were sky-watchers that to see the spots on the sun's pelt would bring luck or turn aside any ill fortune that might be stalking the hunter.

Kenket blinked, trying to clear bright flashes from her eyes. She looked back the way she had come. Behind her lay rugged hills, once green and now turning barren from lack of rain. Beyond the hills the river ran, bending to flow north and then east again, curving around a jutting foot of land as smoothly and sinuously as the rock python would glide around a boulder. She had come to know the great river. As uncertain rainfall dried the plain, game animals drifted into the hills above the riverbank and the cheetahs moved their hunting range to follow.

Something shimmered briefly above the horizon. Kenket watched it draw a pale streak of light along the sky before vanishing in sunglare. Her ears twitched back. She had seen such things often enough so that they did not distress her, but she felt faintly annoyed. By rights the sky belonged to the sun-cheetah and her prey, who moved in regular and familiar paths. These unknown sky-animals appeared suddenly and unpredictably, violating the rules of territory that even celestial creatures should obey.

Kenket looked back at her sisters, who climbed the slope after her. She recognized them by the shape of their heads and the cant and form of their ears, but most of all by the markings on their faces. Many other cheetah females shared her sister Nasseken's burnt-orange coat color with distinct black spots, but Kenket knew her sister by the broad band of her tearline that began at each eye, arching over the cheek to end in a black patch behind the whiskers.

The other sister, Beshon, was light tan, with creamy highlights in her coat and dark brown spots. Her tearlines were narrow and wandering, losing themselves in the yellow fur of her face before reaching her muzzle.

Kenket knew she was darker than either one of her sisters. Her spots fused together in irregular patches, and along her back they melted into a single heavy line running from the crown of her head to the base of her tail.

As she waited for Nasseken and Beshon, she sensed the ties that bound her to her sisters, but she also felt ill at ease. It was strange to be hunting again with her kin-group. She had gone to den with cubs, but game was too scarce near her lair. One litterling died and the other had grown weaker, forcing the young mother to abandon the traditional role of solitary hunter. She knew that males who were brothers often banded together to pull down larger game than could be taken by one cheetah alone. Perhaps this was a way that could be used by females, she decided, and so asked to hunt with her sisters.

To leave and rejoin the kinship group was something a female rarely did, for once she left to have her own family she gave up her membership, never expecting to regain her place among her sisters. It was Nasseken who argued Beshon into accepting her back. Kenket felt grateful, but she knew this was not the proper way among her people and might well displease the sun-cheetah, who always coursed her prey alone.

"Perhaps that is why she refused to show me her spots," Kenket said sadly to herself and tried not to think of the tiny cub lying in a lair dug beneath an outcropping.

She turned down the ragged crest of the escarpment. Farther on, shadowed clumps of scrub vegetation began to appear, showing the presence of underground water. Here the thorny acacia formed thickets where antelope and gazelle browsed. Kenket looked for the spoor of her own kind as well as that of prey, turning away when she found evidence that others might be close. As a cub she had been taught never to come within sight of anyone outside her own group, and this prohibition had grown more severe as the hunting range shrank. Only the messengers, those who were chosen to carry news between otherwise isolated cheetah groups, were allowed to disobey.

The stalking cheetahs moved silently, eyes searching for a flicker of movement, a puff of dust, a swaying branch that might betray a victim. When Kenket and her sisters found nothing, she leaped up into the limbs of a stunted tree to survey the plain beyond.

She saw the gazelles as graceful silhouettes against a fading rose-and-gray sky. They moved slowly, trailing long shadows. Now the evening wind tantalized Kenket's nose with the acrid musk of young bucks and the milky mother-scent of does with fawns. The herd was small and many animals looked thin, but from their smell, Kenket knew they were still healthy and would yield enough meat. They would also give her a good chase, and her body quivered eagerly in anticipation.

The cheetah's muscles felt a need as strong as the hunger in her belly—a need to pour out effort into an explosive sprint that would overrun her chosen victim almost before it had begun to flee. She lowered herself into a half-crouch, her shoulders hunched, her head straining up. With her attention now focused on the prey, she was only peripherally aware that Nasseken and Beshon had dropped down on their chests behind her. Their action told her that this was her hunt. It was too soon to expect either sister to abandon the traditional way of the cheetah female: the belief that she who began the chase must finish it.

The gazelles grazed, tearing up the scattered tufts of grass. Although they raised their heads at intervals to search for hunters, their flicking tails and ambling gait told Kenket they hadn't seen her. She rose from her half-crouch and began a slow controlled approach. The vegetation was too scattered and sparse for a hidden stalk, but she hoped the setting sun's glare would discourage any long glances in her direction. She kept her eyes fixed on the prey, continuously judging their level of alertness. She was able to freeze her movement before a suspicious head popped up and was locked still in her stride by the time the buck's gaze turned her way.

Only once did Kenket fail to anticipate discovery. A keen-eyed doe honked an alarm call, and dust whirled beneath galloping hooves as the prey took flight. Annoyed, the cheetah broke off her approach and retreated. She thought then that the hunt was lost, but the gazelles had only gone a short distance. She waited and then backtracked, glancing over her shoulder. Tails flicking uncertainly, the gazelles stood bunched together, heads up, showing a row of sinuously curved horns.

A doe lowered her head and stalked purposefully after Kenket, who waited, knowing the rest of the herd would soon follow. Soon the gazelles all trailed after the venturesome doe, yielding, as Kenket knew, to curiosity and the need to keep an enemy within sight.

They came close enough for her to hear the noise of their hooves and their bleating calls to one another. Soon their markings became visible; she saw their buff-colored upper bodies and pale underparts. A black stripe over the animals' hipbones accented their startling white rump.

7

The gazelles' bright black eyes beneath the horns seemed too large for the delicately modeled skull, but the cheetah knew that those eyes, with their elongated pupils, could catch the slightest movement.

Kenket scanned the herd, looking for any signs of injury, age, or excessive nervousness that might mark an animal as vulnerable. The group was a small one, for which she was grateful. More than once her charge had faltered as she lost her targeted quarry amidst a confusion of milling animals. She sat down and averted her head, a gesture she knew would draw the fascinated gazelle even closer.

Again she waited, monitoring the prey with her ears and nose while her eyes searched for her sisters. She spotted their slender shapes outlined atop a knoll in the red-gold light of sunset. One turned her head, and ruby fire glinted at the center of her eyes.

Excitement rose in the hunter, starting her heart leaping. It was always so in the moment before the chase began. Kenket's body sang, her muscles shivering with joy as she prepared to unleash herself in an intoxicating burst of speed. Yet she remained still, facing away and letting the tension build within her until the right instant.

Kenket snapped her head around and sprang into a gallop. During her first few strides, the prey stood rigidly as if trapped. Then a doe brayed in fear and broke from the edge of the herd. The rest wheeled to follow, but they disappeared from the cheetah's mind. Between the two sighting stripes along her nose, she saw only the one gazelle whose premature flight announced its vulnerability.

As if an invisible cord had been strung and drawn taut between hunter and fleeing prey, Kenket was drawn after the gazelle. She could neither halt her charge nor choose another victim. Instinct drove her now and her intelligence could only observe from the sidelines. Later she might judge whether the choice was best, but now, in the heat of the chase, she could neither change nor question it.

The gazelle tore across the plain, its churning legs throwing up a line of dust. Kenket sprinted after it, increasing the length of her stride with each step. Her breath surged in and out of her chest and the great muscles in her loins flexed and bowed her spine until her hind feet struck the ground ahead of her forepaws. She flung out her tail to balance herself through swift turns as the gazelle dashed back and forth in a path made ragged by panic. The cheetah felt the horny ridges of her pads bite into the dirt, keeping her on the quarry's track. The dust-blurred image of fleeing prey remained locked between the sighting stripes on her nose.

She drew close enough to hear its hoarse whistling breath and see the white of the eye as it rolled back in terror. The slender legs shook, and Kenket didn't need the acrid tang of exhaustion in the quarry's smell to tell her that it was weakening. The cheetah called on her body's great reserves, pouring effort into her run until her straining muscles nearly cramped with intensity. Grit stung her eyes and breath burned in her throat, but through the haze she saw the bobbing hindquarters of the prey drawing nearer.

And then she saw the scars on the animal's rump. Two raised and puckered streaks showed where a cheetah's dewclaw had torn through flesh. Yet the gazelle still lived to run from her. The hunter, not the hunted, had lost that attack. Doubt sprang up in Kenket's mind, but she pushed it aside savagely. She had lost several strides and the animal was drawing ahead.

Quickly she regained the distance until she was alongside the gazelle's flank. Her hindquarters bunched and extended, launching her at the prey. She struck down with rigid fore-legs, driving her own dewclaws deep into the coarse fur. Throwing her weight backward, she lashed her tail, feeling the fierce pull in her shoulders as her dewclaws sank and held.

Staggering off-balance, the animal thrust its way forward a few paces before its rear legs folded and it collapsed beneath her. The cheetah ripped her dewclaws loose, dodging frantic kicks. Before the prey could scramble to its feet, she at-tacked again, diving at the head and seizing it from behind with her fangs. Kenket pressed down its front quarters with her own forelegs and chest, holding herself stiff against heaves and jerks. The sweat-damp pelt slipped beneath her paws while the rise and fall of the gazelle's ribs rocked her up and down.

At last the prey subsided, sinking into lethargy. Kenket waited, panting between her teeth without releasing her bite. Now the chase was ended, but she still had to finish the kill. She knew her jaws were not powerful enough to break the neck of an animal this large. The throat was the vulnerable area. Even with her smaller gape and short fangs, she could gain an effective grip. Then, by twisting the gazelle's neck, she could crush its windpipe. She paused briefly before unlocking her jaws and lifting a forepaw to claw at the animal's head.

She felt herself flying backwards as the prey bucked and writhed in one last frantic struggle. Now she knew what those scars on the gazelle's flank meant. As she rolled and thrashed to escape the deadly hooves, she cursed the instinct that had chosen this creature as prey. Weak and nervous as it was, the animal had survived a previous attack. Its wounds were made by the dewclaws of another hunter, one who might have lost more than just a meal. Now Kenket's intelligence told her too late how dangerous a quarry she had chosen. The creature had known she would have to loosen her grip to catch and turn its head with her forepaw and that her momentary shift would make her vulnerable.

A sudden blow and numbness in her left foreleg startled Kenket so violently that she reeled back, letting the gazelle lurch to its feet. Rage and hunger flooded through her, sweeping away the awareness of her injury. She sprang onto the animal's back, bouncing savagely on its rump to force the beast down. As it threw its head back, trying to impale her with a rearward jab of its horns, she flung her forelegs around its neck and seized its throat.

The animal plunged. She kept her jaws locked in its throat, squeezing hard and twisting the head to one side. It landed heavily on its side and gave a last stiff back-kick with two feet together. The cheetah felt the taut muscles beneath her relax as the gazelle fell into the trance that most prey animals assumed before death overtook them. It no longer seemed to feel her claws in its flesh or her suffocating grip on its throat. The gazelle became still long before it died, and Kenket knew that its life was gone only when she felt the full weight of the head sag in her jaws.

She let the head drop and panted, soothing her aching lungs with rapid breaths of air. Weariness overwhelmed her. She knew that the chase and the extended battle had nearly drained her, but she couldn't rest yet. She must drag her kill under cover, out of sight of scavengers and thieves. Only then would her sisters come to share it with her, for her people never ate the kill where it had fallen.

Kenket seized the carcass by its neck, but as she took a step, a flash of severe pain from the middle of her foreleg made her gasp and drop her catch. Again she attempted to move her prey, this time taking it by the hock and balancing on three legs. The cheetah tugged it a distance equivalent to the length of her body before she gave up and sank on her chest to wait for her sisters.

Beshon arrived at a fast lope, scattering the vultures and kites gathering about Kenket's kill. "Why aren't you taking your prey to cover?" she asked. Impatiently Beshon grabbed the dead gazelle by its nape and hauled it away. Kenket growled and limped after her but halted as the other sister reached them.

"Beshon, she's hurt." Nasseken was beside Kenket, nosing the lifted foreleg. "Sister, I thought I saw something go wrong in your hunt."

"The beast kicked me. Like a silly gray-mantled cub, I released it too soon. Ah!" She had tried to stand on the leg again. The pain was too intense to be only a bruise. A fearful realization drew cold streaks along her back and down her shoulders as she heard and felt the ends of broken bones grind together.

She saw Nasseken gave Beshon a cuff. "Greedy one, eat first at your own kill. Kenket has a cub to feed as well as herself."

Beshon pulled the gazelle farther away before she dropped

12

it and retorted, "She won't eat much of it if she leaves it out in the open. There are lions nearby. Hurry and help me get it under that thornbush."

Kenket heard the grunts of her sisters and the brittle snap of dry brush as the prey was secured. Again she tried to put weight on the injured leg, but the alarming way it gave and the sudden flare of pain made her draw a harsh breath. She shivered and grimaced, trying to put together the words she had to say. "Nasseken, tell Beshon she can eat," she began slowly. "And you also."

"What?" Nasseken put her muzzle close to Kenket's and her large topaz eyes went wide with astonishment. "You're not that badly hurt, are you?"

Kenket lowered her head and spoke dully. "It's broken, Nasseken."

"Oh lion-dung! I got kicked once and I thought my running days were through, but I healed. Let me look."

Kenket lay down and gingerly extended the leg. She clamped her teeth as Nasseken touched the tender swelling with her tongue. When the other cheetah pressed hard enough to shift the bone ends, Kenket jerked and gave a muffled howl. Nasseken raised her head slowly and there was shock and sorrow in her eyes. Behind her, in the growing darkness, came the sounds of Beshon tearing at the prey.

"Both of you, eat now. Before the scavengers find us," said Kenket, not looking at Nasseken.

"Kenket . . ."

"My leg is broken, Nasseken. The same thing happened to Jarun last season and her kin-group . . . had to leave her to die. It makes no sense for me to eat now."

"Kenket's right, Nasseken," came Beshon's voice from the prey. "Fill your belly while you have the chance and while you still have four good legs."

Kenket flattened her ears and snarled silently at the night. It was difficult enough to face the truth without having it flung at her in words.

"May you trip over an ant mound at full gallop, sister," Nasseken hissed as the sounds of eating ended the conversation with Beshon. "Never mind her, Kenket. Lie still and perhaps the pain will ease."

"I can't rest, listening to your belly growl. Go on. You're hungry."

With evident reluctance Nasseken left her side. Kenket stifled a strong pang of fear and resentment. What she wanted most of all, and what she could not bear to admit, was for Nasseken to stay beside her and warm her against the chill of the evening wind. She wished her sister could soothe the throbbing leg with gentle strokes of her tongue and say that it was just a sprain after all; the injury might hurt but it would heal. She almost wished that Nasseken would invite her to eat with them, for that gesture might instantly erase the fate that had befallen her the moment the gazelle's hoof fractured her leg.

And her one remaining cub? Was the little one also fated to die? If she attempted to return, injured as she was, she wouldn't reach the den for at least a day. By then jackals would have discovered her lair. Having eaten nothing herself, how was she going to feed her litterling? The pain of those thoughts hurt her as much as her leg. She laid her head on the ground and moaned.

Nasseken left the prey and returned to her, gently licking

her cheek as Kenket said, "Nassi, I don't want to go away from you to die. I know that is the way of our kind, but I am afraid of the pain and the thoughts of my little one . . . I am so afraid of being alone. . . ." Her voice caught.

"Don't think of it now," said Nasseken softly and Kenket knew that was the only comfort her sister could offer.

"I am ashamed. So many of our kind have faced this bravely, while I . . . it is all I can do not to beg you to stay with me, Nassi. Why I am this way I do not know. I feel I am cheetah only outside, not inside."

"You have always hated being by yourself. I remember even when we were cubs how you howled when you were left behind." Beshon's voice came unexpectedly from beneath the thornbush.

"Oh, keep your nose buried in gazelle guts," snapped Nasseken. "Feelings have never troubled you, you furred crocodile. Take what's left of the carcass and go somewhere else before I swat you."

There was the noise of the gazelle being dragged away. Nasseken sighed. Kenket swallowed. "I want to ask you to stay with me, Nassi, but you can't, can you?"

"Beshon and I have to keep to our trail, and I must hunt again tomorrow even if she isn't hungry. Kenket, I know this is hard, but you said yourself it is the custom of our people. You must believe you are strong enough to do what you must. You are cheetah all through and I should know, shouldn't I?"

Kenket butted her head softly against her sister, making the slender body sway. "You have always been strong, Nasseken."

"Beshon is strong, too."

"Nassi," Kenket hesitated. "I know you can't stay, but there is something else you can do. Go to my lair. See if she is still alive."

"Your cub?" Nasseken's eyes widened. "Kenket, you're not asking me. . . ."

"Save her, please. Is it right that she should starve because of my mistake? Yes, I know it is the way of our people that she should die, but is it right?"

"By the sun-cheetah's spots, Kenket!" Nasseken's voice was harsh.

"Sister," Kenket pleaded, "you just lost your own litter. You know what I feel. And she is the only surviving cub from any of us. Do you want our mother's line to be lost?"

Nasseken gave a low growl. "Or worse still, to be carried on by Beshon and her bunch of little crocodiles when and if she has them."

"I won't ask you for anything else. Just save her before the hyenas get to her. Maybe you can find another nursing mother who might take her."

"Kenket, you know no one whose pelt is on straight would even consider such a thing. I know she means a lot to you. Perhaps too much. When things get better, I will have another litter. One can always have cubs."

"I can't," Kenket said sullenly. "This one is my last."

Nasseken remained silent for a long time. Kenket could hear the faraway snap of a rib bone and knew that Beshon was enjoying herself.

"Where is your den?" Nasseken's voice made Kenket start. Quickly, before Nasseken could change her mind, she told her sister the location of the lair.

"Well, now I know you're serious," said the other cheetah, and Kenket knew what she meant. Only under great duress would a mother reveal where she had hidden her cubs. Despite her closeness to Nasseken, Kenket experienced a moment of uneasiness. Never had she shown her young to anyone, not even her sister. "All right. I'll do what I can," said Nasseken wearily. "You're the only one I'd ever do it for, so remember that."

"I will," whispered Kenket as she felt Nasseken's tongue on her face. "And it will give me strength on my journey to meet the sun-cheetah."

"Ask her to show her spots to me and send me strength as well," answered Nasseken, with a tremor in her voice. "And forgive Beshon. It isn't her fault she was born a crocodile."

Kenket leaned toward Nasseken to make the last nose-touch. Then her sister was gone and she sat alone in the night with her pain and her fragile hope.

She gazed up at the familiar star patterns she had known since she had first staggered out of her mother's lair to blink and stare into the night. She sharpened her gaze. One star was out of place, unfamiliar, an intruder. It burned with a cold, steady light that made her shiver. As she watched, she could see it sweep past the others through the sky before disappearing behind the horizon.

Hunger cramps in Kenket's belly and the fierce ache in her leg kept her from sleep and at last she got up and hobbled around on three legs. At first, she turned back the way she and her sisters had come, guided by her old scent-marks and driven by the irrational hope that she could still travel fast enough to reach her abandoned cub. The youngster had to survive. Even if Nasseken didn't honor her promise, Kenket herself could. . . .

No. Her own pace was hopeless. She would have to depend on Nasseken. Kenket turned and found her sister's trail where Nasseken had left with Beshon. They couldn't have gone far, not in the brief time since they departed. Perhaps if she hurried, she could catch up.

A deep roar sounded in the distance and was answered by other calls. Kenket drew back her whiskers. Lions! If she followed Nasseken's trail, she would have to travel toward those roars. If the lions found her trail, they would know she was injured, and if she did reach Nasseken and Beshon, the lions would track her to her sisters.

Her only choice was the open plain. Slowly she limped in a large circle and set her face into the wind blowing from the east.

Weariness had overwhelmed the pain at last and had let her sleep, but Kenket was awake now. She shifted, rubbing her back against the face of an outcropping that had given her shelter from the wind. The sun was moving up from the horizon, in pursuit of the white gazelle grazing at the top of the dawn sky. The wind spit sand into her face, making her sneeze.

Kenket got up and shook the dust from her pelt. Something caught her eye at the crest of a nearby dune and she froze, tensing her hindquarters to spring away. Now she could hear a low undertone beneath the sound of the wind. At first the deep rumble made her think of lions and she

18

searched for their tawny forms, almost grateful that her end would be quick if they caught her.

The smell on the wind had a harsh, unfamiliar tang. The sound was a continuous drone, too constant to be coming from any living creature. Kenket sensed the approach of something entirely alien. She retreated, trembling, into the diminishing shadow of the rock face, blinking against the sun's glare. A dazzling burst of light on the horizon made her start. As she gathered herself to spring, she caught sight of moving forms outlined against the sky and shrank back.

Now the invaders surrounded her and their smell cornered her. Part of it was animal, reminding her of baboon, but much of it was strange—not dead but never alive. Nor was it the smell of rock or sand, whose scents were faded by age and weathering. It was raw, new, and harsh.

And the forms themselves were upright, swaying like acacia trees and extending their limbs to move like animals. But they moved across the bare ground in a manner unlike any creature she knew. For an instant Kenket's terror turned to rage. She readied herself for an attack on the nearest one. She bared her fangs and lunged, but her injured leg gave beneath her and she sprawled on her front, her muzzle buried in sand.

As she leaped up and whirled around, seeking an escape, her mind plunged into confusion. The sun's light seemed to jump at her from many places at once, making her duck and narrow her eyes. The sound grew louder and deeper until it vibrated through her. The forms themselves made noises like the shrill cries of apes. Everything blurred before her eyes, and the sounds became a meaningless clamor in her ears.

The smells assaulted her mind through her nose, bringing waves of helpless panic.

She reeled as something smacked into her flank and she found herself on her side. Everything stopped. The sound ceased. Her eyes focused again, bringing the scene into a clarity that she did not want. The nearest of her captors stood within a tail-length of her. Its smell told her it was animal and could be killed, but as she tried to lash out with her good foreleg, she felt weak and sleepy.

Her head fell back and she stared up at the figure standing over her. It had a covering that flapped in the wind and it stared down at her from a flat simian face, lacking whiskers or markings. Behind it stood a larger, motionless shape that shone like river water in the sunlight. Emblazoned on that gleaming surface was a figure that Kenket knew. Its color was wrong. It had been made solid black with odd, golden face markings instead of being spotted as she was, but she recognized the outline of a coursing cheetah.

Her bewilderment fought with overwhelming weariness as her eyes began to close and her head wobbled. She lost the struggle to remain alert and at last lay still, letting the muffled sound of the wind pull her down into darkness.

TWO

The tiny cub's growing dismay at being left alone mounted into terror as hunger gnawed and cramped her belly. Her flailing paws met cold, stale earth whose stink was the smell of betrayal and abandonment. She thrashed around in the dry litter of the den, finding only the brittle shells of dead insects. She cried, first in fear and then in rage, but no one came. She almost welcomed the exhaustion dulling her senses. Still no one came. Then she heard noises and scrambled desperately toward them but found that the eager whine and scraping paws were not those of her mother.

The harsh jackal-smell warned the little cheetah, but before she could retreat, a hairy muzzle drove deep into the den. Fangs seized her. She fought back as she was dragged into the blazing sunlight, rending the bony face with sharp young claws. She felt herself being shaken wildly, but she held on, biting with needle teeth. Her small fangs scored the jackal's muzzle as he pawed her off.

Staggering to her feet, she made a clumsy but determined lunge, stamping down with both little forepaws and hissing.

The jackal pounced, clamping his jaws on her hindquarters and began to drag her away.

Over his eager growls, she heard a hoarse screech. An orange-and-black spotted blur sped past her, then whirled, lashing its tail. Another creature landed behind the jackal as she felt the jackal's teeth dig deeper into her back, his jaws threatening to crush her spine. Then abruptly she was free, sprawling in the dirt where he had dropped her.

Ignoring fierce pain and blood welling from her bitten flanks, she staggered to her feet, hissing defiance both at the jackal and the two female cheetahs attacking him. Her vision blurred by rage and exhaustion, she saw one knock the scavenger's hind legs out from beneath him with a powerful sweep of her foreleg. Ears flat and howling, the jackal scrambled to his feet and took off in another direction with the cheetah after him. Another forepaw strike sent the predator tumbling tail over muzzle. Each time the jackal recovered, the cheetah chased him to full gallop and then tripped the beast, sending him flying.

A shadow fell across the cub, startling her. A muzzle bent to nose her. Even as she looked up with a sudden surge of hope, she knew by the smell that this was not her mother. Yet the newcomer's scent reminded her of her mother, and at last she huddled against the sinewy forelegs and let the rough tongue comfort her.

When the female lay down, instinct made the cub bump against the furred belly in search of milk. When her nose touched a swollen teat, she forgot everything else, suckling frantically and savoring the warm, rich flow.

She had no idea who her rescuers were, only that they

bore smells like her mother's. They fed her, washed her, and soothed the pain of the jackal's bite with soft tongue-strokes. Still haunted by her abandonment, she watched with dismay when they rose to go, but just as a whimper was building in her throat, a gentle mouth picked her up by the scruff and took her to a dry cave in a hillside.

The same female always nursed her, fed her, and tended her. Soon the delicate narrow-nosed face with its distinct dark tearlines replaced the fading image of her mother's. The first word the cub spoke was her foster-parent's name, Nasseken. The other partner, Beshon, seemed more aloof, and the little cheetah often sensed in her a mixture of affection mixed with irritation. Beshon frequently would disappear and return panting, dusty, and sometimes dragging prey.

Although the cub knew she had a name, the shock of abandonment and the jackal's attack had stricken it from her memory. For lack of anything else, Beshon had started using the name Burua, which meant exactly what she was, a motherless orphan. At first the cub didn't understand Nasseken's dislike of the name, but as she grew older and learned the usual fate of burua-cubs, she began to resent Beshon's choice.

When the time came for her to shed her baby fur, she was eager and excited, but as the days passed, she became anxious, looking at herself often in the river. She had looked forward to getting her spotted coat, but except for the juvenile cape of silvery gray fur about her neck and down her back, the new fur coming in appeared to be a solid ebony black. The most startling change was in her face, where charcoal patches appeared and gradually merged to cover her head. A light-beige streak appeared in the center of each dark tearline, growing outward and displacing the original black fur. Similar streaks appeared along the edges of her ears and on her muzzle, deepening from tan to gold as she grew older.

She sensed her two guardians were watching this change with growing dismay. When the black patches first appeared on her muzzle, Beshon tried to wash them off, thinking that they were just stubborn remnants of river mud. Her sister had to stop her before she licked the cub's face raw, but Beshon wasn't convinced until she caught Burua and scrubbed her hard with a callused pad. The cub fled, squalling.

As little Burua began learning to hunt under Nasseken's guidance, it became obvious that she couldn't ignore her variant coloration. Against the bleached reeds of the drying marsh or the dusty hillside above the lair, she stood out like a shadow at noon. If she hid carefully, Nasseken couldn't spot her, but the slightest movement betrayed her position. She practiced stalking frogs, but they would croak and plunk into the water before she even got close. Her clumsy attempts seemed to alert the entire riverside and she often sat scowling while ducks and coots mocked her with raucous cries.

As the cub grew older, Nasseken taught her to lie motionless in the high grass for long periods of time. If Burua contained her impatience enough to remain hidden for an entire morning, Nasseken would reward her with an expedition along the riverbank. She used the outing to show her adopted daughter the animals she would learn to catch and the ones she should avoid, such as hippos and crocodiles.

24

Living along a river whose seasonal rise often flooded the land meant that one had to know how to swim. Not all the resident cheetahs could, but Nasseken told the cub how her own mother had forced her daughters to learn, despite their instinctive dislike of water. When the little cheetah gained sufficient coordination, Nasseken led her into a marshy inlet where bulrushes stood at the edges of quiet pools. For the first lesson, she chose a pond with an island sufficiently close to shore to be reached with a bound, but distant enough to force the youngster to paddle. Burua watched Nasseken as she sat in the reeds on the island, chirping encouragement. Frantically the cub scampered back and forth, touching the water with a tentative paw and giving Nasseken resentful glares.

Just as she became resigned to getting herself soaked, a nearby splash distracted her. She trotted along the shore of the pool and stared into the water. What she saw made her dance with excitement on the mud flat, ignoring the mud clinging to her paws. "Look! Look! Whiskers, like me! Like me! What is it, Nassi-mother? What is it?"

Nasseken perched on the bank and craned her neck. Just beneath the surface the cub had seen a fat catfish, flipping its tail idly as it glided across the pond. Fleshy barbels on the blunt nose trailed in the water.

"Like me," Burua said again. "Same color as me and whiskers too! What do you call it?"

"Kichebo, or river catfish," replied Nasseken, totally mystified by the cub's fascination.

"Kichebo," the youngster repeated, staring so intently her reflection looked cross-eyed. "That's what I am. Not Burua, as Beshon-mother calls me."

Nasseken's jaw sagged open. Her wet tail gave a sharp twitch. "You're not a fish," she stammered. "You're a cheetah, like Beshon and me."

Burua looked down, scuffing one forepaw against the other. "I only smell like you. I don't look like you. You have spots and I'm the same all over, like the kichebo."

The catfish slapped the water with its tail, sending up spray into Burua's face. It curled around and shot away across the pool. On the bank, the cub sprang up and chased it, yelling, "I don't care, I'm a kichebo!"

She came back, mud-spattered and whiskers down, eyeing Nasseken, who grinned and said, "Well, if you're a kichebo, then let's see you swim." She hopped back to the island. The cub wriggled her hindquarters, clamped her jaws together, and launched herself into the pond.

She thrashed and sputtered, but her determination got her across. As Nasseken licked her face in praise, she said fiercely, "There! You can tell Beshon I'm Kichebo, not Burua."

"Kichebo you are, then," Nasseken answered. The cub thought Nassi-mother was secretly glad that she had at last rebelled against the name Beshon had given her.

Her triumph over choosing her name was short-lived, for she still had to face the problem of learning to stalk. Discouraged, she turned to Nasseken, who suggested that she might improve her speed enough to compensate for her visibility. Kichebo spent time practicing sprints before Nasseken and Beshon took her to course gazelles.

"She's fast enough," she heard Beshon remark acidly as the three made their way home just before dusk after a failed hunt. "She's fast enough to send the whole herd stampeding across the plain beyond our reach!"

Kichebo lagged behind the other two, her head bowed and her step heavy. She had no need of Beshon's words; she was well aware of her deficiencies.

"Beshon, perhaps we tried to take her too soon. If she hadn't become excited and rushed the heard. . . ." Nasseken began.

Beshon stopped and shook the dust from her coat. Kichebo couldn't help seeing how her ribs showed in the patchy fur along her side. She, too, felt drained by the fruitless chase after fleeing prey; her lungs ached and her legs shook. She fell further behind, hoping not to hear any more, but the wind carried the voices to her.

"Oh, Nassi, it wasn't her fault. I wish it had been. Bad timing is something you can train out of a cub." Beshon paced on in silence for a while before her twitching tail warned Kichebo she had more to say. "It's that coat of hers. Not even a dull black, but glossy like a raven's feathers! And if the gazelles miss that, those marks on her ears and face stand out to them like a mother's white tail-tip to a six-week cub. She's hopeless!"

Nasseken flattened her ears and gave a quick glance behind at Kichebo. "Sshh. She's discouraged enough. Do you have to make her feel worse? She did try."

"Trying doesn't fill our bellies," grumbled Beshon, and the cub could feel her own stomach growl in agreement.

"Couldn't we teach her to hunt at night?" Nasseken persisted.

"You can, if you want her to break a leg in a hole you can't see, or run smack into a termite mound."

"All right, she can't chase at night, but she can ambush," Nasseken retorted.

"Like a leopard," Beshon said, and the open disgust in her voice clawed at Kichebo. "Why don't you teach her how to climb trees and pounce on warthogs as they root in the ground below? Or fight the vultures for rotting meat!"

"She would starve rather than do that. She is a cheetah, after all, Beshon."

"Is she?" The other sister snorted. "I'm beginning to wonder. I'd like to see the male that Kenket took in her courting circle. He must have been a sight."

Nasseken fell silent and slowed her pace, letting Beshon have the lead. Kichebo knew she was trying not to blame her sister for being irritable. Hunger frayed tempers, and everyone's was wearing down. Nasseken paused to let Kichebo catch up and walked beside her. The cub badly needed comfort, but one glance at Nasseken's face told her that Nassimother had nothing left to offer. The two walked in silence.

In spite of her weariness from the failed chase, Kichebo woke before dawn. She laid her head down on her forepaws and tried to sleep again but couldn't. Perhaps it was the rough floor of the hastily dug den that disturbed her, or perhaps the brilliance of moonlight streaming through the entrance. She curled up near the den mouth so that she could see the sky outside. The gazelle-moon rested just above the palm fronds, having grown full and fat from its heavenly pasturage. In its light, everything cast long, faint shadows. Kichebo sighed quietly to herself, wishing she, like the sun-cheetah, could chase such prey as the white gazelle.

Even more, she wished that she, too, could glow in rich gold like the disk of the sun. She would even be grateful for a washed-out fawn or dirty tan—anything close to the usual cheetah background color. But no amount of wishing seemed to affect her wretched pelt, which grew blacker every day. Nassi-mother had told her that each female of their kind was a daughter of the sun. When each had run her final chase, the sun-cheetah would take her back into herself. Their pelts would meld with hers and their spots would become hers. But how then could the sun accept a dark cheetah, Kichebo had asked. Nasseken had no answer to that question.

I'd probably make a horrible blotch that would ruin the sun's beauty, the cub thought. From the corner of her eye she caught sight of Nasseken, who slept outside the lair. She badly wanted to wake her and ask the question again, but she also knew Nasseken needed what rest she could get. Moonlight cloaked the sleeping cheetah in silver, disguising her thinness and her rough coat. She was turned so that the moon lit her face, and Kichebo could see how the spots on her brow fused together into a line between her eyes, giving her a faintly worried look even as she slept.

As Kichebo watched, the sleeper stirred. Afraid she had somehow disturbed Nasseken, the cub scuttled backward into the den, but when she poked her head out again, she realized she wasn't the cause of Nasseken's wakening. The adult cheetah stood up and stared into the night. Then she raised her muzzle and gave a breathy hiss.

Following Nasseken's gaze, Kichebo searched the horizon, looking among the silhouettes of palms and bulrushes for something that didn't belong there.

And then she saw what Nasseken had found. An arched surface, too smooth to be a hill or boulder, was outlined in moonlight. So low and still was it that the cub stared hard to be sure her eyes weren't tricking her. She started to crawl forward to get a better view, but then halted, staring up with a mixture of awe and delight.

A ring of fireflies circled in the air above her. When she crept out of the den they didn't dance and flit away but continued their steady descent. Fascinated, she lifted up a paw to bat at the tiny lights. She had played with fireflies before, but never had they come so close or displayed so little fear. A touch of uncertainty crept into her mind. Fireflies usually blinked. These didn't. Their motion seemed too regular, and they didn't dart in and out among each other. When Kichebo stared harder, she saw the fine threads forming a net amid the sparks. The lacy weave billowed as the circling lights carried it down around her.

"No!" Nasseken's hoarse cry burst in her ears, shocking her into full awareness. Startled, she ducked and tried to scramble out from beneath the web, but it expanded to cover her. When she tried to paw the net, its strands drifted out of reach. Perplexed, she stood, looking at the lights and the strange meshwork that floated about her, confining her without touching her. She shook her head, trying to fend off a wave of overwhelming sleepiness.

As if from a distance, she watched Nasseken charge the net, rearing and striking out with her forepaws. The web evaded her blows. When Nassi-mother snagged a dewclaw and jerked back, the net stretched without distorting its weave. Almost too groggy to feel alarmed at the net's strange effect on her, Kichebo swayed, trying to stay on her feet.

Beshon came flying into view with a startled hiss. "Sister! Over there! Look!" she yowled at Nasseken. Kichebo staggered around, nearly losing her balance, and peered between the encircling lights. In the dim glow of early dawn, she saw that the low metallic form had come closer. As she watched, part of it swung aside and apelike two-legged figures climbed out.

She heard an angry snarl, and the sharp slap of a callused pad on her rump nearly knocked her over. "Kichebo, wake up!" Nasseken's face was before her, ears flat, fangs bared and gleaming. The adult cheetah threw herself at the net and attacked it with her teeth, gathering a mouthful of threads and yanking hard. The nearest light spark flared an incandescent purple, frightening Nasseken back.

"Run, sister," Kichebo heard Beshon cry. "You've lost her; save yourself!"

Now she could hear the approaching figures' footsteps and a soft, dry rustle, unlike the sound of fur or feathers. Now she smelled their odor, animal and at the same time not. She saw Beshon whirl to face them, stamping down and lashing her tail in helpless anger. Again Nasseken flung herself at the web, biting and clawing. Her jaws closed on one of the firefly lights.

The flash and muffled concussion jolted Kichebo out of her lethargy as Nasseken reeled backwards on her hind legs, white smoke spilling from her jaws. "Nassi-mother!" the cub cried, straining against the web. For an instant Nasseken lay motionless, then she staggered to her feet, shaking her head fiercely in a daze. Only then did Kichebo see that the lights were gone. Frayed strands floated around a large gap in the mesh.

Snarling her defiance, Nasseken lunged at the group of approaching figures while Kichebo stumbled through the torn web. Beshon was behind her in an instant, and another sharp slap on the rump jolted her out of her lethargy entirely. One of the figures raised a long stick and pointed it at Nasseken. There was a muffled crack and then a thud as a dart slammed into the bole of a palm tree. With a hoarse screech, the cheetah sprang away. Another dart drove into the ground in front of Kichebo, making her start and shy. Nasseken caught up quickly and the three ran as hard as they could, leaving the enemy far behind.

Spent and frightened, the cheetahs took shelter beneath an overhang until dawn. Exhaustion kept Kichebo mute, but she overcame her terror enough to creep to Nasseken and lick her gently behind the ears. The adult cheetah panted, stretching her scorched jaws wide and grimacing with pain. Saliva ran down her jowls and dripped from her chin. Feeling helpless, Kichebo continued to lick and nuzzle until Nasseken gingerly closed her mouth. She squeezed her eyes shut and leaned against the cub.

"We'll go back to the hunting trails," she said thickly to Beshon. "Kichebo's old enough to travel with us. We don't need to keep her in a den anymore."

Kichebo looked to the other sister for help, but the sudden anger that flared up in her eyes made the cub shrink back. Beshon didn't reply.

"Milk-stealer!" she spat at Kichebo. "Carrion-eating black leopard! I'm tired of running and hiding and not being able to hunt because of you." She turned on Nasseken. "And you, my fool of a sister. You think you can bring her into the hunting range? A cub who can't stalk because her black coat betrays her? You'll have to kill for her all her life and even if you don't hate her now, you will soon."

Kichebo felt a paralyzing chill sweep through her from her muzzle to the end of her tail. The pale dawn sunlight did nothing to warm her. She couldn't even flinch when Beshon sent her another poisonous glare, then jumped at her, aiming a bite at her cheek. Bewildered and miserable, Kichebo scrambled backward, away from Beshon's frenzied assault.

"Get out of here! Go die in the desert!" Beshon screamed. "It is you who brought those cursed two-legged things down on us. It is you they want, not us. Go back and let them take you!"

Dust and pebbles spurted up into the cub's face and two pelts seemed to blur together in front of her. In the next instant, Beshon lay on her side with Nasseken standing over her. Both cheetahs made threat-grimaces at each other, their black jowls and tearlines emphasizing the gleaming white teeth. Beshon leaped up and went after Kichebo again, but Nasseken knocked Beshon's foreleg aside before she could strike the club with her dewclaw. The two held their positions, each staring hard into the other's eyes. For a moment, Kichebo thought the two sisters would attack each other, but at last Beshon turned aside, her fur bristling in a ridge down her spine. Her legs shook with exhaustion and rage. She laid her ears so far back she looked as if she had lost them.

Nasseken lifted a forepaw to block another strike at the cub. She swayed and spoke with difficulty, but she made her words clear enough. "Sister, you don't hate her. You wouldn't have stayed with me this long if you did. Lie down and rest."

For an instant, Beshon succumbed to her weariness, let-

33

ting her hindquarters drop. A glance at Kichebo seemed to refuel her anger.

"No. Like a fool I listened to you, Nasseken, but I've finally come to my senses. Look at her. She's not Kenket's cub. She's not even one of us, although she runs and speaks as we do. There has never been anyone like her; not even in the oldest messenger-tales. And there has never been a cub who couldn't learn to hunt. She can't be one of us. She has to belong to those two-legged creatures."

Kichebo wanted to scream aloud to cut Beshon off, but she knew that those painful words contained some truth. She choked back the cry in her throat and breathed hard.

"Sister, they weren't trying to capture you or me. The net was for her. They wanted her," Beshon said hoarsely. "You saw that, didn't you?"

"Yes, I did," Nasseken confessed.

"Then she belongs to them. You must have made a mistake and gone to the wrong lair."

There was a long silence, much longer than Kichebo expected. Nasseken looked defeated. Could it be she was finally admitting that Beshon was right? If so, Kichebo refused to hear the words that must come next. She stalked away from both of them, her tail stiff.

"No. That was Kenket's den, Beshon. I don't know why Kichebo looks the way she does, but it doesn't change anything. She is still our sister's cub and that's what matters to me." Kichebo heard footsteps behind her and Nasseken's scent grew stronger. She lifted her chin higher as her legs began to shake.

She felt Nasseken's cheek rub against hers, but she only squeezed her eyes shut and begged her legs to stop trembling.

Unable to accept comfort, Kichebo choked, "Beshon doesn't want me. And you shouldn't want me, either."

"I shouldn't, but I do. That makes me a bit strange, I suppose."

She opened her eyes. "Why do you want me to stay?"

Nasseken met her gaze. "Because I want you to survive. Remember how you fought for your life against that jackal? Did you struggle so hard only to end up dying of starvation or being taken by those two-legged creatures? Kichebo, I took you in for Kenket's sake, but you have come to mean more."

Kichebo whimpered and buried her head under Nasseken's chin. She felt damp fur against the top of her head and remembered how fiercely Nasseken had attacked the web that imprisoned her. She pressed close to the warm, pulsing throat and cried softly, "Nassi-mother, why am I this strange color? Why do those two-legged animals hunt me?"

"I don't know," she heard Nasseken answer.

"Will your tongue be better soon?"

"I think so."

"Then will you stay with me?"

Kichebo felt Nasseken hesitate.

"Kichebo, I don't want to make a promise I can't keep. If I can, I will stay with you until you are able to live on your own. Is that enough?"

The cub swallowed to ease her dry throat. "Yes, Nassi-mother."

THREE

Kichebo sat in a clump of dry grass on a knoll, waiting for dusk. She shifted to ease the growing stiffness in her legs and squinted up at the sun. It would be a long time before the celestial hunter chased her prey beyond the horizon and Nasseken came to fetch the cub to the day's kill, if there was one.

Kichebo groaned unhappily to herself. She might be safe in hiding, but this was no life for a cheetah cub. Sitting still in one place all day to avoid being found made her legs stiff and weak. She began to fear that even if Nassi-mother taught her to hunt, she would no longer have sufficient strength or speed. She longed to stretch her cramped muscles in a fast sprint across open ground, but she knew that her black pelt and gold tearlines made her visible not only to prey but to those mysterious creatures who had tried to capture her. If she was seen, she would be taken; her only safety lay in concealment.

Once she had tried to run at night, ignoring Nasseken's

warning and her own inability to see far enough ahead. One forefoot went into the mouth of a burrow, flipping her onto her chest and knocking her breathless. The top of her forepaw still ached and so did the knowledge that she had nearly crippled herself. She knew she was enough of a burden to Nasseken without that.

The cub grimaced as the hateful thought crossed her mind again. Nasseken and Beshon would be much better off without me and they must know it. Perhaps it might have been better if the light-borne net had closed around her, freeing the two sisters from the duty of caring for such a misfit. . . .

The rumble of galloping hooves distracted Kichebo from her dismal thoughts. Her refuge on the hill gave her a good vantage point over the dusty plain below. Often the land stood still and bare, but sometimes a few antelope straggled across, searching for sparse grazing. They attracted other hunters—sometimes cheetahs, but, more often, lions.

The cub knew she was as much lion-prey as the antelope, but fascination defeated her fear. Curling in tightly to hold in her scent, she watched two lionesses chase prey into the claws of a third. At first Kichebo had disdained the lionesses' hunting methods. In comparison to Nasseken's swift charge, their attacks were ponderous and they brought down their victim with raw strength rather than a cheetah's high-speed grace and precision.

Nasseken had told Kichebo about lions: they couldn't speak to each other as cheetahs did, nor did they have the wit or need to give each other names. Lions worshipped nothing, thought only of their bellies, and had no ability to imagine either past or future. In that lack, Nasseken had said, they were like most creatures. Only cheetahs differed, having been created by the sun in her image and gifted with her light in their minds.

The lionesses opened and ate their kill, growling and slapping at each other. Shadows lengthened across the plain as they tore at the carcass with snarls and grunts. Watching the feast made Kichebo feel hungry, and she hoped Nasseken would soon come with news of a kill. When at last she caught sight of the familiar triangular face with its bold tear-lines, the lionesses had finished their meal and wandered away.

With nervous glances to either side, Nasseken trotted up the crest of the knoll. Kichebo sprang up to greet her and staggered on unsteady legs. Nasseken shied back from the near-collision and gave the cub a puzzled glance.

The other cheetah sniffed along her from nose to tail. "Kichebo, you also stumbled yesterday when I came to get you. Does your foot still hurt?"

The cub squeezed her eyes shut, feeling shame and anger wash over her. "No, Nassi-mother. My legs . . . get so cramped from sitting all day. How much longer will I have to stay hidden while you and Beshon hunt?"

"Until those animals who tried to capture you have gone away. I don't know how long that will be. I'm sorry, Kichebo, but this is the only way I know to keep you safe."

Kichebo knew Nasseken was offering the only comfort she could, but knowing that only added to the resentment boiling inside. She followed her away from the knoll, keeping quiet until they were beyond the scent of the lions. Annoyed by the stiffness in her legs that hampered her trot, she burst out, "Safe for what, Nassi-mother? For a life of eating what others have killed and staying still and hidden until my legs are as brittle as dry acacia twigs?" The bitter words were all too ready on her tongue and she spat them out.

The other cheetah stood rigidly, her head low, her ears flat. She looked away from Kichebo.

"Do you keep me for my sake or yours?" the cub hissed, letting the force of her anger carry her. She saw Nasseken flinch and knew she had struck tender flesh. "Will I be your litterling all my life, to be hidden and fed like a newborn? If so, I have as little freedom as if the net had closed around me. Perhaps things might have been better if it had."

She saw the other cheetah's eyes widen in shock. Nasseken's hindquarters tensed and trembled as if she would spring away, even if the pain attacking her was one she could not run from.

"Stop talking nonsense!" she spat back, and Kichebo braced herself for a cuff or a tongue-lashing. Instead, Nasseken stayed quiet and then hung her head. "No," she said after a long silence. "No, it isn't nonsense. I haven't been honest with myself or with you." She sighed, and it was so weary a sound that the cub's anger fled. Frightened and guilty, she pressed up against Nasseken, trying to offer comfort.

"Nassi-mother, I'm sorry . . . I didn't mean . . . I'll sit in the grass and I won't complain . . . please don't be sad."

Nasseken lifted her head and gave Kichebo a long, searching stare. "Yes, you did mean what you said," she answered crisply. "Follow behind me and be quiet for a while. I need to do some thinking."

The crack of breaking branches met Kichebo's ears when

39

they reached the site where Beshon had made a kill. Her hunger came in a rush and she attacked the carcass, ignoring thorns and dry twigs that had caught in its fur.

"Where were you, sister?" she heard Beshon complain to Nasseken. "I had to stuff my catch under this bush to keep off some pesky jackals."

"We had to avoid lions," Nasseken replied.

A short time later, Kichebo heard footsteps and felt a soft nudge from a damp nose. "Enough, little hunter. You don't want a full belly for this night's work." Surprised, the cub backed away, letting Nasseken have her place. The adult cheetah ate briefly, then wiped her muzzle against her foreleg. She walked away, her tail swinging, and the cub followed.

Daylight was gone, but the moon gave enough light for Kichebo to cast a soft shadow. "All right," Nasseken said, stopping in the center of a clear patch of ground. "Now then, I've been thinking about what you said, and you're right, you can't depend on me all your life. You must learn to hunt, and I know how to teach you."

The cub sat, pricking her ears.

"This is the way, little hunter. I am a young antelope that has strayed too far from its dam. I am your prey. Bring me down."

Kichebo crouched while Nasseken lifted her head and imitated the abrupt jerky stride of a young grass-eater. It was so unlike her usual fluid gait and so good a mimic that Kichebo imagined she could see the fawn grazing before her. Eagerly she sprang, lifting her forepaw for a swat at the other cheetah's hindquarters. When Nasseken broke into a trot, Kichebo seized her nape and tried to tumble her over.

The first time the cub was dragged several tail-lengths before she lost her hold; the second time she clung tenaciously until she felt Nasseken collapse gracefully beneath her weight.

It became a game, and Kichebo played avidly. Lacking siblings, she had never tussled with a littermate or fended off mock attacks. Her two guardians had been too preoccupied with survival to devote much time to play. The hunting game became part of every evening's activities and Kichebo looked forward to it each day as she sat hidden in the dry grass.

Yet it was not just play. Even when there was no kill to sate the cub's hunger, Nasseken called her to the hunting game. Her empty belly gave her mock attacks the edge of reality. She did not understand the intensity of her training until one night she stepped back from pummeling the adult cheetah, realizing she had drawn blood.

Remorse flooded over her as she watched Nasseken lick a small wound on her neck. "You didn't hurt me," she said quickly, but the cub had already heard the involuntary hiss of pain. After the next few rounds, Nasseken backed off and shook herself. "Kichebo, you were doing very well. Now you're holding yourself back. I told you, you can't hurt me. Now let's try again."

Kichebo tried, but it became clear that she was keeping her dewclaws sheathed and her bite shallow in order not to wound Nasseken.

"Is that how you will hunt, cub? You'll never fill your belly if you pity your prey," the other cheetah mocked, and Kichebo knew she was being goaded into a more reckless attack. But the goad was not sharp enough to ignite real anger and Kichebo could see Nasseken hated what she had to do. They broke off the game and sat apart, not looking at each other.

Kichebo felt despair creeping over her again. She had to learn to hunt and if this was the only way, she must do it. But to strike at Nassi-mother with fully bared claws . . . that was meat almost too tainted to swallow. Footsteps sounded nearby and Kichebo looked up, expecting to see Nasseken.

It was Beshon who stood over her, looking down with narrowed eyes. The cub shrank back, retreating from the contempt that seemed to fill those amber slits.

"You want to be a hunter, do you, little carrion-eater?" Beshon sneered. "I'll give you worthy prey."

Kichebo's jaw sagged. "Y—you?"

"Whose meat fills your belly? Whose pads are worn with the chase? Now you'll earn the food you get, black leopard. Come on, show *me* your claws!"

The slap of a pad stung Kichebo's cheek. With an angry yowl, the cub leaped at Beshon, only to be thrown off by a casual shake. As Kichebo gathered her breath, Beshon walked back and forth in front of her, wagging her hind-quarters insolently. She raised her tail as if the cub was no more than a tree or a rock on which she could leave her mark. Kichebo lashed out, but Beshon was already gone, loping away with an easy gait, her tongue lolling out.

Digging her claws in the dirt, Kichebo scrambled after Beshon. Fury choked her throat, giving her new strength, and her lunge carried her further than she expected. She brought her dewclaws down on Beshon's hindquarters hard enough to make the other cheetah's rear legs splay apart.

She clung as Beshon dragged her in circles on the moonlit ground, favoring her with occasional kicks. Kichebo's dewclaws ripped free and she lay on her back in the dust, grimacing.

"Not bad, black leopard. That might have brought down a young warthog. A weakling young warthog," Beshon added, taunting Kichebo again. A growl bubbled in the cub's throat, but she became aware of Nasseken nearby.

"If you think you're going to interfere, my softhearted sister, think again," Beshon said sharply to Nasseken. "You tried to teach her your way. Now I'm going to teach her my way. And it's working. She has her claws out and she's using them."

Nasseken's expression was doubtful, but she sat down again. "I may have to do your hunting for you tomorrow, you crocodile," she said wryly, but Beshon ignored her, turning on Kichebo once again. "If I had been a gazelle, my kicks would have broken your jaw. You have to hit me hard enough to knock me down. All right? Go!"

Again Kichebo attacked and again, until the moon hung just above the horizon and she was yawning with weariness. When Beshon finally let her go, she staggered to Nasseken and collapsed against her, asleep before she slid to the ground.

She awoke to the sting of a slap on her flank and whiskers tickling her ear. "Up, black leopard. It's not yet dawn, but the sun-cheetah's approach gives us enough light to practice." The cub groaned and rolled over, feeling cold, stiff, and grumpy. She tried to bury her head against Nasseken's flank, but Nasseken wasn't there. Beshon seized Kichebo's tail in her teeth and gave it a sharp yank. In an instant, the cub was after her, threatening to chew hers off at the root. Beshon slowed enough to flick her tail-tip in Kichebo's face and sprinted away.

Now that there was enough light to see by, Kichebo could use her full speed. She caught up with Beshon and ran beside her, trying to seize the other's nape and bring her down. Each time, the adult cheetah nimbly avoided the cub's attack and taunted her into trying again. At last, Kichebo slowed, panting. She was never going to catch Beshon if she kept this up. Perhaps if she did something unexpected. . . . She thought for a minute, making a plan in her mind, then broke into a trot toward Beshon, who was jogging in a large circle.

Instead of chasing Beshon, Kichebo waited for her to come around again before she launched her next attempt. As before, she paced Beshon, but instead of trying to seize her nape or throat, the cub slipped a paw between Beshon's two front feet. With a grunt of surprise, the older cheetah catapulted forward onto her chest. Her momentum flipped her over and she skidded on her side for several tail-lengths before coming to rest in a cloud of dust.

Kichebo watched her regain her feet and shake the dust from her coat. "You little daughter of a jackal, where'd you learn that trick?"

"A hole in the ground taught me," the cub retorted, cocky with success. "I thought I'd pass the lesson along."

Beshon's ears flattened, then twitched and came forward as she eyed Kichebo. "You have spirit, black leopard. That I'll admit. See what else you can teach me when you come back tonight."

"I'll teach you not to pull my tail," Kichebo snapped, but

Beshon was sauntering away and Nasseken had come to take the cub to her daily refuge in the high grass.

Kichebo's instruction continued in much the same manner as it had begun. Each morning Beshon prodded her awake before dawn for practice. When the moon gave enough light to see, Nasseken's sister worked Kichebo until the cub rebelled from exhaustion. Now she almost welcomed the necessity of remaining hidden during the day, for she could spend some of those hours catching up on lost sleep. Yet she hungered to use her growing skill in a real hunt. Perhaps if I shred Beshon's pelt, she'll decide she's had enough of being prey, the cub decided and nursed that hope.

She knew without being told that game animals were growing scarce enough so that each chase required the best efforts of the hunter. Mistakes were too costly to allow the success of a hunt to depend on an inexperienced cub. So she continued to eat from the two sisters' kills even while she longed to bring down prey of her own.

It was Nasseken who suggested that she start by hiding in ambush and attacking a small animal as Beshon chased it past. The latter grimaced at the idea but at last agreed, and the three set off to find game.

Through distorting waves of heat rising from the ground, Kichebo saw a tawny blur and then a sudden puff of dust. Nasseken, crouched with her behind the crumbling edge of sandstone, eased forward. The cub felt whiskers brush her ear. "Get ready. Beshon's flushed a hare."

Kichebo gathered for a lunge that would knock the hare down as it passed. She could see the prey as a dot at the front of a plume of dust. As if the hare sensed the waiting ambush, it swerved away from its path. Behind it, Beshon flung out her tail to aid her swift turn. The pursuing cheetah cut off the hare's escape and drove it back toward the outcropping.

Now the prey was close, streaking along the ground at a speed much greater than Kichebo had anticipated. For a moment she panicked, afraid she would be unprepared. Then she was sure again and she leaped. Her forepaws struck air as she searched for the prey that she thought was ahead of her. Something brushed her rear leg and a rush of air fanned her belly. She caught a brief glimpse of Nasseken, charging out from behind the outcropping, before she was startled by an angry yowl from close behind her.

"Look out!" Beshon screeched. Kichebo lurched aside, barely avoiding a collision with her. Flying gravel pelted the cub's coat as Beshon flew past. She heard a high squeal interrupted by a muffled growl. Beshon bounced to a stop, dust swirling around her. Kichebo's gaze went to Nasseken who crouched a short distance away, the hare hanging limply from her jaws.

Kichebo shook her head in confusion. It had all happened too fast. She had lunged too soon; the hare had run under her belly and Nasseken had caught it. The cub's first impulse was to duck behind the outcropping before Beshon could regain breath enough to send some stinging comments flying in her direction. With a penetrating glance at Kichebo, Nasseken carried the prize over to her panting sister and laid it down in front of her.

The cub swallowed, her hunger making her resent Nasseken's action, but she knew very well why she had done so. Because of my ineptness, Beshon will have to run again,

46

Kichebo thought and felt like hiding herself in shame, especially when Nasseken's eye caught hers. Beshon carried the hare away into the shade while Nasseken turned to the cub.

Kichebo braced herself for a reprimand, but all Nasseken said was, "Well, you slowed it down enough for *me* to catch it. Next time, make your leap so you are slightly behind the prey as it passes."

The cub kept Nasseken's advice well in mind. She quickly caught and killed the next hare that streaked by the outcropping. It made a few mouthfuls, but it was all she got that day.

The following day went as had the one before and so did those that followed. Each morning before sunrise, Nasseken woke Kichebo and took her to a rock or thicket bordering open ground. There the two hid while Beshon scouted for game. As Kichebo's ambushing skills improved, she no longer needed the help of an adult, and Nasseken could join Beshon in the search. Often the cub waited the entire day until she saw the two sisters returning with empty jaws and matted coats. On these days, the cheetahs ate nothing except a few bites of tsama melon, to ease their thirst.

But there were also days when a dusty haze just over the horizon would announce that the two sisters were on the chase. Wild battles with prey taught Kichebo that size was no measure of ferocity and that even small animals could fight furiously enough to wound her if she did not take them swiftly.

Soon she knew she was becoming a valued member of the hunting group. The ambush technique worked well enough; even Beshon had to admit that. Yet the cub felt a vague sense of dissatisfaction. To hide and pounce on an animal chased by someone else was not the traditional cheetah way of hunting. Beshon had already made it abundantly clear that she would accept this way only as a temporary measure to cope with scarce game. A true daughter of the sun, she said, chased and caught her own prey and when things got better, she would hunt according to ancient ways. Kichebo noticed that at such times, Nasseken's faintly worried look would deepen and she would fall silent.

Beshon also continued to call Kichebo "black leopard." Although the cub knew she was doing it out of habit rather than malice, the name still hurt. Because it is the truth, the cub thought bitterly to herself when she couldn't keep her feelings at bay. Why should it matter how I take prey if I can catch it, she often argued with herself, but each time she peered from behind her rock or thicket to see the two sisters coursing, a strange ache came into her throat and chest. Her legs trembled with the urge to run and she hungered to launch herself in pursuit. To feel the wind of her own swiftness blow her whiskers back against her face as her strides consumed the distance between herself and her fleeing prey was something she longed for deeply yet never dared admit.

She envied the adults their freedom to chase prey in the open. Beshon might look thin and ragged while standing still, but once she began to run, the patchy coat and bony hips disappeared into the fluid beauty of motion. Kichebo knew this was her heritage, yet she was barred from it by the color of her pelt and the mysterious creatures on two legs that still hunted her. Again and again she tried to persuade herself that she had all she wanted. She was with

Nasseken and had gained Beshon's grudging respect as a working member of the hunting group. What more could she want?

The answer came too swiftly. To run across the plains free and unafraid. She tasted bitterness in her mouth at the thought of springing out on a driven victim, making the kill, and then scurrying back to cover as if what she had done was somehow shameful.

The feeling began as a small one, but it grew larger each day. Kichebo said nothing to Nasseken, for there was nothing Nassi-mother could do except sympathize, and that somehow made the feeling worse. Trying to put it aside was like trying to squash a frog in a mud puddle, which she had tried once when young. No matter how hard she stepped on the creature, it slipped from beneath her paw and popped back up, staring at her with big goggle eyes.

"Be content, black leopard," she growled to herself, but there was a part of her that refused to listen.

It was still early morning and dew dampened the shaded side of the boulder where she crouched. She had expected to have to wait until well past midday, as the two sisters often ranged far in their search for game. Carefully she peered around the edge of the rock. The billowing dust on the horizon and the sound of galloping hooves told her the two adults had found something better than a hare. She started and tensed as a head bearing a sinuously curved pair of horns appeared over the rise. Such prey would fill more than one belly . . . if she could catch it.

First Nasseken and then Beshon charged over the hill after the antelope. Neither sister was using her full speed and

49

their heaving chests and lolling tongues told Kichebo they had run as far as they could. Neither one could aid her if her first attack failed.

As the sounds of the chase grew louder, the cub prepared herself, trying to recall everything she knew. She coiled her body in a tight crouch. She caught a glimpse of the ribbed horns and a blurred body with a black streak; the sharp scent of fear-sweat hit her nose. As the antelope's forequarters flashed into view behind the rock, Kichebo sprang.

Her bared dewclaws struck the prey's back. One caught and held in coarse fur, but the other tore loose. For an instant the young cheetah flailed wildly with one foreleg as she was dragged along by the other. The antelope's hocks battered her ribs.

She lost her hold and tumbled into the dirt, knowing that she had failed and should creep back into shelter before she was seen in open daylight. But, as she regained her feet, she saw the prey ahead of her, its image hovering between the two gold sighting stripes on her nose. An unknown part of her seemed to take control and she found herself racing after the antelope.

Her sense narrowed until only the smell and sight of her quarry had any meaning. Dimly she heard Nasseken cry out, but the call was lost in the wind of the chase. She drank air in huge gulps, feeling her breath expand her chest, sending new strength to her legs. She increased her stride, rejoicing at how each bound carried her farther than the previous one and how fast she was closing on her prey.

Again she prepared for the lunge with bared dewclaws, but the antelope dodged to one side, cutting directly across her path. For an instant, she skidded, whipping her tail and throwing her weight backward to avoid a broadside collision. When she knew she couldn't stop, she kicked off with her hind feet, extending and stiffening her forelegs.

The young cheetah hit the antelope hard enough to knock it sideways from its path. The two went down together in a thrashing tangle of hooves and paws. Kichebo forgot everything she had been taught as she sought for a hold on the animal. She bit at anything that stayed still long enough to be seized. She caught the antelope's tail and hung on while it wriggled and bucked, trying to free its hindquarters.

With hard yank on its tail, the cub pulled the antelope backward and scrambled up its back, biting its nape. It bleated and flailed, then rolled over, pressing the young cheetah's muzzle into the dust. Choking and sneezing, Kichebo wrenched her head free and scrabbled for a claw-hold. After another short flurry, she found herself dancing around with the antelope, its twisted ear clamped in her mouth and the sharp horn-tips waving close to her face. A bony knee punched her in the chest, but she kept her jaws locked in the stiff cartilage of the animal's ear.

Slowly she began to back, pulling the antelope with her in a series of sharp jerks. A sudden wrench of its head to the side toppled it over, exposing its white throat. She bit there, feeling her fangs slip through coarse, dry fur to meet the resistance of flesh beneath. The muscles in her cheeks strained and her fangtips broke through.

A great weariness swept over the cub and she was suddenly hungrier for breath than meat. Her legs gave. She fell into a crouch on the prey, drawing as much air as she could through her nose and between her teeth. She concentrated on her jaws, pulling them tighter and tighter as the antelope's struggles grew more feeble.

And then, abruptly, it was over. Kichebo loosened her bite, stretching her jaws wide to ease the cramped muscles in her cheeks. Panting heavily, she stepped back. The antelope lay before her, limp and glaze-eyed, strangely transformed from the lively animal it had been. For an instant she saw the dead creature as something more than just food. It marked the frightening but necessary transition from movement to stillness, from color and depth to dullness, from life to death.

Confused, the young cheetah blinked and shook her head. The rest of the world, which had disappeared during the intensity of the chase, sprang back into being around her. Now the sounds of the other two cheetahs penetrated her hearing, and the words they said once again had meaning.

She saw Beshon canter up, her eyes wide and her whiskers raised. "A good catch, little hunter!" the adult cheetah said briskly. "But you can't stand and stare at it until the vultures pluck the meat from beneath your nose. Let me help you drag it to cover."

As the cub watched Beshon sniff the carcass, she felt a surge of possessiveness that grew quickly to anger. "My kill," she said sharply, half-amazed at her boldness. "Stay away."

Beshon narrowed her eyes and switched her tail-tip. For a moment, Kichebo feared she had earned a cuff for her impudence, but Beshon only cocked her head to one side. "Who's been pulling your whiskers, youngster? Nasseken and I have often helped you get your catch under cover."

Kichebo looked back, slightly ashamed at her defiance of

an adult, yet she couldn't help feeling an odd satisfaction that was new to her. "Those were ambush kills, black-leopard kills. This antelope was my first catch as . . . as—"

"As a cheetah." Nasseken's voice came softly from behind her. Kichebo spun around, forgetting Beshon. She read a mixture of emotions in Nasseken's deep amber eyes. The adult cheetah's whiskers trembled as if they didn't know whether to bristle or droop. Kichebo hurried to fill the uncomfortable silence with words.

"I know I disobeyed you, Nassi-mother. When I missed my first lunge, I should have gone back to cover immediately. I should say I'm sorry, but—"

"You're not." Nasseken's voice was dry. As Kichebo looked down at her forepaws and struggled for an answer, Nasseken said, "No. Don't try to explain why. You made a choice. To catch that antelope, you risked being seen and you probably were. . . ." Kichebo felt her exultation begin to drain away, but Nasseken wasn't finished. "You probably were," she continued, "but right now, that doesn't matter. What matters is that bellies that would have been empty will be filled. Take your kill to cover. That right is yours alone. We will come when we are bid."

Nasseken nudged Beshon and both withdrew to a distance. Pride warmed the young cheetah as she straddled the antelope's carcass. It was not a clean kill; it bore too many bites and scratches. One ear was chewed to shreds, but that made no difference. What mattered was that Nasseken understood, and that, despite everything else, she was proud. Kichebo seized the white throat, hauled the antelope's head upright and let the rest of the body trail down her chest and between her forelegs. Hampered by its bulk, she strutted awkwardly, curling her tail high over her back as she carried her prize to the shade of the boulder.

By late afternoon, the carcass had been stripped and the remains abandoned to vultures and jackals. To escape the quarrelsome clamor of scavengers, the cheetahs retreated to the patchy shade of an acacia, where they lay in a circle with muzzles facing in and forepaws touching, talking and licking each others' faces.

Kichebo had eaten first and she was so full she could hardly bear to lie on her belly. At last she rolled onto her side, feeling the pleasant distention of her stomach. A mild ache in her legs reminded her of the chase. Next to her, Nasseken rolled onto her back, lazily paddling her feet in the air. With an impish gleam in her eye, Beshon poked a blunt claw in Nasseken's ribs and the two began to play-wrestle.

Kichebo groaned with dismay as they jostled her, for she was far too stuffed to join in and it was too much of an effort to get up and move away. She closed her eyes, but then opened them as the muffled growls and slaps of the adults ceased.

"What, by the sun-cheetah's mark, is *that*?"

At the sound of Beshon's voice, Kichebo lifted her head. Beshon stood over Nasseken, one paw raised, but she was no longer paying attention to her sister. Instead she stared out of the shade toward the site of the kill, where scavengers still squabbled over scraps.

"Is that a vulture?" Beshon asked.

Nasseken craned her head around to look. "It must be a bird of some sort; it's hovering over the carrion." Kichebo sat up, ignoring the drag of her bulging stomach. Through

54

the rippling waves that rose from the sun-baked plain, she saw the crowd of vultures and maribou storks surrounding the leavings of her kill. Above them, hanging motionless in the air, was something she had no name for. It was the same size as a vulture and had twin projections that reminded her of wings, but, unlike a large bird, it remained absolutely still as it hovered.

Fascinated, she crept forward. A paw came down on her back cautioning her to go no further, but she had no intention of leaving the acacia's shade for the open. She stared hard at the object, whose dull color made it hard to see against the dusty hills. It looked like a rock hanging suspended from the sky, except for the strange smoothness of its surface. On its underside, something spun and fluttered.

The vultures refused to accept the intruder as one of their own kind, for they hissed and mantled their wings as it drifted lower among them. Kichebo thought then that the creature would descend to feed on the carcass, but instead it drifted purposefully, clearing a path through the jostling flock. It wasn't until the intruder had gotten beyond the scavengers that the cub realized with a shock that it was traveling toward the acacia that shaded her and her companions.

At the thought, her jaw fell open in dismay. Nasseken, always careful, had scuffed out their prints, and the arid soil did not hold scents. How then was the intruder tracking them, if indeed it was? As it approached, following the same route they had taken, Kichebo became more certain that by some means unknown to her kind, the creature was seeking her out.

The fullness of her belly became a leaden lump that

dragged at her middle. She had eaten far too much to run any distance; all of them had gorged like lions, for they knew such opportunities were rare.

Wordlessly, Nasseken and Beshon crouched beside her on either side, their action telling her they had also read the intruder's intentions. It drifted closer and stopped, thrusting out an eye on a thick stalk, a glassy black eye with no pupil. No bird ever had eyes like that, the cub thought, and the hair began to rise along her back.

"Nasseken, stay with Kichebo," Beshon hissed. Before the cub could react, Beshon had slipped out from beneath the sheltering branches. Kichebo's throat grew tight with the fear that Beshon was deserting them and that Nasseken would be the next to go. She tracked Beshon with her gaze and saw with envy how well the adult cheetah's spotted pelt concealed her at a distance among the rocks and litter on the ground.

She retreated behind Nasseken, trying to get into the deeper part of the shade. Crouching, she curled up tightly, drawing in her scent. Yet the hovering seeker came on with deliberate slowness as if challenging her to break from cover. Her tongue was dry from fear-panting and her legs twitched with the desire to run.

As she looked again for Beshon, movement in a patch of withered grass caught her attention and she had a glimpse of a spotted back. Her heart jumped wildly with the knowledge that Beshon wasn't deserting them. Instead, Nasseken's sister had circled behind the intruder and was stalking it.

Now Kichebo could hear a soft whirr and a keening that was almost beyond her range of hearing but so intense it set her teeth on edge. There was a cicada-chirp as the seeker's

56

eye moved back and forth. Beshon scuttled from one clump of brush to another until she was a short distance behind and below the intruder.

Kichebo felt her breath coming faster, until she was dizzy with fright. Nasseken's hindquarters, rigid and trembling, pressed her against the base of the thorn tree. The intruder had nearly reached the pool of shade thrown by the acacia when its eye stopped searching. It seemed to stare past Nasseken, directly at Kichebo. With a sound like the trill of a bird, it opened a little mouth.

At the same instant, Beshon, squatting almost directly beneath the seeker, threw herself high into the air. She moved so fast Kichebo saw only a blur, heard a slap and a strange squawk. Something whined past her ears and lodged in the gray flaking bark. Sunlight flashed from the seeker as it spun wildly away from its path into the branches of the acacia. Broken twigs and brittle flowers rained down on the young cheetah as she scrambled to her feet.

Beshon was suddenly with them again and Kichebo found herself loping between the two sisters, fleeing across open ground. Behind them, the thorn tree shook with the seeker's attempts to free itself from entangling boughs.

The fugitives' full bellies kept them from running very far. Soon they found shelter and hid. When they emerged, there was no sign of pursuit.

Beshon shook herself, glanced back over her shoulder and gave a self-satisfied grunt. The cub, feeling as though she should show gratitude for her escape, asked, "Where did you learn to do that?"

"You're not the only one who watches other animals hunt,

youngster," she replied. "I once saw a serval cat use such a trick to catch low-flying birds. That one-eyed thing was no bird. It felt like a flying stone the way it stung my paw pad." She grimaced and shook her foot.

"It must have belonged to the two-legged creatures who have been hunting Kichebo," Nasseken answered. "They have strange animals to do their tracking for them." She turned to Kichebo, her expression troubled.

"Nassi-mother," the cub blurted, before Nasseken could speak, "I can't go back to hiding behind rocks and waiting for you to drive animals to me. When I chased and killed that antelope, something in me changed . . . I don't know what."

Nasseken's eyes softened. "I was going to ask you to go back to ambush hunting, but I know now you can't and I know why."

"It makes things hard for you and Beshon, doesn't it?"

Nasseken sighed. "Yes, it does."

"Maybe I should go and live by myself. I'm almost old enough."

"Almost, but not quite. You have many more things to learn if you are going to hunt like a cheetah." She hesitated and said, "Little sun-daughter, it will be hard. Each time you start to chase, you must judge whether the prey is worth the risk of being seen and caught. Do you understand that?"

Kichebo's throat tightened again, but she forced the words out past her fear. "Yes, Nassi-mother."

"And one thing more," Nasseken added as she started to turn away. "Despite the problems your choice will cause, I am glad you made it. I am as proud of you as I would be of a daughter I birthed myself. Keep that in your heart as you run, even when the time comes for you to leave us."

Kichebo stood still and let the meaning of Nasseken's words fill her. She felt happiness send new strength to her weary limbs and push away the threat that often seemed to close in. For a few moments, she let herself bask in the warmth of the older cheetah's love and respect.

"When you two are finished licking each other's faces, we should probably think about where to go next." Beshon's acid voice cut into the cub's thoughts.

"I have thought about it," Nasseken replied calmly. "There is a place called the Broken Caves. I have never been there, but I heard about it once from a messenger. There are good places to hide and open ground for the chase. It lies far downriver; perhaps farther than the two-legged ones will go in seeking us out."

Beshon looked pensive for a moment. "Your idea sounds like prey worth chasing. Kichebo?"

The cub almost tumbled over herself in her eagerness to agree. The cheetahs groomed themselves briefly and made ready to leave. Before they went, however, Beshon hopped up on a desiccated log and looked out over the dry landscape. "How it has changed since we were cubs, Nasseken," she said and fell silent.

"Sand blows across the old hunting trails and the land will never be the same as it was before. Perhaps that is why I can find it easy to go," Nasseken answered. Beshon jumped down without leaving her usual mark.

"Come," Nasseken said softly and led the way toward the river.

FOUR

The three cheetahs came out of the hills onto tablelands atop cliffs overlooking the eastern bank of the great river. It took a day of travel before wind-scoured sandstone bluffs gave way to broken slopes, allowing the cheetahs to find a way down. Once the river valley had been choked with lush growth, but now desert palms grew amid the brittle remains of fallen trees and vines. Kichebo could see, as she descended, how the carpet of green foliage that had once covered the valley was now withdrawing to the river margin. Nasseken told her how, with each year's dwindling rainfall, the land came more and more to depend on the river's seasonal flood.

On the valley floor, the cheetahs made their way through fields of high grass that had edges sharp enough to sting or cut a tender nose. It was heavy going and soon everyone was panting and leaving sweat-damp pawprints. Despite the suffocating closeness of the grass and the insects that droned about her ears, Kichebo preferred the lowlands to the dry cliff-tops. Here, at least, there was shade and a small breeze from the river.

Abruptly Nasseken emerged into what appeared to be an overgrown clearing. A fitful wind carried to Kichebo the sound and smell of the river, telling her they were close. But instead of plunging once again into the wall of saw-edged grass that barred the way to the water, Nasseken turned and followed the clearing.

After a while, Kichebo realized that this was not just an extended clearing, but an overgrown trail. It was much wider than any path she had previously traveled, taking several good bounds to cross, and she grew uncomfortable at the thought of what might have made such a trailway. She noticed that the grass carpet often thinned enough to expose jagged chunks of gray stone that were flat on one side. Some of these had white stripes. Roots thrust these fragments up at sharp angles, and Kichebo learned to keep watch in order not to trip over them.

Soon the stands of trees and grasses that seemed to form walls on each side of the trailway began to thin out, giving a more open view. A wind from the river blew into the cheetahs' faces and ruffled their fur as they reached the crest of a small hill and started down the other side.

Kichebo noticed that Nasseken became more cautious, slowing her pace and keeping to the edge of the path. Beshon soon followed her example. The trail broadened even further and numerous little side paths joined it. Ahead lay something Kichebo had never seen.

To her eyes, it was a slab of stone, standing strangely upright. Another slab stood against the first at an angle, meeting it at a corner and propping it up. In the slab's center was a square hole. Kichebo stared at the structure, trying to relate its form to things she knew. Instinctively she sensed that no natural object could have such rigid lines or such an absolutely vertical stance. Flattening her ears, she crossed to the far side of the path to pass by, but she soon encountered another strange construction. Again she saw the unsettling symmetry of straight lines and sharp corners.

There was more of this wall than of the first; it had a slab across the top, roofing it over. It also had an opening in front that reminded Kichebo of a den entrance. Ahead of them, Beshon broke into a gallop, running straight down the center of the path and keeping as far away as possible from the structures that rose on both sides. Some were concealed by grass or palms, and others had tumbled down into the more natural configurations of fallen stones. Some, however, stood bare, marked only by streaks and cracks. Sunlight reflected from white walls into Kichebo's eyes, making her duck her head against glare.

On the path side away from the nearby river stood more crumbling walls, half-hidden by vines that had dried and were starting to fall away. Metal bars, ribbed like antelope horns, formed twisted skeletons to which pieces of stone still clung. The sight frightened the cheetahs back to the river-bank and the concealing shade of the trees.

Soon the river shore took another bend to run almost parallel with the current. Here the wide trail ended in a spreading papyrus marsh, and the cheetahs turned inland to seek drier footing.

Kichebo had one forepaw in shade before she realized this shadow was much too solid and dark to be cast by a grove of palms. She gazed up and her fur rose. Before her stood a wall, but one much higher than any she had yet seen. Staring up at it made her feel as if she were at the foot of a cliff, confronted by a soaring rock face. For an instant the young cheetah cowered, frozen in place by terror and awe.

When nothing happened, she uncurled and studied the stone slabs rearing back before her. She looked more closely and saw that the rock had been deeply scored in parallel lines, as if some great lion had drawn its claws across the face of it. Between the lines were other markings. As she stared at these carvings, she had the unsettling feeling that she should know what they meant.

Shaking her head in confusion, she backed away. Now Nasseken and Beshon were far ahead of her. She knew she should catch up to them, but there was something compelling as well as frightening about this place.

She retreated a short distance and saw two huge rectangular pillars, topped by a capstone to form a square arch. Again, it seemed like an entranceway to some great den, yet there was nothing behind it. An entrance with no den behind it, she thought, and for a moment felt scornful toward the kind of creature who would make such a strange thing. Yet it was an entrance, and it seemed to beckon her through.

Perhaps her sudden emergence from deep shade on one side into brilliant sun on the other side made her dizzy or blurred her vision. Her fur prickled with the sudden sense that she was not here alone, although she couldn't hear or smell anyone else. Quickly she glanced back, wondering if anyone had followed her through the inscribed gateway.

No. She was utterly alone, with only the faraway sound of the river, the hiss of the wind, and the still, silent stones.

Kichebo took several wary steps forward, fighting the odd feeling that was starting to creep over her. Vague images hovered at the edge of her vision, vanishing if she turned her head to stare directly at them. She had the impression of bare, brown-skinned bodies, each wrapped in some strange thin pelt of dazzling white . . . not just a few but a great herd pressing together to form an endless mass on either side of her.

The sound of the river seemed to swell in her ears to a deep roar—not the voice of any beast she knew, but stronger and more powerful than a pride of lions calling together. And then she knew that the sound was coming not from the river, but from the throats of the ghostly myriads surrounding her.

The figures became more substantial. Sweat and gold gleamed on bared chests. Faces watched her, their eyes outlined in black. The sound spilled from open mouths, filling her ears and making her tremble. In a daze, she walked forward until she stood before the next wall that loomed in front of her.

She had thought the gateway huge, but beside this soaring monolith, it seemed like a pebble next to a mountain. The young cheetah lifted her chin high to see the top, but not until she sat up on her rear paws and threw back her head until her ears touched her nape could she catch sight of it.

For an instant, the voices faded and she saw the great pylon wall as it was: worn, pitted, one side partially collapsed into rubble. Then her eyes clouded and when she could see again, the wall stood whole—symmetrical, majestic, and brilliant with color. Atop its heights, banners snapped in the wind, adding their noise to the swelling cry of the crowd.

And at the center of it all, Kichebo stood, alone.

No, she was not alone. She sensed, without knowing how, that she had a companion. From the corner of her eye, she saw the faint image of an upright form wrapped in white. Its ghostly head was elongated and partially covered with a strange blue crest. It was not one of her own kind, for it strode beside her on two feet and reached out another limb to touch her. Somehow she knew it meant only kindness, but when the hand touched her. . . .

Kichebo shied away violently, but even as she retreated, she recognized the nudge of a familiar nose. The sound in her ears ceased abruptly and the wavering images gave way to an annoyed cheetah face.

"You'd think I was a crocodile by the way you jumped when I nosed you," Beshon grumbled. "What possessed you to go wandering away from us and roam about in here?"

Kichebo was grateful for the irritation that flared up and overwhelmed her sudden desire to explain everything. No. It would be better to keep the experience to herself, at least for a while. Except . . . that there were a few things she wanted to know.

The first was whether her passage through the great archway had somehow caused her to see and hear what she had.

"Did . . . did you go through the entranceway or around it?" she asked suddenly. Beshon eyed her and retorted, "Around, and at a good distance, too. I don't like walking under things that might collapse."

"Go through it," Kichebo said, surprised at her own impulsiveness.

"Why?"

"Are you afraid?"

"Afraid? Even if it did start to fall, I'm fast enough so that I'd be through before the first stone hit the ground. You just watch, black leopard."

With a defiant glance back at the cub, Beshon entered the shadowed side of the gateway and sprinted through into sunlight. "There," she snapped, shaking herself. "Satisfied?"

Kichebo eyed her, resisting the impulse to ask if she had seen or heard anything unusual. Obviously, she hadn't, for neither her expression nor her manner had altered.

Nasseken, who followed Beshon through the archway a short time later, didn't seem to be bothered by what she had seen or heard after she went through. She did look angry, though, and Kichebo half regretted lingering behind. "Don't frighten me like that again!" Nasseken snapped. "We were walking by the riverbank and Beshon noticed you were gone. I thought you'd been taken by a crocodile."

Beshon added, "I tracked her into here. I have no idea why she came."

Kichebo heard them only with half an ear. Her remorse for alarming Nasseken faded so fast she felt a pang of guilt, but it quickly vanished. The young cheetah lifted her eyes to the mass of piled and tumbled stone around her. The great ruins drew her gaze in a compelling way, especially the imposing pylon that soared up before her. Now the feeling was not just one of awe, but of new and unwanted familiarity. In her head, a thought whispered, You have known this place.

Kichebo's tongue formed the question before she was aware she wanted to ask it. "Nassi-mother, did you ever bring me here before?" she blurted. Beshon's glower made the cub wish she had kept her question to herself, but Nasseken gave her a puzzled stare before answering, "No, Kichebo. I never brought you here."

"Even when I was very young?" the cub persisted. Again Nasseken answered no.

Kichebo's next question surprised her as much as any of them. "Then who ... did?"

She saw Nasseken exchange glances with her sister. "No one, not that I know of. Beshon, what do you think?"

The other cheetah grunted. "I think she's been standing in the open sun too long. That black coat of hers picks up more heat than ours. Come on, youngster," she said, butting Kichebo's flank. "Go cool yourself in the river."

To avoid argument, Kichebo let herself be escorted to the riverbank. While Nasseken and Beshon watched for crocodiles, she bathed, even ducking her head under at Beshon's insistence. But no amount of tepid river water would wash away her experience. At last she pulled herself out, shivering and streaming. With one last glance at the silhouette of the distant ruin, backlit by the sun-cheetah's glow, she made her soggy way after the two sisters.

Hunting on this new ground wasn't as good as Nasseken had hoped, but conditions were enough of an improvement that the three decided to explore. Kichebo felt glad when they chose an area away from the great ruin with its carved gate. She sensed there was something waiting for her within the place, something she had no wish to confront.

Freed from harrassment and provided with better hunting, the cheetahs settled into their usual routine. All should have been well, but Kichebo sensed it wasn't. Nasseken, who had been snappish on the journey, grew restless and irritable. Often she would wander alone and call in a mournful voice, rubbing against trees and stones. Thinking she was itchy, Kichebo tried to groom her, but she ducked away, shivering and hissing.

Bewildered and miserable, the cub asked Beshon if she knew what was wrong with Nassi-mother, but Nasseken's sister was of little help. Kichebo suspected that Beshon knew but was unable or unwilling to tell her. She also suspected it had something to do with her own presence in the group.

One evening, when Nasseken's ragged howls echoed through the trees, Beshon sat up and glared in that direction. Kichebo heard her growl under her breath, "By the sun-cheetah's mark, Nasseken, quit worrying about Kichebo and go do what you must." Before the cub could open her mouth, Beshon was on her feet, ordering Kichebo to stay there while she went to find her sister.

When Beshon came back, she lay down moodily and refused to answer any questions. Kichebo gave up. Listening to Nasseken's voice in the distance kept her awake until late, but at last she fell into an uneasy slumber.

When she woke, she noticed something odd. It was quiet for the first time in days. That had to mean. . . . Suddenly frightened, she nipped Beshon awake.

"Nassi-mother's gone," she blurted as Beshon blinked and gave an annoyed shake.

"She'll be back soon enough. Now don't you flatten your ears at me," the other cheetah added as Kichebo's uneasiness grew into anger.

"Why? Why did she go? What is wrong with her?"

"What's wrong with her is she's too scatting stubborn to admit that she can't keep you forever." Beshon paused, eyeing the cub. "Look, just don't worry about it for now. When she comes back, she'll talk to you. I'm going hunting. Are you coming or not?"

Kichebo couldn't think about hunting. The ache in her belly wasn't hunger. Miserably she laid her chin on her forepaws.

"Please yourself," said Beshon, starting to pace away. She stopped and looked back over her shoulder. "Don't even think of trying to go after my sister. She isn't in the mood for dealing with cubs. And—" Beshon cut herself off.

"And what?"

"Nothing. You just do as I say. Understand?"

Kichebo muttered agreement and Beshon left. The cub sat, feeling frightened and rebellious. Why would Nassi-mother disappear so suddenly without explanation or warning? Why had she changed so abruptly from being patient and gentle to being nervous and easily irritated?

When Kichebo was sure Beshon was out of sight and far downwind, she got up carefully and cast about for Nasseken's trail.

Kichebo trotted all morning and late into afternoon, refusing to slacken speed to ease her tired legs. Nasseken's smell filled her nose and drew her onward. Somewhere in the back of her mind a voice told her how much she was risking, traveling in the open daylight like this, but the danger seemed remote compared to her need.

"Even if Nassi-mother scolds me for following her; even if she bites me, I won't care," the cub told herself fiercely as she scrambled over boulders and forced her shaking paws to find secure footing on the trail. She glanced back over her shoulder, begging the sun-cheetah not to disappear beyond the horizon before she had found Nasseken.

She noticed the other smells accompanying Nasseken's fresh scent but was too intent on trailing her to give these much attention. She did notice that the bearers of these scents often stopped to mark rocks or outcroppings. When she once stopped to smell a marking, the aggressive musk made her grimace and sneeze. Distasteful as she found the odor, she knew it, for she had smelled faint remnants of it near the trails where a band of male cheetahs had gone ahead. A small fear started, but she did not allow it to grow. She wanted Nasseken too much to imagine she might not find her alone.

Kichebo trotted wearily up a long slope, coaxing her aching paws to carry her to the crest. She did not linger there, for fear she would be seen. Quickly she descended to a crumbling ledge on the hillside and paused in its shadow while she studied the dried stream bed beneath. At first she thought that the spotted figure there was a trick of the fading sunlight, but her nose caught Nasseken's smell. Caution halted her eager dive downhill, for she could tell that the adult was uneasy. Then she saw the other shadows stretching across the ground and traced them back to their owners. A group of strangers sat or lay in a wide circle around Nasseken.

A growl started in the cub's throat. Whoever they were, they had no right to come between her and Nassi-mother. Why didn't Nasseken chase them all away?

One of those who sat in the circle got up and approached Nasseken. Kichebo studied the figure, whose deeper chest, longer legs, and heavier neck ruff gave it a form different from that of the two females she knew. She felt the sweat break from her paw pads. The scent drifting to her was the same as that of the trail markings, but now it carried threat and a strange, intense hunger.

She expected Nasseken to retreat before the oncoming male, but the female cheetah held her ground. Her ears were laid back, but her eyes held more than anger. She, too, was hungry, in the same way as the male. Stiffly she crouched, lifting her chin. Then she cried out, a mournful pleading call that made Kichebo shiver. Its harshness and longing shook her to the depths of herself. For an instant she wondered if she had somehow made a mistake and tracked a strange female; Nassi-mother would never crouch and beg like that. Yet as hateful as the cry was in Kichebo's ears, she knew the voice that made it.

Another cheetah started from the circle to intercept the first. The big male snarled and lunged. Kichebo heard the double slap of his paws on the ground. The other reared, lifting his nape in challenge. The two males danced back and forth on their hind paws, sparring with each other. Tufts of fur flew with the blowing dust.

The challenger sprang away and retreated, pausing to squabble briefly with another who took his place. The next fight was over in a flurry of blows and the big male cheetah paused, eyeing the circle, before he again approached Nasseken.

Kichebo's legs threw her downhill, her outrage and anger building with each stride. This was wrong! Why didn't Nassi-mother chase them all away? Why did she just crouch and howl in that terrible voice?

The cheetahs to either side jumped back from her as she

burst through the circle. She heard startled hisses and mutters but paid no attention to them. Her quarry was that hateful spotted pelt ahead of her.

"A leopard!" someone cried.

Kichebo grinned fiercely as she ran. Good. Let them think she was a savage night-hunter. That would put them all to flight quickly enough.

She leaped on the large male, fastening her teeth in his nape and dragging him over. She dived for his furred throat but found her bite blocked by his foreleg. He shoved his leg sideways in her mouth, stretching her jowls and pinning her tongue. She tried to bite, but he forced her mouth so far open that she could only gnaw his leg with her back teeth. Gagging and twisting her head sharply she scrambled away from him. Around her she heard startled exclamations.

"That's not a leopard. No leopard ever had legs like that. A cheetah. A black cheetah!"

"Hey, you carrion-eating spawn of a panther, don't you know how to behave in a courting circle?"

She only half heard them as she wrenched her mouth free of her opponent's choking foreleg. Panting, she faced him, and his wide face with its broad tearlines filled her vision. He lunged at her with startling speed. She tried to slip a paw between his forepaws to trip him, but he swerved and used his remaining momentum to ram her with his shoulder. Breathless, she went sprawling. He pounced on her, wrapping her in a close musky scent that nearly choked her. His chest and forelegs pinned her to the ground as if she were his prey.

With an angry grunt, he seized the side of her neck. His jaws closed and the tips of his fangs speared her skin, but suddenly he froze in his attack. She felt his jaw go rigid and she heard a sudden pause in his breathing. The teeth loosened. A callused pad slapped her away.

"By the scats of the sun, it's a female!" he growled as Kichebo staggered to her feet, feeling blood ooze from shallow punctures on her neck.

"A female?" called another cheetah in a high, mocking voice. "You must be confused, Rahepsi. The female's the one at the center, crying love songs at you. Better hurry or I'll have her first."

"No!" the cub screeched, nearly choking on her rage. "None of you can have Nassi-mother. She's mine!"

A sudden stillness fell over the group. Rahepsi turned his head to one side and muttered "Nassi . . . mother?"

"Kichebo," said a strained voice behind her. The cub forgot everything else as she started to run to Nasseken, but the wild stare in that delicate and gentle face froze her paws to the ground. She could smell and feel the compulsion that drove the adult female to crouch and call. The way Nasseken's gaze strayed unwillingly from her to the males told Kichebo that however much Nassi-mother might care for an adopted cub, this new urge was overwhelming.

She is sick, she is wounded, she has eaten something that makes her look at me in that strange way, the cub thought frantically, but she knew that the answer was none of those things but something else whose nature still eluded her but which threatened to cut her off from the one who meant the most to her. A black haze seemed to descend over her vision and the smell of stale earth filled her nose. The cold of memory struck her, bringing a paroxysm of shivering.

Shaking her head, Kichebo fought the spasm away. She

73

strode stiff-legged to the crouching female and stood over her protectively, glaring out at the assembled males. She held fiercely to her anger, using it against feelings of loss and a bitter longing that drew a dark veil across her eyes. Long ago, she had scrabbled hopelessly in the blackness of an abandoned den, seeking the warm and comfort that had once been there. . . .

New mutters broke out among the male cheetahs, forcing her attention back to them.

"Rahepsi, are you going to let a crazy black she-cub disrupt the circle?" she heard one complain.

"I don't fight females," Rahepsi snapped back. He stared at Kichebo, his expression a mixture of annoyance and bewilderment. The hard amber of his eyes softened as he studied her. "You are a cub, aren't you? That is why you don't understand this. You will, when your time comes. Now you must go away."

His gaze lingered on her before he turned again to Nasseken. Instantly, Kichebo flung herself between the two, stretching her mouth wide in a hiss whose savagery tore her throat. Eyes wide, Rahepsi retreated, but she scarcely saw him. Her rage seemed to blind her, and her flailing paws met cold soil whose stink was the smell of betrayal and abandonment.

She became again the tiny cub, crying her misery to an empty lair until a jackal's jaws seized her. Torn from the den's shelter into blinding sunlight, she had fought back. She remembered how the jackal yelped in pain as she fed her vengeance on his howls by driving her claws deep and ripping them through his pelt.

Dimly Kichebo knew she was attacking not the scavenger

74

who had pulled her from her mother's den but the male Rahepsi, who was seeking Nasseken. Yet it was the old memory that was real to her, that possessed her with an intensity that the present could not match.

There were cries in her ears, not jackal howls but the frightened snarls of a wounded cheetah. Fur and flesh filled her mouth. Her teeth dragged the bony line of a shoulder, and the sensation was the same as when she had scored the jackal's muzzle with her tiny fangs. The body beneath struggled as her claws continued to pierce and rip steadily, almost without direction from her mind. She opened her eyes and saw red-stained spiky fur crushed beneath her paw.

Her anger did not give way entirely to shock. Rahepsi deserved whatever she had given him. But the knowledge she had attacked without knowing what she was doing was enough to make her falter.

A sharp blow on the head knocked her loose from her victim. As everything stopped spinning before her eyes, the dark haze cleared from her vision and the bitter earth-scent left her nose. The young cheetah's legs threatened to crumple beneath her as she regained her feet. No one was near her; they had all drawn away. The males all grouped together, their shoulders hunched, their heads lowered. "She has the biting sickness," said one nervously.

The victim himself stood apart from the other males, the skin of his shoulder hanging down in a furry flap along his foreleg. The wound was an ugly mess of torn and chewed flesh, oozing blood.

Kichebo looked to Nasseken, but even she had withdrawn, shocked out of the courting-circle trance by the cub's frenzied attack. The stricken look in her eyes and the still-uplifted paw told the cub who had cuffed her free of Rahepsi.

"Nassi-mother," Kichebo said hoarsely and staggered one step toward the other female before a sudden twitch of Nasseken's ears warned her back. Something seemed to shatter inside her at the sight of the bewilderment and revulsion that flickered across Nasseken's face. She wanted to throw herself down in front of Nassi-mother and cry out that it was not sickness that made her do as she did but another kind of pain. Yet she stood still, held by doubt. Perhaps she was mad after all. Perhaps she did have the terrible illness she had once heard about; perhaps this was the beginning, and later her mouth would foam and her legs turn wooden. . . .

Why else would she have mauled Rahepsi, fighting like the leopard she had so often been called, instead of sparring fairly with front paws?

Nasseken's eyes began to glaze with a strange fever. Her gaze strayed once again to the males in the courting circle. Though Rahepsi hung back, another suitor edged toward her. Shaking with rage, Kichebo lunged at him. Instantly the other cheetahs closed around her, growling.

"Let me in!" said a sharp voice. Nasseken butted her way through the males and glared at Kichebo. "Beshon told me I've let you stay with me too long, but I refused to listen. By the sun-cheetah's dung, cub, you have not only proved me wrong but rubbed my face in it."

Kichebo thought she was numb to any further hurt, but Nasseken's words drove deeper than claws or teeth could reach. "No, Nassi-mother," she cried.

"I am not Nassi-mother to you anymore," Nasseken said furiously, but Kichebo saw the pain that couldn't be hidden by anger in those burning eyes. "My time with you is done. Go."

"No," Kichebo whispered. "You don't mean it."

Nasseken gave a strangled howl that wrenched the cub's belly. Kichebo was unprepared for the sudden pounce and the teeth that sank into her cheek. Nasseken withdrew, breathing raggedly.

Blindly the cub staggered away, feeling the throb of her bitten cheek. The other cheetahs drew back their whiskers as they moved aside from her, but their disdain meant little now. She wanted only to be away from them; away from Nasseken, Beshon, and a life she had been born to but somehow could not live.

She began to run, driving her feelings into her body. There was no grief choking her throat; it powered the thrust and sweep of her legs. Her mind was dead to rage, but her body was filled with it and she ran under the rising moon, not looking where she was going, or caring.

FIVE

The white gazelle finished grazing among the stars and descended to the western horizon. Still the young cheetah ran, no longer continuously but in short spurts soon ended by exhaustion. She had abandoned the idea of trying to run herself to death. Each time she felt as though the pounding of her heart threatened to split her breastbone, her legs gave beneath her.

When Kichebo could no longer sprint, she jogged, and and when her feet grew too heavy for that pace, she walked. The coolness of night surrounded her, letting her ease her thirst from dew that formed on her whiskers. She did not think about what lay ahead or behind; it took all her concentration to keep to a straight path and lift one foot after another.

She had gone a long way, knowing only that gravel had turned to sand beneath her pads, when she lifted her muzzle and saw a fiery glow lighting the horizon ahead. Emboldened by a reckless curiosity born of despair, she approached.

Sharp, orange snake-tongues licked the night sky. The light flickered and danced hypnotically before her eyes, drawing her despite her instinctive distrust. A pungent, ashy smell stung the inside of her nose. Frightened by the fierce glare and the hot wind on her face, she was turning away when she heard a faint cry.

Something about it made her pause. Could other creatures be here? Perhaps hurt or lost? The call could have been the wail of a cub, abandoned, as she had been. Over a dune and down into a hollow beyond she went, keeping a wary eye on the writhing flame-animal, which seemed to change shape endlessly to reach even higher toward the stars. Yes, it was a creature, for she heard its voice—a deep rumble and hiss interspersed with sharp cracks and groans. A gust of smoke made her eyes sting and water. She coughed and was about to turn away when the cry came again.

This time she knew it wasn't a cheetah voice. She halted, swiveling her ears and twitching her tail, wondering why the strange sound made her brave the fire-creature to listen for it. The wail came again, a strangled monkeylike call. She followed it, tracking the noise.

As she circled outward, keeping her distance from the blasting heat, she saw that the fire-creature fed on a crumpled shape, half buried in sand. She could see the shadowed track the thing had made, rutting and gouging the desert floor before coming to rest.

Torn edges gleamed, their metal sheen reminding Kichebo of the humped silver forms she had seen by moonlight when the firefly net had nearly taken her. She remembered, too, the sinister one-eyed bird that had tracked her from her kill to her refuge beneath a thorn tree. She trembled, knowing that this burning wreck also had to belong to the two-legged hunters who had tried to capture her.

She was gathering herself to spring away into the night when the cry came once again. It was not just the screech of a monkey but a voice that held the same kind of desperation that had driven her so far out into the desert. Setting her face against the fire's heat, Kichebo began to search. She found only charred forms that rolled limply when she touched them and whose substance gave like rotten wood beneath her paw. She retreated, grimacing at the burned-meat smell that hung about them.

The wreck had scattered pieces of itself over the sand, and it was from one of these that the cry came. Kichebo recognized panic in the quavering scream. It burst at her once again as she prepared to dash past a twisted chunk of metal that held its own fire-nest. A chunk of blackened debris lay on the tail of a long, flat tether, stretched taut, its other end wrapped about a struggling body.

Narrow feet churned sand in a clumsy effort to escape flames licking close to bare skin. Small hands beat the air, and the face contorted in another scream. Kichebo slid to a stop, having no idea why she had come or what she meant to do. Her first thought was to flee the fire, her second to sink her teeth into the fat, brown flesh and eat as much of this trapped prey as she could before fire took it from her. Yet she did neither, staring again at the furless creature whose cries assaulted her ears. A memory rose, the memory of the place of tumbled stones.

There she had seen a ghostly form who stood beside her on feet such as those that now kicked sand. With ape-hands like those clenched before her face, he had reached out, not to seize or kill, but to touch. . . .

A snake-lash of fire licked close, nearly scorching her. The naked creature reared, straining against the tether, tossing its head so that the black mane covering its skull flew wildly. Tears spilled from its eyes, mixing with drool from its mouth to run down its neck and chest. The stretched tether strap quivered before Kichebo's face. Recklessly, she lunged and bit, gnawing the strap until it frayed. It snapped, and she fell aside with the end in her mouth.

Kichebo retreated as fast as she could, dragging the furless animal with her. Impatient with its clumsy floundering, she seized it by the straps still binding its body. The little creature writhed and twisted in its harness. It battered her chest with its heels, seized fistfuls of fur, and kept up a continuous screeching yowl that deafened her. One of her fangs scored its back, and the flavor of its flesh seeped into her mouth, reminding her again that this was prey.

A sharp explosion from the wreck put those thoughts to flight. Hissing sparks fell around her as she wrestled her captive across the sand, over the crest of a shallow dune, and down the other side.

Kichebo's teeth ached down to the roots by the time she released her burden. Having lost her night vision to the fire's glare, she could only keep track of the creature by its angry howls. She took advantage of its efforts to escape her by letting it stagger, nudging it the way she wanted it to go. Each shove of her nose was met by a piercing scream and a flailing fist, but the creature was not strong enough to force its way past her. Its cries lost force and volume as she drove it further on. Soon she heard only mournful burbling punctuated with an occasional hiccup.

The cheetah's night vision recovered, but the moon had set and starlight alone couldn't show the way. Knowing she must wait until dawn, she cast about until she found shelter behind an outcropping.

By pulling its legs out from under her sniffling companion, she forced it to lie down, bringing forth a renewed torrent of screams that reminded her of the harsh cries of baboons. This tailless monkey was even noisier, and she wondered what had made her rescue it. The crying subsided into weary panting and other peculiar choking noises, as if a bone had caught in its throat. Well, the night was too dark to look, even if she could get the animal to open its mouth. It would survive until sunrise and if it didn't, she would be saved the trouble of killing her prey. Right now she was too tired to think of eating.

She retreated from it, lay down against a rock face, and placed her chin on her paws. Left alone, the creature gulped and moaned to itself. Alien as such sounds were to her, she couldn't help hearing the misery in them. It woke her own loss and she curled up angrily, wishing she had a warm flank to rest on and a soft purr to sooth her. No. All that was behind her now. She must forget she ever wanted or needed such comfort. Yet she couldn't forget and she lay awake, hating the night for being so empty.

Kichebo huddled, moaning softly. Last evening's run had taught her that no amount of exhaustion could purge her mind of the grief. Never had she thought the parting from her foster-mother would be so sudden, so brutal, or so bitter.

The blood from Nasseken's bite crusted on her cheek, but the wound in her soul still bled.

She waited a long time for sleep, and just as she began to drowse she heard the little animal's teeth chattering. Then came a whimper. Tired and annoyed, she yawned widely, but when she felt fingers on her hind leg, she shut her mouth so fast she nearly bit her tongue in half. She drew her leg back, hoping the little ape would retreat, but it crawled closer and grabbed her again.

She could feel how it shivered. No pelt, she thought, and the idea disgusted her so much she wanted to shove the thing away. Yet she herself was chilly despite her coat, so what must this ape cub be feeling? She remembered how much she longed for warmth when she had been left alone in an abandoned den. Pity overcame revulsion. She let the shivering creature crawl to her and settle itself against her belly, forcing herself to remain still even when it wiped its wet face on her coat.

At first she kept her legs and tail rigidly away from it, but, as it continued to quiver and huddle against her, she curled gingerly around the creature, hoping to warm it enough to keep it still. When she touched it with her nose, she found that the bare skin was smooth, soft, and somehow comforting. The cheetah wondered again what she was doing and why, but the answers didn't seem important any more.

Kichebo came awake suddenly, alarmed by the unfamiliar scent of her surroundings and the unaccustomed weight of a strange, black-maned head pillowed on her flank. Her start woke the creature. With a sharp hiss of indrawn breath, it

83

scuttled away from the cheetah as she scrambled to her feet. Both blinked and gaped at each other in the morning brilliance. Kichebo had to shake her head twice before everything fell into place. From the astonishment on the face that looked back at her, she guessed her companion was trying to do the same.

The ape creature sat on narrow haunches, its thumb jammed into its mouth and one knuckle flattening its nose. Sand speckled its arms and clung to tumbled black hair that hung over its eyes. A few scorched rags clung around its waist. Kichebo inspected it closely, trying to determine its gender. It had no obvious male genitalia so she decided it must be female, like herself. For some odd reason the discovery pleased her, at least until she wondered why she cared. To her, the sex of her prey had never mattered, unless it made the animal more or less vulnerable to attack.

She blinked and sat down on her haunches. This creature was prey, wasn't it? What other reason would she have for capturing it? She hadn't eaten it last night because she had been too tired. Now that she was rested and hungry. . . .

Even as she rose to stalk her prey, she remembered what had stopped her the previous night. She recalled again her vision in the place of tumbled stones and her memory of the otherworldly companion whose clay-brown skin was swathed in white. She remembered the sheen of sweat on bare chests and the gaze of eyes outlined in black.

What these animals were, she didn't know, and she wondered if she had dreamed or imagined them. Perhaps her mind had made up these images from her fleeting glimpses of the two-legged hunters who might still be tracking her.

Yet if this was so, why wasn't she more afraid of the upright creature now in her vision, and why did this noisy, clumsy ape litterling rouse that memory so strongly?

A spray of grit made her flinch and snarl. The creature sat, making high-pitched bird noises as white sand dribbled out of one closed fist. At Kichebo's glare, it grew solemn and pouted, thrusting out its small chin along with its lower lip.

The cheetah shook the sand out of her coat and squinted up at the sky. It was not a good time to start traveling. Her black pelt would show against the sand and even if it did not draw the attention of the hunters, it would gather in more heat from the fierce sunlight than would a spotted coat. No, she would have to wait until dusk.

In the shade of the rock, she dozed, waiting out the day. She thought the animal might wander away, but it stayed near the outcropping, digging in the sand or following beetles that crawled over the rocks. At last it sprawled out in the shade-cooled sand and fell asleep.

When dusk came, the animal still slumbered. Kichebo felt the sharp sting of hunger in her belly along with her growing thirst. She stared at the brown-skinned chest, rising and falling in a gentle rhythm. It would be such an easy kill. The pangs from her belly and throat made her bare her teeth and brought her one step toward the little creature. Such an easy kill. . . .

She stopped, furious because she couldn't attack and she didn't know why. She raged at the memory of the hand reaching out to her and the eyes that looked at her from a strange, flattened face that somehow held its own beauty. And those eyes held the same depth of gaze as the eyes of a cheetah. Could it be that the mind behind them was gifted in the same way as those of her kind?

As she knelt down for a last sniff at the creature, it stirred and woke, gazing back at her. She expected to see the hard, beady stare of a monkey or baboon, but these eyes were softer and held the same qualities as the eyes of her visionary companion. Despite her hunger, she knew she could never think of this animal as prey.

A little hand came up to stroke her cheek fur, adding further turmoil to her feelings. Angrily she jerked her head away and looked out across the shadowed sand. She would go now and leave this ape thing for another hunter who would not be deterred by pity for his prey. She lowered her head and padded away from the outcropping. -

A sorrowful sound made her glance back. The furless ape was kneeling by the rock, one thumb in its mouth and the other hand clutching its ribs. Wet streaks ran down its face, reminding the cheetah how thirsty she was, but she turned back and kept pacing.

The soft swish of feet in loose sand made her turn again to see the creature following. It stumbled awkwardly, floundering in dunes that sifted away beneath its feet. She put her back to it and kept on walking, thinking that it would soon give up. But each time she looked back, it was there, staggering across the plain or struggling up a dune on hands and knees.

At last Kichebo's patience broke and she tried to drive it away, growling and showing her fangs. The animal cowered, but when she resumed her trail it came after her. She knew she could lose it easily by increasing her speed, but the creature's determination challenged her and she wondered how far she could lead it before it gave up or collapsed.

The creature kept on, but in the darkness it fell further and further behind until she could no longer see it in the moonlight. She thought no more about it and traveled until moonset. Yawning with weariness, she found shelter and settled to sleep, only to find herself listening for the faint sounds that would tell her if the animal was still seeking her. At long last, she heard them, but they grew no louder, indicating that it was wandering around aimlessly, unable to find her.

Stubbornly, she put her head down on her paws and tried again to sleep. The moving sounds ceased and were replaced by the odd choking noise she had heard the previous night. Unable to lie still, she got up and paced in a circle. What was wrong with her, she wondered. Why did those ape noises disturb her so? And why couldn't she make the kill that would sate both her hunger and her thirst?

The cheetah found herself widening her circle, guiding herself with her ears. Although she wouldn't admit she was searching for the furless animal, she wasn't surprised when she found it sprawled on its front, its face buried in its arms. When she nudged the creature once, it pushed her away, but another nudge stopped its crying. She waited for it to come after her, but it hesitated and then crawled blindly the wrong way, telling her it could see nothing in the moon-less dark.

Again she thought she should leave it, but something made her offer her tail and not pull away when a little hand closed on it. Slowly she led the animal to her shelter and curled around it as it snuggled against her belly. It sighed once and then soft, even breathing lulled her to sleep.

Kichebo woke, feeling weak and dizzy. She knew she had to kill this day or she would no longer be able to travel. Carefully she uncurled herself from her companion, letting its head slide gently from her belly. It murmured once, then sank again into slumber. Sand clung to its dry lips, making her wonder if it was also feeling the effects of thirst. It must be hungry as well, she thought, but not as ravenous as she. She sniffed an outstretched arm and thought again how easy a kill this would be. Saliva flooded her mouth, and her lips pulled back from her teeth. She was crouching to pounce when she caught a flicker of movement at the edge of her vision.

A scaly tail disappeared behind a stone. In an instant she was after the rock lizard, seizing him by the nape and holding tight as he writhed in her jaws, slapping her face with his tail. At last, when the lizard ended his struggles and hung limp between her teeth, she took him back to her shelter.

The young cheetah ate her prey carefully, squeezing the meat between her teeth to let the juices sooth her parched throat. Blood seeped into the gut cavity of the carcass and she lapped eagerly. It was not as good as water for quenching thirst, but it was good enough. She was starting to devour the rest when a small, brown hand appeared under her nose and grabbed a fistful of flesh.

Immediately, Kichebo seized her prize and yanked it back, but not before the ape creature stuffed a handful of meat into its mouth. It grimaced as if the taste were not one it was accustomed to. It chewed, eyeing her with wary defiance.

88

Outraged at this thievery, Kichebo flattened her ears and spat. The creature's eyes grew wide with fright, its face crumpled, and tears spilled down its cheeks, but after a moment of uncertainty, it tried again. This time Kichebo responded with an angry yowl and a threat-grimace. Among cheetahs, that usually sufficed to warn off a would-be thief, but the furless ape was more difficult to discourage. It crawled after her, snatching at the carcass and pouting through the tears that ran down its face.

When she thought the creature had given up and she would be able to eat in peace, two hands closed around her tail and gave it a fierce tug. She spun around to punish the offender only to find it had scrambled past her and flung itself on top of the half-eaten lizard. She pawed at the creature, but it only curled up tighter around its booty .

At last Kichebo gave up. She had eaten enough to take the edge off her hunger. She lay down, watching as her companion shredded the remains and sucked fluid from the meat.

At dusk, the cheetah set off again and the little ape followed. She kept to a slower pace, often doubling back, although she still wouldn't admit to herself that she wanted a companion. When day came, she slept through it, allowing the creature to join her. The following night, she traveled, keeping to a pace that allowed it to stay just behind her tail.

Desert gave way to scrub plain, bringing Kichebo back to the land she knew, but instead of returning on familiar hunting trails, she skirted the area, circling north and east toward the river. Now she knew where she wanted to go.

Drawing on her memory of the journey made with Nasseken and Beshon, she found her way to the strange wide trails that led past crumbled buildings. She followed them to the same great gateway through which she had passed once before. Instead of entering the ruin again, Kichebo went to the river, where she could soak her weary pads while the water's flow softly groomed dust from her coat.

Her small companion came, too, and made the discovery that river mud was wonderful stuff to sit in, wiggle toes in, make mud-pies out of, and squeeze through pudgy fingers. For a while it seemed to Kichebo that the animal had found its true home, for it refused to be coaxed out of its wallow. It squealed with delight, slapping its palms down in the mud and making a sound that Kichebo heard as "Menk, menk, menk."

It said this so often that the cheetah wondered if the sound might be a word. She lay in the shallow water that lapped the shore, keeping watch for crocodiles and puzzling over the antics of this odd animal. "Menk," it said again, grinning at her and showing its blunt, even teeth as it slapped its chest.

"Is that what I should call you, little mud ape?" Kichebo said, lazing in the tepid water. The creature made a series of high-pitched shrieks and tossed fistfuls of muck over itself. The cheetah made sure she was well out of range, as the little wallower was so engaged in play it took no notice of where the mud spattered.

Kichebo watched it, remembering how she had chosen her own name. "Well, Menk you will be, then."

Once she had refreshed herself, she set out to explore. A mud-caked Menk followed reluctantly as she made her first patrol of the area she claimed. Again she avoided entering the great ruin, feeling still unprepared for whatever might await her there. Instead she went around it, walking slowly and looking for marks made by others of her kind. There were none. Nasseken had been right when she said no other cheetahs hunted this far downriver. There were no marks from hunters of any kind, which puzzled her, although she did not waste time wondering why.

There was also prey, a family of warthogs that had made a burrow in the rubble of a fallen building and a small herd of waterbuck that roamed up and down the riverbank in search of grazing. There were rodents, marsh birds, and the ever-present crocodiles. She was even treated to the rare sight of a female hippo and her calf ploughing ponderously through the shallow water near shore. She could not help noticing, however, that all these animals kept to the edges of her new hunting ground. Few approached the massive ruin that lay in the middle, and she wondered whether the ancient place was as unsettling to them as it had been for her.

Providing food for herself and Menk was the first challenge. She found that her small companion would try to eat almost anything she gave it, although its blunt teeth were too weak to crack a bone for marrow or pierce the tough shell of a river turtle. Sometimes she had to tear apart the prey for Menk, although she was often surprised at how well the creature could use its clever hands as a replacement for teeth.

As the days passed, Kichebo settled into a regular routine. She would sleep during most of the daylight hours, arising just before dusk to hunt and patrol. Even though she believed herself to be far from the two-legged hunters who sought her, she knew how easily she could be seen from a distance. Menk would shamble along beside her, stopping to squat and mark as Kichebo did along the borders of her territory.

Although the young cheetah stayed away from the ruin, memories of her experience within it remained with her. She found herself straying toward the square-arched entrance, turning away only with an effort of will. It was as if the ancient stones called to her and a part of her recognized the summons. When she gazed up at the carvings on the face of the gateway, something in her mind stirred, as if she had once known the meaning of these things but had forgotten. Often she sat quietly in the shadow cast by the great arch, waiting for whatever stirred in her mind to rise to the surface. Each time it seemed about to emerge, it sank away again, leaving only bewilderment.

At last she grew impatient with herself and tried to ignore the ruin, but one day she woke long before dusk. Knowing it was too early to begin her hunt, she wandered aimlessly until at last she found herself at the gateway, the call so strong within her that it seemed like a voice in her ears. Trembling, she passed beneath and, once through, looked warily about her. This time she felt no light-headedness, nor did her vision blur. There was no strange shift in time or place as she had experienced previously.

Relieved, yet slightly disappointed, Kichebo waited for Menk to follow her through the archway. When they were together on the sunlit side, the cheetah approached the great wall that reared up before her, the gap between its weathered pylons beckoning as a second gateway into the depths of the ruin. Beyond it lay an open area, girded by pillars of sandstone as a clearing would be surrounded by trees. Kichebo's hackles rose at the sight of what seemed at first to be a reclining lioness atop a square stone block. She shadowed Menk with her body and tensed, but the form remained motionless. She looked again and saw that the head was unlike that of a lion or lioness but more like that of a prey-beast. Horns curled back from the head, and it bore a goatlike muzzle.

Puzzled, the cheetah ventured closer, daring to rear up and place her paws on the stone base to sniff at the creature atop it. Her nose told her it, too, was stone. She dropped back to all fours, wondering how rock could have taken on such form and why the head of a grass-eater was attached to the body and legs of a hunter. Nothing about the figure made any sense to her, yet again came the odd feeling that she should understand what it was.

Grimacing with frustration, she left the stone beast behind and padded further into the ruin. Menk scrambled after her on all fours as she entered a place where pillars stood in rows like the boles of huge trees. Sand gave way to slabs of sandstone beneath her feet and she walked quietly, not letting her claws click, for she sensed here an emptiness and silence that would not easily be broken. Even Menk's noisy chatter ceased as the two passed columns whose girth took many steps to circle. Kichebo gazed up at beams that seemed to vault from the top of one great stone tree to the next and whose shadows striped the sunlit floor. She recognized the fan shape of papyrus worked into the tops of some columns and the form of the lotus bud in others, yet she couldn't say how the knowledge had come.

There were scribings everywhere: strange chiseled marks

that covered the squat bases of the pillars, the columns themselves, and even the crossbeams high above where no creature but a bird could reach. It was these carvings that drew her attention and wakened again the strange itch in her mind. She stared at them, seeing single eyes without faces, and the heads of jackals and hawks atop stiff two-legged forms. There were other carvings that meant nothing to her, yet a voice inside insisted that somehow they should.

The feeling grew so strong that Kichebo backed away, frightened. "No," she breathed, speaking her thoughts, as if hearing her own words could drown the other voice in her head. "I don't know what those marks are. Stop asking me!" She found herself crying aloud, and her wail seemed to echo back and forth among the pillars until it faded.

Menk crept to her and huddled against her as she crouched. A little hand stroked her fur; a voice cooed in her ear, calming her. With Menk nearby, the demand in her mind seemed to grow less intense, or perhaps just less threatening, as if perhaps she could meet it without betraying too much of herself. This in itself was an odd feeling, and she decided that she had experienced enough. Whatever was in store for her here could wait until she was ready, she decided and left the strange stone forest to itself.

SIX

Kichebo kept to the fringes of her territory, avoiding any sight of the ruin. Often she thought of leaving to journey farther downriver, but instinct told her that any hunting ground there would be claimed. The area about the ruin was hers by default, for none of her kind would come near it.

She pushed all thoughts of her experience within the ruin from her mind, concentrating fiercely on hunting, patroling, and marking the bounds of her land. Even as she made each sign of possession, she felt a twinge of bitter loneliness, knowing how useless it was to leave such marks where no other cheetah would find them.

It was Menk who made Kichebo's outcast existence bearable. The odd furless creature could sense when her companion was at her gloomiest, for at such times she would crawl close and put her arms around Kichebo's neck. Sometimes the hug was too tight, but it gave a rough kind of comfort that warmed even as it half choked her.

Menk surprised her by imitating growls and gestures,

often using them back to her. The creature often abandoned her upright stance to scramble on all fours, tried to sharpen her blunt fingernails against a tree as Kichebo did her dewclaws, and kept looking at her bare backside as if wondering why it did not sprout a tail. Her brown eyes were so deep and alive that Kichebo often wondered whether the mind that lay behind them might contain more than the reckless inquisitiveness of a monkey or baboon. The way Menk repeated sounds as if they might be meaningful words tempted Kichebo to teach her to speak.

The shape of Menk's face and mouth made it difficult to reproduce the exact sounds that made up Kichebo's language. Having no whiskers, tail, or facial markings was even more of a handicap. Kichebo realized for the first time how much of what she thought of as speech among her kind was actually gesture or expression. It seemed so natural to combine a spoken word with a certain wave of the tail or twitch of the whiskers that she had never thought the sound itself could not carry the full meaning of what she said.

However much Menk might struggle to achieve the exact pitch and tone of a yowl or chirr, the best she could do seemed painfully crude. Adding tearline stripes to her face with black mud helped a little until the mud cracked and fell off. And a ropy vine Menk tied around her waist could not curl and wave like a real tail.

It soon became clear to Kichebo that any spoken communication between them could serve only the most basic of needs. She could warn, scold, or direct her companion, but any exchange more subtle or complex was impossible. Menk's hands in part made up for her rudimentary speech, for they were eloquent in the language of touch. The feel of little fingers stroking Kichebo's cheek fur with delicacy and tenderness said what words, even those of her own kind, could not.

Even so, Menk could not state the cheetah's hunger for the sight or smell of her own breed. At times her longing grew so strong that Menk's clumsy tongue, questioning eyes, and strange, exploring hands seemed alien and repulsive. At such times, she had to retreat and be by herself.

Sometimes, when she had left Menk asleep or hidden in some safe place, she would wander upriver at twilight. She never expected to encounter another cheetah, for she was far from their hunting grounds. Gradually, as these expeditions led her farther afield from her territory, she crossed trails used by messengers. Some had fallen into disuse, for they smelled only of gravel and dust, but some still bore the faint scents of those who traveled them.

And so it was that one evening found her several miles upriver from her territory, hidden in a thorn thicket on a hill overlooking a messenger trail. She wasn't sure why she had come or what she would do. It was the smell on the trail itself that held her, for the scent told of someone recently passing, someone who might return the same way.

Her hiding place gave her a long view up and down the trail. Wind blew across the path before it ruffled her fur, taking her scent away from anyone approaching. The sun sat on the western hills, fat and complacent from the daily hunt. At last, when the last light was starting to fade and the wind hissed through the thorns, Kichebo heard a faint patter of feet on the trail.

She tensed with wariness and impatience. The light was growing so dim she feared she wouldn't be able to see and

97

she strained her neck, pushing her nose further between spiny branches. The wind shifted, bringing to her the stranger's female scent. Only once before had she known a similar odor; she had found it on a trail taken by one who, Nasseken said, had lived many years and was soon to die. A harsh, dusty, dry smell, telling of gauntness, worn teeth, and the weariness of age. Kichebo had retreated from it then and she wanted to retreat now, but it was too late, for the traveler was drawing close.

The stranger's legs moved in a stiff but steady trot, her neck was thin, but her head was carried high. Yet on the nape and down the back of this one who smelled so old was the smoky gray mantle borne by young cubs. And the sun's last light briefly lit eyes that were neither orange nor amber but blue.

Surely this was just a great overgrown cub that was late in shedding its cape of gray fur, the young cheetah thought, but the stranger's scent and gait said otherwise. Kichebo became so caught up in the conflict between her different senses that she almost failed to notice when the other slowed her pace and began swinging her head around warily.

At this, Kichebo grew still inside her nest of thorns, and at last the stranger passed on, leaving a faint haze of dust and another mystery for the cub to puzzle over. She stayed by the trail for a long time after the traveler had gone, almost hoping and dreading at the same time that she would return.

At last Kichebo wandered back downriver by moonlight, her mind chewing on the experience as if it were a bone between her jaws. Try as she might, she couldn't crack it. She was certain of only one thing: whoever she had seen on the messenger trail was as different from other cheetahs as she.

By the time she reached her own territory once again, weariness and hunger pushed all thoughts of the stranger aside. She spent the following evenings hunting, playing with Menk, and walking the boundaries of her land.

Kichebo was snoozing in the long shadows of late afternoon when a burst of noise woke her. From the riverbank came the quarrelsome sound of shrieks interspersed with snarling and spitting. As she shot out of her resting place, her nape fur erect, she heard the unmistakable slap of mud hitting a wet pelt. Kichebo crashed through a clump of reeds, yowling an answer to Menk's angry screams. A fistful of muck flew past her nose to land squarely on the flank of Menk's opponent. It was followed immediately by a speckled egg that splattered high on the other cheetah's shoulder, painting the gray mantle fur with yolk.

Kichebo tried to stop but slid in the mud-slick grass, frantically backpedaling her hind feet. She halted almost nose to nose with the stranger. Her gaze traveled down to the prominent ribs and drawn belly. She met the stranger's gaze once more and read the unwillingly told story of debility and growing starvation.

"You!" she blurted.

The blue eyes widened, then narrowed. For an instant, Kichebo could only stare. Then the other flinched as another mudball disintegrated at her feet. Even as Kichebo spun around to face Menk, she knew the last throw had been halfhearted. A warning hiss was enough to make the creature put down a second egg she was hefting.

"I suppose I should thank you for calling off your egg-flinging baboon," said the other cheetah tartly. "I assume it is yours, although I must say your taste in companions leaves much to be desired. I've never seen such a hairless, vicious—"

"Menk's not vicious," Kichebo retorted, but the other continued, "You yourself are a sight not seen hereabouts. By the scats of the sun, for once the messenger-tales are true. A black cheetah."

The stare from the old eyes was surprisingly keen, making Kichebo feel uncomfortable. She twitched her ears back. "I don't know who you are, old one, but you talk too freely for one who hunts on my ground without my leave."

"And you speak too self-righteously for one who hides beside messenger-trails and spies on those who travel them."

"You knew I was there? But the wind blew my scent away. . . ."

"There are other things besides scent that can betray you, youngster. A great many things," the aged cheetah answered. She swung around toward the water. Immediately Menk tensed and groped for the discarded egg.

"Tell that bare-rumped ape of yours that I just want to wash off before I go on my way."

Kichebo quieted Menk while the old one bathed herself in the river and shook dry. As she gazed around at the scene of the fight, she could read what had happened. A nest containing one broken egg lay amid flattened reeds. Menk often ate eggs and she was good at finding them. In pursuit of these delicacies, she went where a cheetah couldn't, aloft into the trees or across boggy ground. The nest looked as if it had been moved some distance by hands, not jaws. Menk had found this prize and almost lost it to the intruder.

"Thief," said Kichebo under her breath.

"What was that, youngster? I didn't quite hear you."

Kichebo spun around, suddenly regretting her accusation. "I'm sorry." The word slipped out before she could stop it.

The other only eyed Kichebo with that sharp blue gaze. "Sorry that you called me a thief or that I am one?"

The young cheetah was suddenly overwhelmed by pity so strong it was almost disgust. To be reduced to filching eggs from a furless ape to survive. . . .

"Who are you? Why did you come here," she asked sharply.

"My curiosity chooses the trails I take. You wanted to know about me, so I wanted to know about you. I tracked you back from where you left the messenger-trail. The incident with the eggs was . . . an opportunity. As for a name, I have one, but since everyone calls me Gray Cape, I've almost forgotten it myself."

"Are you a messenger?"

"I suppose I am, although the news those who call themselves my hunting-group give me to carry is largely useless, since they are convinced I'm going to drop dead in my tracks before I get there." Gray Cape ended her sentence with a grunt, as if the idea was too ridiculous for words, but a slightly strained look on her face said it wasn't.

Kichebo swallowed, unable to think of anything more to say. She caught Gray Cape's glance at the nest containing the one remaining egg, but the old female made no move toward it. She only lowered her head and began plodding away along the shore.

From the yellow smears around Menk's mouth and the pieces of shell sticking to her muddy hands, Kichebo knew that she had managed to consume at least part of her booty before being interrupted. Would it really hurt to let Gray Cape have what remained? Quickly Kichebo made Menk return the other egg to the nest and called the old cheetah back.

Menk squirmed and grimaced as Gray Cape crouched beside the nest, carefully maneuvered an egg between her forepaws and punctured the top with her teeth. After scooping out the contents with her tongue, she ate some shell fragments, spitting out the rest. Kichebo kept the restive Menk at bay while their unexpected guest finished her meal and scrubbed egg-white from her muzzle.

The aged cheetah stretched out on her side, lifted her head, and gave Menk an appraising stare. The creature lowered her brows, crossed her arms, and glared back.

"Doesn't like me. Baboons never do. Silly business anyway, carrying one about on your back. Can't really talk to them as though they had any sense, but they're better than talking to yourself, I suppose."

"I think Menk has some . . . sense," said Kichebo carefully.

"Of course you do. Everyone who's addled enough to want one thinks his or her companion is the cleverest thing on four feet."

Despite the old cheetah's abrasive manner and abrupt replies, she was a good listener. Kichebo spoke hesitantly at first but soon found herself eagerly sharing the story of how she had found Menk amid a burning pile of wreckage. She found, to her annoyance, that Gray Cape was much more interested in her description of the object itself than how Menk had been freed from it.

"Hah," said the aged cheetah after Kichebo had dredged her mind for what details she could remember. "I think I know what it was. I've seen them from far away. Shiny things like big bugs, running along without legs."

Kichebo remembered the night the firefly net had nearly descended on her and what she had seen reflecting the moonlight. Her nape prickled at the memory of the creatures that had emerged from it, with their strange way of moving on two legs and their sticks that could strike from afar. This was easier to describe, for terror had etched the scene in her memory. Her ears twitched back as she told it.

"Two legs, two legs," Gray Cape muttered, turning her gaze to Menk, who was down on hands and knees. For an instant Kichebo felt bewildered, then she knew. To hurl eggs and mud at Gray Cape, the little creature had to rear up on her hind feet. Was the other cheetah suggesting that Menk was kin to the two-legged hunters who had tried to capture her? The thought made her fur rise.

"No! She only gets up on her hind paws to throw things," Kichebo said quickly, wanting to cut off Gray Cape's speculation before it could alarm her. Even as she spoke, she didn't believe her own argument and ended lamely, "If you're thinking she's one of those creatures, you're wrong. And she's too small."

"I'm not saying that she is one. But after all, you did find her in one of their burned-out beetle shells." Gray Cape paused, eyeing Kichebo curiously. "She may be some sort of monkey, but she's not a baboon. They all have tails of some kind, but she doesn't; not even a stump."

"I don't care what she is. I found her, I like her, and I'm going to keep her." Kichebo began to bristle.

Gray Cape, however, only grinned. "Keep your dewclaws sheathed, youngster."

Kichebo took a long breath and smoothed her fur, annoyed at herself for getting defensive. This rickety old female was no threat to her or Menk. Why did it matter what Gray Cape thought or said?

The latter gathered her feet beneath her and stood up stiffly. Catching sight of the huge archway in the distance, she padded over to it and looked up at the carvings while the breeze teased the long silver fur along her back. She glanced back at Kichebo as if expecting her to follow.

"You go," said the young cheetah quickly, hoping her sudden reluctance didn't show. "I've seen it many times before."

Gray Cape, however, wasn't fooled. "Scared, youngster? I suppose you have heard the silly tales that say this is supposed to be forbidden ground. I'm surprised you believe such nonsense."

"I don't," said Kichebo sharply. "Menk and I came here so no one would bother us."

"Obviously because they believe the stories they tell. But you don't, do you?"

Kichebo's tail gave an involuntary twitch. She felt caught between wanting to prove that she was not frightened by old superstitions and her knowledge that something strange had indeed happened to her here. With a start she realized that Gray Cape had gone through the archway and was standing in the shadow of a crumbling wall that soared above her. She was looking around intently, with no change in manner or signs of uneasiness. Just like Nasseken and Beshon, Kichebo thought. The place didn't affect them either. I wonder why I'm the only one who seems to feel it.

Gray Cape was still waiting. Torn between her wish to earn the old one's respect and her reluctance to face whatever waited for her within the ruin, Kichebo hesitated. Impatience made the decision for her. Lowering her head and clenching her teeth together, she dashed through the archway, hoping that Gray Cape's presence would keep any more strange happenings at bay.

Even as she emerged from the shadow of the gateway and ran toward the other cheetah, the feeling began again, this time much stronger. Gray Cape's form seemed to dim before her eyes and she felt she was slowing down, then falling sideways in a long, slow topple. She tried to call out, but she no longer had a voice to use. Her feet seemed to leave the ground and her eyes could see only swirling white, like early morning mist rising from the river. She wondered, with an oddly dulled fear, whether she had somehow fallen sick or was this death? What she didn't expect was the voice that spoke to her directly through her mind rather than her ears.

I'm sorry, it said, trying to sound apologetic, although she sensed a barely controlled eagerness. *I did not mean to upset you. You are much more sensitive to my touch than I imagined.*

Your touch? she thought, bewildered.

The way I reach to you through your mind, as I am doing now.

Who are you? Kichebo was suddenly frightened at this part of her that had started to speak in such an independent manner.

One very much like yourself, came the answer. *At least, that is my hope.* It paused. *Let me withdraw a little. I feel I am overwhelming you.* Even as the voice spoke, the feeling of total disorientation retreated and Kichebo thought her senses were returning. Dimly she sensed that she lay on warm sand, with Gray Cape standing over her.

That's better, said her unseen companion, although the young cheetah wasn't sure she agreed. She lay tensely with her heart thrashing against her ribs, wondering if this was madness.

Daughter of the sun, I have never before reached one such as you. Surely you are one of my kind, but I must be sure. Show yourself to me.

How? Kichebo was completely baffled.

Through your own eyes. There is still water nearby. Let us go to it.

She blinked and found herself able to see, but the face of Gray Cape above her seemed strangely distant and she couldn't hear what she said. Relieved that her body belonged in part to her again, Kichebo lurched to her feet and staggered toward the river.

No, said the voice softly. *Hapi's current muddies its flow. There is a pool. I will show you.*

Kichebo found herself picking her way between fallen stones and over hillocky ground with a knowledge that wasn't hers. Her inward guide let her halt for an instant to glance back at Gray Cape, who was shadowing her closely. Her feet took her through a copse of willow trees whose roots wove through broken sandstone blocks to reach the water of a pool. There in a sunlit patch on the edge, she leaned out and gazed at her reflection.

As she gazed at the outline of her head, made to seem even darker by the brilliant blue of the sky behind it, she felt as though another were looking out through her eyes and seeing a sight much longed for. It was not she who felt pleasure as she noticed in the still water the form and shape of her face, the curve of gold tearlines against a coal-black muzzle and the delicate amber markings on the edges of both ears.

Bidden by the inward prompting, she turned sideways so that the length of her body lay before her in the pool. Something made her lift her chin and the gold tip of her tail.

Pleased you are with your beauty, sun-daughter, and it is right, said the voice again. Kichebo caught her breath. Never before had her color and markings brought her anything but trouble. Not even Nasseken, who had loved her, called her beautiful. Yet she looked at herself, knowing she was. She suddenly dared to hope that the one who spoke within her mind shared the same beauty.

Her wish was answered without words. The reflection before her seemed to lift and shimmer, as if a ripple had passed across it. When the image became clear again, Kichebo saw not her own reflection but that of another. It bore the same black pelt, the same sun-colored markings on face, ears, and tail-tip, but the body was larger and more angular than hers. Amber-brown eyes looked out at her from a wider face that was definitely male.

His image dissolved. The quiet rustling of leaves in her ears made her aware of her own senses once again. He had gone. For an instant Kichebo continued to gaze into the pool as if she could find him there. She raised her head as Gray Cape came alongside and peered suspiciously into the water.

"You won't see him. He's gone," said Kichebo, without thinking.

"What?" The sharp voice and even keener gaze jolted

the young cheetah out of her daze. "Youngster, there's no one here except you and me. At least I know I am. I'm not so sure about you."

Unable to reply, Kichebo stared again into the pool.

"Why don't you come out of the sun? That black coat of yours probably gathers too much heat."

Kichebo grimaced at the memory of a similar request. "I suppose you want me to go soak myself in Hapi's water."

Gray Cape paused with one paw lifted. "In what?"

"Hapi. The river. It has a name," Kichebo added patiently.

"Hmph. Never heard that before," Gray Cape grunted and Kichebo, with a mild shock, realized she hadn't known either until. . . .

"Come on, youngster. A soak wouldn't be such a bad idea." Obediently Kichebo followed as the old cheetah led her to the shore. Menk joined them and trailed behind.

"Now," said Gray Cape, once Kichebo was reclining in the tepid flow, "when you begin a hunt, you follow tracks, one at a time. To start with, I don't even know your name."

Kichebo told her.

"That's better. You nearly frightened the fur off me when you ran through the arch and then started weaving back and forth until you fell over. Thought I'd killed you, though how I didn't know. What happened?"

Carefully she told Gray Cape how the ruin had haunted her ever since she had come to it, and perhaps even before. She described the strange sensation that descended on her whenever she passed beneath the arch that led to the place of tumbled stones.

"The feeling doesn't always come over me when I go near the ruin, but it has happened more than once." She brooded, gazing at the wavering image of her forepaws beneath the shallow current. "This is the first time I've heard the voice. His voice," she added, glancing up at Gray Cape, who sat just out of the water. At the aged cheetah's answering look, Kichebo turned her head away. "You must think I've been bitten by someone with the foaming sickness."

"I've seen that illness before and you haven't got it. If you are mad, it is madness of a different sort."

"But it is madness."

"Not necessarily, youngster. What you tell me is outside anything I know, but that doesn't mean it isn't real. This place isn't anything made by wind or water, but it is here and someone made it. I suspect that someone was not of our kind either, unless the sun-cheetah was in the mood for playing with rocks. Who is the one who speaks to you? Is he a cheetah?"

"Yes," said Kichebo eagerly. "He's dark, like me, with the same markings."

"Is that what you saw in that lake? I thought you were just admiring yourself."

With some difficulty, Kichebo managed to tell Gray Cape why she had gone to the hidden pool and what she had seen there. The other fell silent, and Kichebo listened to the sound of the great river. Hapi's voice, she thought to herself. He knows this river. He told me its name.

After a long time, Gray Cape said something unexpected. "Your . . . friend. Do you think he'll come back?"

Kichebo rolled over in the water to glare at the old one, suspicious that she was being humored after all. One look at the other's face told her the question was honest. She felt a surge of affection for this newcomer. Gray Cape didn't

think she was mad or so lonely as to make an imaginary companion out of her own reflection and give him a voice . . .
all of which could have easily happened and perhaps had?
No. She wasn't going to believe her experience was self-
delusion. His voice had been too . . . different.

I will come back, he said softly, as if from far away. *I
have much more to tell you.*

SEVEN

After recovering from her encounter, Kichebo went hunting, leaving Gray Cape asleep on the riverbank. Although there was no spoken agreement, Kichebo brought back her catch, a young warthog, and shared it with her new friend. Neither said anything further, but when the meal was finished, she knew Gray Cape would stay.

Although Kichebo was initially eager for her other strange companion to return, her desire faded into ambivalence and then uncertainty. Yes, he was one such as she, one she thought could never exist, for wasn't she alone in her difference from the rest of her kind? He satisfied a deep longing in her to know she wasn't unique. At last there was another who would know how she felt, who shared her difficulties and might help her understand them.

Even so, she felt afraid. It was one thing to welcome as companion someone you could see, smell, and listen to through your own ears. It was quite another to accept a disembodied voice who could take control of your body and plunge you into alien and terrifying experiences. She remembered well what had happened when she first entered the great gateway.

Half hoping and half dreading such a thought, she chased it away and tried to keep it at a distance by throwing herself almost feverishly into the experience of the moment. She tried to convince herself that hunting, marking, playing with Menk, and talking with Gray Cape were all that constituted her life.

Try as she might, however, she couldn't shut him out of her mind. Often she woke from dreams not her own, with strange remnants of another's thoughts left in her mind. Sometimes these little pieces were parts of answers to questions she could not help asking. She thought she asked them only of herself and was annoyed to find that he had overheard.

Who was he? Where was he? Here, the answer came, in one of the leftover thoughts. In this place. Then why don't I see you, she asked. Because although I am here in space, I am far distant in time. What is time, she asked, and woke from a dream with her head full of strange ideas.

So puzzled was she that she broke her self-imposed silence and spoke about it to Gray Cape, saying, "This thing he calls time is like a series of tracks that you can follow either forward or backward. Each footprint is a 'now' and they all go in one direction. We are all at a certain footprint. When I was young, I was in a footprint that was farther back. When I am old, I will be in a footprint farther ahead. I'm not used to thinking about such things, but I understand. Does it make sense to you, Gray Cape?"

The old cheetah only looked at her in a way that made

her wonder whether she should have even mentioned the subject. After first suggesting that Kichebo might benefit from another soaking in the river, Gray Cape agreed that the thought was reasonable, if a little outlandish.

"It convinces me that your friend does indeed exist. From what I know of you, Kichebo, you wouldn't come up with such thoughts by yourself. Not that you aren't clever enough, but he seems to have had more . . . experience . . . in these sorts of things, whatever they are."

Kichebo looked back at her with a strange mixture of annoyance and relief. Admitting her fear was hard, even to one who understood. Explaining it was even harder, but Gray Cape listened patiently.

"Youngster, you're fighting something, and I think I know what. You haven't gone near the pool, and you won't admit you're thinking of your strange friend even though he's leaving his footprints all over your mind."

The young cheetah hung her head, unable to answer.

"Perhaps what is hardest for you about this is that it reminds you again of your difference from others. Deep down, I think you do believe he exists, even though you have tried to convince yourself it is madness. I have seen you these last few days, trying to be just an ordinary cheetah. You aren't."

Kichebo stared at the drawn and aged face with its impossibly youthful blue eyes and crown of fine silver-gray fur. These were no empty words, coming from one who had been forced to accept her own differences.

Gray Cape leaned forward and said earnestly, "You believe in him. Do you trust him?"

113

The young cheetah had to search down to the bottom of herself for the answer. "I am afraid, but . . . yes."

"Then everything is simple. I will be there to help you however I can."

Kichebo opened her mouth to protest the foregone conclusion, but, even as she drew breath to speak, she realized Gray Cape was right. Sooner or later she was going to have to face the mystery in the ruin and the even greater mystery of her own self. "Tomorrow," she said and was not surprised when she felt slightly better.

"Tomorrow, then," Gray Cape replied.

In late afternoon of the following day, when the long shadows hid the two cheetahs, they passed beneath the great arch and crossed into the place of tumbled stones. This time Menk was not with them. Earlier that day, Kichebo had purposefully tired her out by rough play and tucked her into a safe hideaway where she would nap until evening.

Remembering how the first contact with her unseen guide had literally knocked her over, Kichebo lay down, waiting for the disorienting sensation that heralded his approach. Gray Cape sat beside her, staring at the huge block wall that cast its shade over them, as if the one they waited for would emerge from its face.

It was some time before Kichebo felt the dimming of her sight and the dulling of her other senses. Instinctively her body fought to repossess them. She tensed and trembled as the mist swirled before her eyes. Gray Cape pressed close as if she knew Kichebo's sense of touch was blunted, saying again and again that she was there and would stay. The old cheetah's voice seemed to become a soothing chant, almost like a purr, and it helped Kichebo to ease out of her fear and let herself go.

As before, she felt as though she were falling, and the fall continued endlessly until the swirling mist before her eyes went to gray and then finally to black.

She did not know how long is was before sensations returned, but she knew at once they were not hers. Everything had changed. Even the air around her had undergone a strange metamorphosis, for it smelled stale and close. The scent reminded her of animal skin, although not the pelt of any creature she had ever caught. As she gained further knowledge of her surroundings, she realized that her head, or rather, the head of the one whose senses she shared, was bound with a covering that cut off sight. She felt a surge of panic.

Do not fear, daughter-of-a-far-time. My masters have only hooded me. The well-remembered voice was quiet yet strong.

"Hooded you?" she asked, although she wasn't sure whether she spoke the answer aloud or just in her thoughts.

Yes. My handler has placed a leather covering over my head so I cannot see. It is done to all the hunting cheetahs, lest we catch sight of prey before our masters are ready to release us.

Much of this Kichebo couldn't understand, but the calm reassurance in the other's reply eased her fears. She allowed the change to complete itself until she was only a thought within his mind. She had left herself to become a dream that walked with his legs, that touched with his whiskers, and saw with his eyes.

His feet were drawn up beneath him and she felt the movement of the platform on which he rode. It lurched and swayed, but he knew how to counter each motion, as if he had done this many times before. Occasionally an unexpected jerk rocked him and made his teeth click together.

To Kichebo, this was utterly strange and terrifying. She started to flee out of his mind to her own self, but he called her back.

My master takes me in an ox-drawn cart. It is uncomfortable, but I have grown used to it. It is the way we are taken to the plains where game is to be coursed.

"Then do you hunt today?"

No, daughter, he answered, and there was gentle amusement in his reply. *The waters of Hapi are rising in the month men call Tekhi. I go to the Temple of Ipet-Sut at Karnak where my master is to be crowned Lord of the Two Lands.*

Kichebo understood almost nothing of this, but, before she could ask, there came a request, not so clearly formed in words, that she observe in silence and not disturb him with questions. By quieting her curiosity, she would focus less on herself and would be able to join him more completely, gaining both his understanding and his experience.

She obeyed, finding herself able to dissolve the final barriers that separated her awareness from his.

The cart creaks and rumbles. Smells of dust and oxen fill my nostrils. My collar is heavy about my neck, for it is not the one I wear for the chase. I am thrown to one side as the oxen grunt and bellow. The cart is turning. A strap is fixed to my collar and I feel a slight pull. My keeper is holding me steady as the cart swings around into place.

A hoarse man-voice calls, "Bring up the pharaoh's escort! Let the crowd give way so that Asu-Kheknemt, the Swift One of Aten, may join the Child of the Sun in procession."

The Swift One of Aten rises to his feet (for it is I they speak of) and waits for the cart to halt. Such names these man creatures have for me and for themselves! If my master were truly the sun's cub, he would be not man but cheetah. Would the celestial mother of my kind bear young who walk on two legs? Of course not! But I let them keep their illusions, for their eyes are not strong enough to see the spots on that bright coat. Perhaps one day I will share the truth with my master and hope that he will be strong enough to accept it and rejoice in it.

I often think of my master. I will see him soon, but he will no longer be the boy who ran beside me in the gardens of the North Palace. The journey from Aten's City here to Thebes must have been longer for him than for me. We have both traveled the same distance, but this day he must step from prince to king while I remain as I have been: his companion in all things and even this.

Hands lift the hood from my head. A tug on my lead bids me to jump down, although I move blindly, dazzled by the sun's light. I blink to regain my sight as warm rays soak into my black coat. My keepers will shade me later with a canopy, but I do not want it now.

The people of the Two Lands are here in massed crowds that stretch along the avenue of ram-headed sphinxes from the temple's gate to Hapi's banks. No other animal I know

117

comes together in such great herds as these men creatures. It is their habit of packing together that makes me still disdain humans, although I have lived all my life among them.

Brown bodies crush together into one mass; voices cry out as one; it seems they have lost their individual selves. Their smells mix and the heady scents of perfumes, unguents, oils, and sweat assault my nose. I narrow my eyes and wrinkle my muzzle. Titters of amusement come from the crowd at the sight of my grimace, but I have no care for their laughter. I lift my head and stand away from them, knowing that as the last sacred black cheetah, I am unique and alone.

And so is he. I can see him now as he comes from the river where the royal barge is docked. The king-to-be of the Two Lands is a shy nine-year-old child who has not grown tall enough that he must bend when he strokes my back. He walks bareheaded, his scalp shaven, showing to all the elongated shape of his skull. At first I thought it a deformity, but he does not think it so and indeed displays it proudly as a mark of his lineage. His narrow chest is also bare and only a starched and pleated loincloth covers his hips. His unshod feet fall softly on the white sand and palm boughs spread for his passing.

I leave my prints in the same sand as I am led forward to the prince. His eyes are outlined in black kohl and his face is remote with the schooled expression royalty must wear. Then he sees me and longing springs forth from his eyes. I know how much he wants to fling his arms around my neck to share his excitement and uncertainty, as he did before we were parted for our separate journeys to Thebes.

But here he must keep his feelings shuttered and play that he is a man, not a shy young boy. It is much easier for me, for I am grown and have the natural dignity of my kind. Yet behind my mask I share his feelings of excitement, uneasiness, and yes, there is also fear.

He has been brought to the throne too early, this little prince, Tutankhaten. He has been pushed forward to repair the hurt done to this land by the one who preceded him, his brother Akhenaten. Yet being a child and one who loved his brother (for I was there and I saw), he may be reluctant to do all that may be asked of him.

I feel trembling fingers slip beneath my collar. Tutankhaten's grasp becomes firm; his hand ceases to shake, and he gives me a small private smile as I press against his legs. He does not enter the kingship alone, for I am with him. For this I was bred from among the hunting cheetahs of the palace. Two years ago, I was taken from the House of the Swift and given as companion to him. I know and love him better than any other. He knows of that love, for he has told me that he will have images of me carved and placed within his tomb. I will be striding, with head lifted, toward the far horizon, bearing his spirit on my back.

I am distracted from these thoughts as two men in rich dress step to either side of us. Aye, the king's uncle and the Divine Father, walks beside the boy. For that I am grateful. Aye is stern, yet kind and one whom I trust. The other, the general Horemheb, takes his place beside me. The man's face is grim and his eyes show a glitter I don't like, for my years among these creatures have taught me how to read the thoughts in their faces. To Horemheb, the boy is an impediment and I am a mere animal.

I think he would be surprised and dismayed if he knew how much I am capable of understanding. I have little fear of him, knowing my teeth are equal to any dagger he may have hidden in the folds of his robe. Both Tut and I know my role as protector is far from being just symbolic.

There comes a gentle pull at my collar and I step forth with the king. I narrow my eyes against the sun's glare on bleached linen and the sharp reflections from gold-lapped pectorals worn by nobles. The smells of the street are all around me and would overwhelm me had I not trained myself to bear them. Again comes the sweat smell of horses and men, combined with incense, perfumes, and the odor of sweetmeats being peddled to the crowd.

As the procession approaches the towering first pylon, the temple gates swing open, the sun flashing on their stud fastenings of plated copper and gold. We pass through this great wall, added to Ipet-Sut at Karnak by my young prince's dead father, and emerge into a courtyard. Here we are accompanied only by high officials, and the crowd gives a massed sigh as we pass from sight.

In the courtyard beyond, General Horemheb raises his eyes to the *tekhen*, the spears of stone that pierce the sky and whose long shadows fall across our path. I know this man would seek to raise another such shaft, mightier than any that stand there now, and dedicate it to himself. Why, exactly, I do not know, for my kind do not have such desires. But I have lived long enough among these human creatures to understand envy. It is hard to keep my fur from rising; I dislike this man.

And what is before us now, half-dancing, half-running, with one arm extended to take the hand of the king? I start and growl, even though I have seen these masked priests before. The feathers of the falcon head rustle, and his beady eyes gleam as the head turns from side to side, mimicking the motions of the real bird. This is their god Horus and he takes my king's little hand, leading us both through a second gate into the temple.

Here another priest bearing the plumes of Amon reaches for my king's other hand. With regret, Tut releases my collar, his fingers lingering for a moment on my head. Aye stays behind and so, I am thankful, does Horemheb. The older man takes the strap attached to my collar and this I permit. Aye knows more of my nature than Horemheb or any of these priests; only the young king himself knows more about the Swift One of Aten than does the Divine Father.

He walks me through a maze of columns to a shallow pool. There, in a shaft of sunlight coming from an opening in the temple roof, the boy stands. He is submerged to his knees and grimaces as the costumed priests pour water over him from golden ewers. More priests stand at the pool's square corners, masked and garbed as gods. There waves the ibis beak of learned Thoth. Those erect ears and that pointed jackal muzzle belong to Set. I see falcon-headed Horus-of-the-Horizon and across from him, another bird-god.

Though these gods are not mine, I know them all from their statues about the palace and their images on papyrus. There is no god bearing the head of a cheetah atop the body of a man. It is not needed, for the humans believe the Aten, in his swift aspect, is here in me, just as the essence of Amon-Ra resides in the nine-year-old boy who tries not to squirm as the priests solemnly douse him repeatedly with sacred water.

Now it is my turn. I don't mind getting wet, and Aye has trained me in the fountain at Malkata Palace. When he releases me, I stride into the pool beside my shivering master and accept my share of the ceremonial deluge. I can see in the eyes of the unmasked priests and General Horemheb, who stands with them to one side, that they dislike this. To these men I am but an animal, whose presence profanes the crowning ritual. They can do nothing about it; Tut wanted me beside him and Aye has so ordered it be done.

The ibis, the jackal, and the two bird-gods assist Tut out and dry him. Acolytes hold a cloth over me so I can shake myself without disrupting the ceremony. I do so, but somehow my tail slips from behind the sheet and sends a sprinkle of droplets toward General Horemheb. I would like to anoint him with a more pungent spray, but Aye would not tolerate that.

By the time the boy is dressed again, my coat is fluffy and the remaining dampness is refreshing against the stuffy heat in the temple. Again the prince takes my collar and, from the gleam in his eye, I know he saw the flick of my tail that showered the general and the priests.

We are then escorted deeper into the recesses of Karnak, across a second courtyard bearing the twin *tekhen* of Hatshepsut, which dazzle us with the sun's brilliance on their sheaths of beaten silver. Trotting to keep up with the fast-striding priests, we pass the sculpted colossi of Osiris and plunge into the dimness of the Hypostyle Hall.

In the north pavilion, we again meet priests disguised as gods. They surround us with chanting and a flurry of hands forming ritual gestures. Then, we are brought to the south pavilion, where carved papyrus fans atop stone pillars support massive roof beams. I know what the king will encounter here, for I listened carefully when Aye told him. He must pay his respects to the god Amon's daughter, "the great in magic," the snake-goddess.

She will be only a costumed priestess, I think, and so does the boy, but as I place my forepaw on the threshold, my sense of smell tells me this is not so. I do not hesitate but walk with him to the raised lintel. A spear of sunlight from a hidden opening strikes the place where the goddess must stand, but, as the boy and I draw closer, I see that the human form we expect is not there.

The scent becomes stronger, a musty smell, speaking to me of coils and scales. My nose does not lie, for she rises before us, swaying gently: a great cobra. The boy pales. Behind us, Aye seizes the high priest and speaks angrily. I hear the whining reply.

"It is no doing of ours, Divine Father. Amon's daughter chooses what aspect she will take." The priest pauses and exchanges glances with Horemheb. "Does the prince then refuse the courtesy due the goddess?"

"No!" the boy cries in a voice made sharp by fear.

"Son of the Sun," begins Aye, but Tut wheels to face him. "No," the young king repeats in a soft, defiant voice. "If this is the test prepared for me, uncle, I must meet it. I will not be shamed before Amon or any other god."

It is then that I long to have a human voice to speak the words the others can't or won't say. This is treachery, young master! This is the way they have planned that you meet your death, with no one to accuse but the goddess herself! My eyes go to Horemheb and the expression in his face answers me. He has no need to carry a concealed dagger. His weapon is there on the lintel before us and she does not fear my teeth.

"I know," the boy says softly, speaking so only I can hear him. He lays his hand on me and kneels before the dais. I can only crouch mutely beside him as he extends his hands toward Amon's daughter in ritual embrace. She opens her hood and rises higher between his two open trembling palms. I fight to control myself, for if I flinch or growl, she will strike. I can do nothing; she is the one creature whose attack is faster than mine.

Sweat from the child's forehead and frightened tears from his eyes run the black kohl in smears down his cheeks, giving him black tearlines like one of my kind. I know then that he is a true son of the sun-cheetah's blessing. Even if he does not share my form, I know that he is not only my companion but my brother.

Slowly his fingertips meet behind the snake's hood, and his eyes stare into hers. No one can come so close to a cobra and not be bitten, I think, but still she does not strike. Gradually Tut's hands part and sink to his sides. Sunlight gleams on burnished copper scales as the snake sways and bows, acknowledging his right to rule.

He rises and backs away from her, drawing me with him. He knows I will move with care, trying not to let my claws click on the polished stone floor. Any abrupt sound or motion might alarm Amon's daughter, and we are still within her striking range.

Once we are away from her, we both draw huge sighs of relief. We notice that the muttering of the priests has ceased, giving way to a tense silence.

Again we two are escorted by Aye, Horemheb, and the priests to the oldest part of the temple where there stands a shrine of rose granite on a sandstone base. There the boy again kneels, with his back to a statue.

Now I lie beside him as the priests recite all the names by which he will be known. Thanks to Aye's foresight and careful training of me, he had lived to claim his throne. Rise, then, little Nebkheprure-Tutankhaten and be invested with the crook and flail of your office. The ibis-god Thoth shall write your name on the leaves of the sacred persea tree and I will walk with you, seeing you whole and untouched, out of this den of king-slayers.

The wearying ceremony draws to an end. Soon he will bestow his blessings on the rejoicing people of the Two Lands. With his own guard and loyal men about him, he will be safe, at least for now. I may relax my watch and let myself be taken back to the cart in which I was brought. But before I go, there is another who must take her leave. She has been here long and subjected to things she does not understand. I will not ask her to face more until she is ready.

Fair journey, daughter-of-a-far-time. Until we choose to seek each other again.

EIGHT

The cool wind ruffling Kichebo's fur felt like the caress of a human hand. The boy had touched her so just as he left. No, it was not she whom he touched, Kichebo realized, coming awake. Not she. The other black cheetah, Asu-Kheknemt.

She lifted her head to the full moon overhead and then looked down to where she stood amid scattered stone blocks in a pallid light. She remembered where she had been before leaving herself. With a slight twinge of alarm, she realized she was no longer in the same place.

"Gray Cape?" she asked, her voice sounding squeaky with uncertainty. The old cheetah was already moving to her side.

"So he brought you back, did he? I was beginning to wonder."

"Where. . . ." Kichebo began but left the question unfinished. "Is this still the ruin?"

Gray Cape's eyes glowed blue-white as she turned to stare at the young cheetah. "You don't remember how you rose from where you sat outside the main wall and walked among these pillars? It is no wonder you're lost."

It was not just the night wind off the river that made Kichebo shiver. She tried to step forward and nearly stumbled over an uptilted block whose edge caught her foreleg.

Again Gray Cape eyed her keenly. "When you came in here, you walked like one asleep or blind, yet you never missed your footing. And when your way was barred, you stood and let me scrape aside the rubble or allowed yourself to be led around it, yet each time you returned to your chosen path."

It is the path I walked with the one from long-ago, when this great place was still new, thought Kichebo. She caught sight of a pale gleam, almost flesh-colored. Moving closer, she saw the time-eaten mass of rose granite atop its sandstone base.

A shuffle and a clatter of pebbles told her someone else had come with Gray Cape. Menk crouched near the old cheetah, gazing at her with a mixture of wariness and a need for comfort. Glittering streaks down her face told Kichebo how painfully bewildered she must have been to see her closest companion stride by in an unseeing trance.

Kichebo chirped softly, bringing Menk to her in a joyful scramble. The arms went around her neck and the smooth face lay against her cheek, hugging away any pangs of remorse. It was no wonder that Asu-Kheknemt looked upon another such face with a love greater than for any of his own kind.

Even as the thought crossed her mind, Kichebo recoiled from it. She warred with two sets of memories: one that saw the boy king as a treasured companion; the other that saw only an upright alien figure with a squashed muzzle and misshapen head lurching about on stick-thin legs. She knew the latter was her own perception, unchanged by whatever feelings Asu-Kheknemt might have had. And to think Menk might be one such. One of those human creatures who were as ugly in spirit as well as body for the way they sought to slay their own kind. No!

Her shudder made her pull away from Menk, but the little creature reclaimed her with a muffled cry and a fierce embrace.

"She's tired and so am I," said Gray Cape, summing up her vigil. Kichebo found her own jaws stretching open in a wide yawn. The old cheetah led the way out of the ruin and Kichebo followed with Menk beside her.

She slept until late the following day and, on waking, found several eggs and a wet catfish near her nose. After she had licked out the eggshells and devoured her namesake, she turned to Gray Cape and Menk, who were lying in the shade nearby. The little creature lay with her head on Gray Cape's ribs, the latter eyeing her with tolerant affection.

"Menk and I thought we would provide you with dinner for a change. We do much better when we cooperate, although there were a few moments when I thought I might end up wearing eggs again."

"Who caught the kichebo?" the young cheetah asked, grinning.

"She laid paws on it, although I had to give it a bite to stop it from thrashing." The elder looked faintly pleased with herself.

With the sharpness taken from her hunger, Kichebo could lie at ease. She wanted to share her experience with Gray Cape, but when she tried, she found herself unable to explain it. At first she thought the difficulty lay in her own inability, but soon she realized that cheetah language lacked the words she needed. Worse still, she realized that she had only borrowed Asu-Kheknemt's experience instead of gaining her own insight.

Yet she had understood some and this she tried to relate to Gray Cape. The old cheetah let her stumble and fall, never showing signs of boredom or impatience. When Kichebo faltered enough to fall silent, the other prodded her on with careful questions.

"So these tumbled stones were once a great above-ground den," said Gray Cape, casting her gaze toward the ruin. "And you say that those of the two-legged kind did not use it as a lair for raising cubs?"

"No. They used it to worship the sun, as we do."

"But we give honor to the sun-cheetah wherever we may be. We don't have to come to a great den raised for such a purpose. What strange creatures you have seen, Kichebo!"

Menk grew restless and wandered away to play in her mudhole by the riverbank. Gray Cape groomed her chest briefly and then asked, "What of this two-legged one who you say was nearly killed? What was it about him that made his kind place him before a cobra coiled to strike?"

Kichebo wrestled with a language that had no word for king and no concept of royal power. "To his kind, he is like a herd-leader among gazelles," she said finally, knowing her description was miserably inadequate. "He holds sway over them and they are a far greater herd than any gathering of prey-beasts. They believe his birth gives him the right to command them, and that they will die if they do not obey."

"And they give that right to one so small and slight as you have described? He sounds like a fawn among bucks." Gray Cape grimaced disdainfully, her tail-tip flopping back and forth.

"Perhaps the choice of such a herd-leader angers some and that is why they would kill him," said the young cheetah thoughtfully, but she knew that simple explanation was not the real answer and she suspected she would be long in learning the truth.

Grap Cape fell silent and Kichebo felt herself drifting to sleep again, lulled by the sound of the river nearby. She woke to the feel of the hot sun on her back and cries that rang in the air. Remembering how such yells had previously torn her from slumber, she sprang up and galloped south along the river, winding her way through palms that shaded the bank. As she charged through a stand of high grass, she glimpsed a mane of long, silvery fur, a patch of brown skin, and then, beyond, a fawn coat with spots. The racket assaulting her ears told her that Gray Cape and Menk were here, but who was with them?

A strange trio met her eyes when she came clear of the grass. Menk was in the middle between Gray Cape and the stranger, her fists wound tight about the ears of the other, who was a rangy male. He danced backward, his head low, snarling in pain, trying to pull away from the bare-skinned ape. Gray Cape had her jaws fastened around Menk's elbow and was trying to drag her free without scoring her skin, but Menk only clung and gave the luckless victim's ears another fierce twist.

With the crown of his head jammed against Menk's stomach, the other cheetah couldn't use his jaws. His fore-paws were free and he had taken some swipes at Menk with blunt claws, judging from the angry red welts on her flank and sides, but he hadn't slashed her with his dewclaws. For some reason, this stranger was holding himself back.

A sharp hiss from Kichebo broke the three apart. Menk hunkered down with her arms about her knees, a sullen expression on her face. Her victim retreated halfway into a thicket, shaking his head and scrubbing at his ears as if to reassure himself they were still attached. Kichebo was beginning to sense something unsettlingly familiar about him when she saw the ragged wound along his neck and shoulder.

For an instant she wanted to vanish back into the grass and let Gray Cape take charge, but her commanding hiss had drawn his attention.

"Well, well," he said after a long stare. "You again. I should know better than to come near you, cub. I seem to end up the worse for it."

"You will, if you try to steal eggs from Menk," Kichebo retorted, but Gray Cape came alongside and interrupted. "It wasn't eggs this time, Kichebo. And he wasn't the thief." Her gaze went to the carcass of a rock hyrax, mangled both by teeth and by hands. The young cheetah stared at it, then at its owner. She couldn't even claim that he had hunted on her ground, for the boundary she had made lay a short distance downriver from where they now stood. Having his rightful prey pilfered was reason enough for making a cheetah strike out to kill, yet he hadn't.

Why, of all the males that roamed the land, did it have to be Rahepsi who showed up here?

"Perhaps," said Gray Cape in a hoarse murmur, "you should train Menk not to attack those she is not familiar with. She wasn't risking much when she fought me, but this male could have killed her."

Even though the old cheetah's words were spoken softly, they seemed to linger in the air and Kichebo had no doubt Rahepsi had heard.

"Yes, I could have killed her, but I didn't," he answered. "I had heard messenger-tales about such a furless ape being taken for a companion by one of our kind. When I saw the creature, I had no wish to anger the one who kept it. I stayed aside until it tried to steal my prey. I have wounds enough," he added, with a penetrating glance at Kichebo.

And the injury got from me may explain why he is here. Unfit to join a hunting group and too weak to hold a place of his own on the trails, he was probably pushed out to wander downriver to a place no one else would want, thought Kichebo, trying to still the old anger that threatened to rise again. She tried to say something, but it was Gray Cape who spoke first.

After asking the newcomer his name, the elderly cheetah said, "Having been greeted by Menk in much the way you were, I compliment you on your restraint. Both Kichebo and I value this creature, strange as it may seem to you, and we appreciate your good judgment. Where do you journey?"

"Nowhere in particular. I am just waiting for this wound

to heal so I may rejoin my brothers in the hunting group," said Rahepsi, confirming Kichebo's guess about his presence this far downriver. He lifted his head, sniffing a breeze that swayed the palm fronds. "You know, this isn't a bad place. I wonder why the messenger-tales say it is unlucky to come here."

You may know soon if you stay around, thought Kichebo, remembering the unsettling events in the ruin. Feeling that she had to make a courteous gesture, she said awkwardly, "If you want to stay and eat your hyrax, I'll keep Menk away. And if you wish to hunt south of my boundary, you may."

Something changed in Rahepsi's eyes as he looked at her. Perhaps he sensed she had done some thinking since the fight in the courting circle, although all he said was, "Thank you, I think I will."

As Kichebo herded Menk away, leaving him to finish his meal in peace, Gray Cape said dryly, "So you know him?"

"I was the one who placed that wound on his shoulder," she answered shortly. "I don't want to talk about it now, but maybe later. . . ."

Gray Cape asked no more questions as she followed Kichebo back to their resting place.

Kichebo did not see Rahepsi that evening or the ones following, but his scent, drifting across the boundary she had marked, told her he had chosen to stay. Her annoyance with him for stirring up unpleasant memories was tempered by the knowledge that she owed him reparation for her attack. It would have been easier for her to deny that debt if he had been brash and forward like the other males in the courting circle, but he wasn't. To Kichebo's dismay, he showed evidence of being not only polite, but kind, and tolerant to the point of being forgiving. It was she who had not forgiven . . . yet.

So she let him stay and hunt the ground downriver from her territory. He marked a boundary alongside hers and she answered back in similar fashion, laying her smell beside his. At first it was done to ensure he did not violate her border, but soon the exchange of marks and smells became a sort of neighborly communication. Once or twice they were not there and Kichebo felt a vague sense of disappointment, dispelled only when she later found fresh evidence of his presence.

Even though she often sought his trace, she would not admit she did so. When she sensed Rahepsi might be hunting or patroling close to her land, she kept away, asking Gray Cape to go instead.

"I don't see why you want to avoid him," said the old cheetah, after Kichebo had made her request once again. "He's pleasant, as well as handsome. I've had some words with him and he doesn't seem to hold a grudge against you for that wound." Gray Cape waited before asking, "If you don't mind my digging into your business, youngster, what did happen?"

Kichebo had to overcome a sharp impulse to bristle and snap back that she did mind. For a moment, she stood fighting herself. Then Gray Cape said, "Let's find a place to talk."

Curled up in a nest of grass near the old one, Kichebo found it easier to speak. Trying to find the words brought back the hateful memories. She found herself racked by anger and grief as she told her story. At the end, Gray Cape said nothing but offered her flank for the young cheetah to bury her head against.

When at last Kichebo looked up, Gray Cape licked her face and said, "Leaving such a thing unsaid is like leaving a hairball in your belly. I'm glad you got rid of it."

"I'm not sure I will ever get rid of it," answered Kichebo in a low voice. "Having Nasseken turn away from me to one such as Rahepsi . . . I went mad."

"You realize she had little choice in what she did."

Kichebo closed her eyes and let her head sink. "I know. If only Nasseken could have told me why. If I had known, I would have obeyed and not followed her to the courting circle."

"And she wouldn't have turned on you and driven you off? No. Kichebo, even if she hadn't done it then, she would have had to soon after. That is what must happen between mothers and grown cubs. Nasseken had to chase you away."

"Why?"

"When a female takes a male in the courting circle, she will bear a litter in the following season. She must devote herself entirely to her new family and can have no thought for anything else, even for her older cubs. If grown cubs don't leave on their own, she must run them off or else they become jealous and might even attack the new litterlings."

"But I wouldn't!" Kichebo protested. "I'd help her care for them."

"So you might think," answered Gray Cape dryly. "I imagine you had no thought of attacking Rahepsi either."

The young cheetah fell silent as the old one continued, "From what you tell me, she and her sister Beshon are extraordinary for females of our kind. To raise an abandoned cub is not easy. Most cheetahs wouldn't do it."

"I know how hard it was for Nasseken. I just wish I hadn't been so . . . ungrateful. But the courting circle—"

"Is no place for cubs," Gray Cape interrupted. "If I fault your Nasseken for anything it is that she allowed you to stay with her too long. I know. I drove away many of my half-grown sons and daughters, though it clawed at my heart to do it. But the hurt would have been worse had they stayed."

"She was afraid for me," answered Kichebo.

"She loved you," said Gray Cape simply.

Somehow there was no need for further words. Kichebo let her head sink back down onto the bony old flank, feeling more at peace with herself. Gray Cape lay quietly and Kichebo relaxed, letting her contentment give way to sleep.

When at last she woke, under the starlight, she knew she hadn't resolved everything, but the bitterness was eased. Perhaps she could even talk to Rahepsi without having her memories intrude. And perhaps, someday, even Nasseken.

Several days later, Kichebo went to the lake within the temple grounds where she had last seen Asu-Kheknemt's reflection. Why she went, she wasn't sure, for there were no words in her mind that commanded her to seek this place. Perhaps she sensed a call that needed no words, or perhaps it was only her own wish to see him. Together with Menk and Gray Cape, she left the shadows of the columned hall and scrambled over rubble to the pool.

This time she found stone steps leading from the high-walled edge down to the water below. Carefully she descended, her two companions crouching on the stairs above her.

Kheknemt was there. Kichebo felt his presence the moment she looked in the water. As she crouched on the stone lip of the last step, her reflection shimmered into his. She stared with longing and fascination. The eyes and face were the same as she had seen before, yet they were not. He had grown older, many years older, but age hadn't weakened him. The amber eyes were wiser than before. Sorrow still lay in their depths, but it was a sorrow tempered by understanding and acceptance.

Now his voice was strong enough for Kichebo to hear words. *Touch your nose to mine, black cheetah.* Slowly she lowered her muzzle. From beneath the surface the other face rose to meet hers. Her eyes closed. With a slight shock she felt the wetness of water become the cool, moist leather of someone's nose.

She sensed a pull, drawing her down and out of herself, into the image floating before her in the lake. Her first thought was to let the whole of her being spring eagerly toward that sweet and astonishing contact, but she thought of the old cheetah and Menk waiting on the upper steps behind her.

"Gray Cape," she said, unable to turn her head, "my . . . friend . . . is here again."

"I gathered as much." At the sound of Gray Cape's voice, Kichebo opened her eyes and caught another reflection, the old cheetah's twitching tail. "Are you sure you want to do this?"

"I have to. And I want to."

"You're going to get mighty stiff crouching on that little bit of rock."

"You should be able to guide me back up the stairs."

"More likely I'll have to haul you," Gray Cape grunted. "All right. I'll manage, I suppose. But tell him not to keep you too long."

Kichebo barely heard the old cheetah. Impatiently she leaned forward, seeking the touch of Kheknemt's nose. "Good-bye, Gray Cape!"

As her spirit dove out of her body, she felt blunt teeth fasten in the nape of her neck, holding her steady so that her corporeal self couldn't accidentally follow her spirit's plunge.

At first, she felt as though she had become the face beneath the water and she was staring up at a bright world above. Then everything seemed to shift and right itself. She found herself standing in a place of dappled sunlight and shade. Sweet flowers tickled her nose. Before her, amid water lilies and the slim shapes of carp, lay a reflection of a black male cheetah face with gold markings.

Welcome again, sister-in-time, Kheknemt greeted her, but before she could answer in kind, another sound came through the ears she now shared with him. It was a young man's voice and one he knew well.

"So, it is not thirst but vanity that makes you linger so long beside the pond, Asu-Kheknemt."

As before, Kichebo let herself blend into the male cheetah's mind, experiencing the flow of his thoughts and feelings as her own.

· · ·

There was laughter in my pharaoh's voice but not the harshness of mockery. I lapped water while a newly arrived part of me tried to find in this resonant man-voice the piping of a child heard not long ago. Is he the companion who was with you before, the new part asked, and I answered, yes. Hapi has flooded and ebbed ten times since. This is now the month men call Khensu. For you, sister-in-time, it has been only days. I do not yet understand this difference, but the feet that walk the trail of time tread at a different pace in your world than in mine.

I lifted my dripping muzzle from the pond, knowing there was no way I could explain to Tutankhaten what had just happened. Even if my tongue were able to form human speech, his language had not the ability to describe the flight of one being to another across the wide desert of ages. It was enough for me that I had reached her and brought her, this one who is more like me than any other whose faraway touch I have felt.

I regretted again that I couldn't share this triumph with him. I knew that soon would come a time when the lack of speech could no longer keep me and my master from sharing selves. That is, if our training at the House of the Swift bore fruit and that fruit were not struck from the branch before it ripened.

I turned my head and regarded him, seeing with new eyes the countenance of a child who has become a man. His eyes were large for his face, shaded by widely arched brows, his nose delicate and slightly hooked, yet still retaining a trace of its boyish upward tilt. The taper of his chin was long, a reminder that Tutankhaten was of the same flesh as the horse-faced Akhenaten, but in him the defect was small and only gave strength to his face.

The hands that ruffled my fur were hard and brown, their palms roughened by spear hafts, bow grips, and the chafing of chariot reins. Inside too, he had toughened, learning to hide the uncertain child from all but me.

He sprang up, impatient with indolence in the pleasure garden. When I leaped to my feet and rubbed against the royal kilt of starched linen, the hidden sparkle in his eyes came to life. "You would go with me to the House of the Swift, *ba meht*, my leopard-of-the-north. Come then!"

His strides were quick but not rapid enough to keep us from being intercepted on the pathway out of the garden. First came worried attendants, wringing their hands in dismay. Then came palace guards, determined that their pharaoh be accompanied to his destination even though it lay within the grounds, but he would have none of it.

"Isn't it enough that I am scrutinized, attended, and fawned on every moment of my life? If the soldiers who keep watch on me by night stay any closer, I will have to bear their onion-breath in my face. Even a king has a right to his own company once in a while. Away, away with you all!"

Tutankhaten flung his arms wide and the crowd scattered with little cries and clucks, but the guard captain, who was more persistent, placed himself in the king's path. "Son of the Sun," said he gravely, "a king has such a right, but Egypt has a right to keep its ruler from harm."

This guard captain I knew as a reasonable and almost kindly man, but such warnings were something else Tutankhaten had heard enough of. The bronze of his face darkened with anger. "What harm lies within these walls save that which you allow?"

At this the captain stiffened and paled. "Assassination?" the young king went on. "I have heard that word since I was old enough to understand it. You all fear for me. More than I fear for myself. But I have also heard the whisperings that say this precious nation of Egypt would be grateful if I were to be struck down from the throne."

Eyes were cast down before his glare. Faces flushed and sweated. "Let us have no more empty words of caution," Tutankhaten said in a lighter tone, but the edge of his laugh was bitter. His hand dropped to my head. "I go with one I trust," he said and turned on his heel. I paced alongside.

"They cannot hide their eagerness to be rid of me," he muttered to himself. "Now they know I can think for myself and not just mouth words in the scrolls that the priests of Amon-Ra set before me, as if I were a child commanded to eat his mush. . . . Is it not enough that I have restored the gods my brother cast down? Or that they have forced me to disown the Aten by stripping it from my name? They call me Tutankh*amen* now, *ba meht*. Only to you and a few others am I known by my birth-name." He broke off and walked in silence.

Even though the House of the Swift lay within the palace grounds, it was a long dusty walk in the glare of the afternoon sun. The speed given by anger faded, and Tut's sandals were scuffing the ground by the time we passed the chariot stables and the kennels where greyhounds set up a frenzied yelping as they scented my presence. Beyond were pens for gazelles, and then at last, the House of the Swift.

No writings above the entryway marked it as such. There were only two incised carvings of seated cheetahs, one on each side of the threshold. It was a low structure of plain mud brick and seemed out of place in company with the stone and tiled walls of the royal compound. From the doorway drifted mingled scents of man and hunting leopard.

I paused there to shake dust from my fur and he to give his high, blue khepresh-crown into the keeping of an attendant and accept in exchange a striped headcloth such as the trainers wore. We passed into an open, airy chamber divided on each side into stalls, as if for stabling horses, but larger and better kept. Each one contained a cot for a keeper as well as a stone ledge for his animal. From each cubicle, a low cattlehide door led outside to one of two common enclosures on each side of the building. A sloped trough ran through each row of stalls, providing fresh flowing water. The sound of it, echoing softly like a stream within a cavern brought memories back to me, for it was in such a place I was birthed and schooled.

On this day it was quiet within the House of the Swift. I knew most of its occupants were outside on the training field. A murmur came from one end where a keeper knelt with his animal at an altar painted with the winged form of the sun disk. Above it was another representation of the Aten, a sun-image whose rays ended in open hands, reaching down to touch all creatures below.

My king paused beside me to let his eyes rest on the image of a god he worshipped when he was a child. This was the only place he could find it, for the Aten had been thrown down by the jealousy of those who worshipped the old gods. Its symbol had been chiseled off columns and temples, along with the name of Akhenaten, he who is now reviled as the Heretic.

And what should all this matter to me, a cheetah? The rise and fall of two-legged gods and the strivings of one pack of human jackals against another? I once thought it was only my love for Tutankhaten that kept me from disdaining the rest of his kind. My love for him is strong, but it is not the only thing that ties me to these upright apes. I would like to think of myself as being a creature of the desert, the river, and the windswept plain, but I know that my nature and my being have been shaped and molded by generations of captive breeding. I have seen many hunting leopards taken from the wild and none had a pelt or markings such as mine. Whether or not I accept or reject it, I am as much a creation of men as the temples they build or the gods in whose names they make war.

From the bright rectangle of the other door, a figure stepped inside and approached us. He was clad in loincloth and sandals, his grizzled hair escaping from beneath a sunfaded headcloth. At his throat the winged disk gleamed in gold while his forearms were sheathed in leather against playful bites.

"Asu-Kheknemt!" he cried, dropping stiffly to his knees and mauling me with rough caresses from his big hands. "How does he, Son of the Sun?"

"He does well, Keeper of the Swift," and another hand descended to stroke me. "He has years enough to show his age, yet he is still fleet and dances like a kitten."

"The best ever bred in Tel Amarna, aren't you, *ba meht*?" the old trainer crooned, taking my head between callused palms. "Pity he's the only one left. The cubs he has sired are promising, but without a female of the Amarna stock. . . ." The keeper shook his head and sighed. "You still intend to send an expedition, don't you, my king? If any of those animals are still alive. . . ."

"Yes, I will, but it is a slender hope at best. Has the Divine Father, Aye, come yet?" Tut asked, and the old keeper didn't question the sudden change of subject.

"My lord, he said he would meet you outside on the training field. I would be honored," he said and led the way.

Aye had not yet arrived and we took advantage of his absence to wander across the training field toward a line of keepers and their companions. The training masters prostrated themselves before my lord and offered him a sunshade made of lashed stakes and hides. Although he was grateful, he bade them put it aside and walked with me to the line as if he were just one more keeper with his animal.

Quietly we took an empty place and watched. Two slaves, their skins gleaming with sweat, bore a trap-cage containing a live gazelle to the far end of the field. Beside us, a young Nubian untied the lacings from the leather hood of my half-grown son, Neba Resu. My son's tail flicked as he caught my scent, but a soft murmur from his Nubian trainer brought his attention back to his schooling. Like many of my cubs, his pelt was dark enough to swallow his spots, but not the true black of mine. Nor did he have my gold tearlines. Neba Resu tensed and strained forward as the trainer's hand poised to slip back his hood. The slave by the trap-cage prepared to release the gazelle.

Even as the small antelope sprang free, the Nubian's hand was on Neba Resu's head, directing him at the quarry as an arrow is aimed from a drawn bow. Then he was gone. Only a spurt of dust and a limp leather hood swinging by its tassel from the trainer's hand marked the spot where he had been. He ran as I run, head held dead level in direct line with the quarry, his spine curving and arching in a whiplash motion, feet covering with each bound a distance many times his nose-to-tail length. Bowling over the racing gazelle, he seized it by the throat, flung it down, and crouched over it, growling.

When Neba Resu's kill was sure, his Nubian trainer crossed the field, but Neba Resu was so absorbed in his prey, he paid no attention to the man's approach nor to the warning scowl. From the band of his loincloth, the trainer took a wooden shell with a stiff piece of metal attached. Pressed between thumb and finger, the thing made a sharp snicking sound. Neba Resu's ears went up, then back, but he retreated from the gazelle, only switching his tail irritably as the man laid hands on his kill.

I didn't scold him. None of us find it easy to surrender our catch to a man, even one who has been a companion since cubhood. Even I know the dull burn of resentment when I must yield my kill, but it passes quickly. I no longer need the scarab-chirp of the training device to rouse me from a panting crouch over my prey. I still remember when that sound bit my ears, stealing my attention whether or not I wished to give it. Neba Resu will learn in time, as I did.

As I sat watching my son, I felt fingers gliding along the fur beneath my throat and my king's voice murmured, "You remember your schooling well, don't you, *ba meht*." With a wave of his hand, he ordered another caged gazelle to be brought and set at a further distance than the one Neba Resu had chased. I began to prance and sidestep with eagerness at the thought of coursing my own meal instead of eating man-killed meat from a dish.

A keeper came forth with my old hunting hood and offered to handle me, but Tut smiled and himself slipped the worn leather cover over my ears. It was he who launched me, guiding my head with a deft turn of his wrist and snatching off the hood in the instant I exploded away from him with the gazelle between my sighting stripes. Even as I left him behind, I felt the intensity of his concentration as if he were still guiding me. I knew his gaze was locked with mine on the animal and part of him ran with me in the chase.

Straight as a cast javelin I went. My bared dewclaws struck the quarry before it could reach full sprint and it struggled only briefly in my jaws. Knowing the prey was mine, I could have kept possession, but I yielded, bowing to my master. I laid my chin on my forepaws and panted, savoring the delicious exhaustion that follows a good run.

I watched a keeper bind the gazelle's feet and place it about the shoulders of a slave to be borne up to the palace. Tut did as I anticipated, ordering the kill not to be dressed for the table but given to me for the evening meal. He also requested a curry brush to clean the training ground dust from my coat.

"Can't bear to see his beauty spoiled, even briefly, eh lad? A treat for the eyes Asu-Kheknemt may be, but he is no palace decoration." Both of us glanced up. Tut grinned at the only man who had the temerity and the station to call the Son of the Sun and Lord of the Red and Black Lands "lad." Aye, my king's uncle and the Divine Father, was a great standing stone of a man, whom age seemed only to set more firmly on its base. It was he who had stood over both of us since the day of the crowning, and it was he who led me from the House of the Swift in Amarna to the palace where a frightened young boy waited amid the chaos created by his brother's death.

"You handle him well. You have learned to stay with him through the charge. But coursing him is not the only thing you must learn."

Tut stroked my head thoughtfully as he replied, "I have begun to study the old papyri of Djoser's reign and I have spoken to those in the House of the Swift who have achieved a high degree of empathy with their animals. Still, I do not understand exactly what the scrolls mean or how to do what they describe." He spread his palms. "Can you offer me no further guidance, Divine Father?"

"I have none to give, Son of the Sun. The farther part of that path of knowledge you must tread yourself. No man of this time can aid you."

Tut heaved a discontented sigh and said, "Oh, I wish there had been less haste when we left Amarna! Had I been of age, I would have ordered that another barge be built to carry the black hunting leopards sacred to Aten."

"Then I, too, would have possessed a companion and perhaps could have taught you what you struggled so hard to master," replied Aye, and a slight smile broke the granite of the Divine Father's face. He knelt stiffly and ran leathery fingers along my back. His touch was almost reverent. I turned my head and looked into his eyes.

"I had a companion, my king," Aye said in a voice like the rolling millstones. "I gave Asu-Kheknemt to you."

As the Divine Father stroked me, I felt the old yearning that has lain within him since I passed from his hands into those of my king. In mind as well as body, I have sensed that Aye is a more powerful man than Tut. In partnership with him I might have gone far beyond what I might do with this slight boy. More than once I have been tempted. But what is given is given and the Divine Father knows that even better than I.

Perhaps it is just as well, for what might have been possible once is no longer. Something tells me Aye has grown too old and the paths of his mind too worn for him to depart from them into a country of which he knows little. Tut may lack Aye's strength, but he is still limber enough in his thoughts to bend as does the willow branch.

"I understand the value of your gift, Divine Father," he said. "I will read the scrolls again . . . and try."

"You may be further toward your destination than you think," rumbled Aye, rising and covering me with his shadow. "You and Asu-Kheknemt are nearly one, judging from the skill with which you course him."

Tut bent his brows as he studied me, only lifting a hand absently to acknowledge Aye's departure. He wiped his brow on the back of his forearm. "All this thinking tires me, *ba meht*. And the sun is hot. I think I will accept the makeshift canopy the attendants have made for me."

When the sunshade was brought, I too, reclined gratefully in its shadow. Tut called for a campstool and sat to watch the activity on the training field. Another handler brought a leashed female followed by several leggy, gamboling cubs. This time the trap-cage held a half-grown bushpig, easier quarry for the young. One flick of the leash freed their mother and she streaked after her squealing victim. Instead of striking the creature down as prey for herself, she drove it toward her young. They ran alongside the snuffling beast, giving it clumsy swats and trying to bite its nape to tumble it over. Each time the harried pig tried to escape, the mother turned it back, forcing it to endure the young cheetah's clumsy attacks.

At last, more by luck than anything else, a cub knocked the pig down and the mother made the kill. Their trainer trotted after his charges, the clicker raised high in his fist. With pricked ears, the cubs watched him, alerted by the sharp noise. But not until their mother gave a warning snarl did they yield the prize and back away with annoyed grimaces. I watched, remembering how, in the same way, my own schooling had begun.

NINE

A short time later, the young pharaoh rose, folded the camp-stool, and handed it back to an attendant. Pausing for me to stretch, Tut went back into the House of the Swift. At its threshold he met again the grizzled old trainer, who then guided both of us into a chamber more suitable for the work of scholars and priests than cheetah trainers. One side was lit by a well-placed gap in the ceiling; the other was dark but held carved brackets for torches. The wall between had light wooden shelves on which lay many scrolls of papyrus. My king selected one stored apart from the others and bound with a black-and-gold cord.

Carefully he spread it on the sloping top of a scribe's table. Leaning on his elbows, he pored over it as he had done many times before. I have long been curious about these sheets made from beaten reeds in which the two-legged ones seem to find great meaning. As Tut sighed and began to reroll it, I reared up and placed my forepaws as gently as I could on the edge of the sloped table. Even so, the awkward thing rocked and Tut frowned, laying hands on the papyrus as if to snatch it away from my claws. He must have seen something more than animal mischievousness in my face, for instead of binding the scroll once again, he stooped beside me and held it open on his knee.

"Would you read it, *ba meht?*" he said in a half-teasing voice. "I wish you could, for you might find more sense in it than I can."

I peered at the papyrus, being careful not to touch my wet nose to the worn and yellowed surface. Countless little tracks like bird-prints walked across it. Softly Tut murmured in my ear, "This is a record of the keeping and training of your kind from the days when King Djoser raised the first pyramid tomb at Sakkara. See, *ba meht,* here is the sign that means hunting leopard." He set his forefinger beneath a bird-track. The longer I stared at it, the more I was able to convince myself that it did portray a slender, striding cheetah shape.

He then pointed out another, an equally crude depiction of a kneeling human figure, and said, "The text speaks of breeding and coursing, but there is something yet more important. It hints that there can be a certain conjoining of man and creature so that both are as one in the light of the Aten. I know we two can approach that when we hunt, but the scribe who wrote this says we can do much more. But, curse it, the papyrus is damaged and the text is incomplete."

Tut pondered the scroll a while longer, then got to his feet and bound it with the black-and-gold tasseled cord. "What knowledge we have lost, *ba meht,*" he said with a sigh, replacing it on the shelf and gazing down at me with a bemused expression. "There may be magic in you, yet I can't touch it."

I gazed up at him and felt much the same frustration. Many times during the hunt, we had drawn so close as to be nearly one mind, yet it was not something we could command at will or keep once the chase was done. Perhaps neither he nor I had the strength of mind to break the bodily shells that held us apart from one another. Again, I thought of Aye but knew the time was past when I could have chosen him.

With that thought quickening my steps, I followed my king from the House of the Swift and took his trailing hand in my mouth.

At the touch of my teeth, he started and nearly snatched his hand away, but a second thought made him stare seriously at me. When I tugged, he followed, and I did not need to keep hold of his hand to lead him to a secluded courtyard. There, on a shade-cooled stone bench, he rested, listening to palm fronds rustle and letting his fingers play up and down my nape as I sat and leaned against him.

The breeze stilled, leaving everything in silence. I became more and more aware of Tut's fingertips ruffling the fur at the back of my neck, and I closed my eyes in pleasure. A humming sound came from him, a noise rather like my purr, although less musical. His hand, traveling in lazy strokes along my spine, lulled me into a trance and I began to feel that a part of me was flowing away into that hand. I was ready to open myself, for I had already accepted another spirit who had left her own habitation to lodge in my mind. But never had I been coaxed from the shield of my self into that of another. Could it be that I was afraid, I, the gifted one, who had sent my senses far ahead in time to seek out others of my kind? Yet in truth, I was, and that made me not only fearful but ashamed.

In the midst of my uncertainty, I felt something within me stir, telling me to throw off shame and fear. Surely my king would receive me much as I had welcomed her at the end of her long journey. After all, mine would take me less than a tail-length from my own body. And I would be sheltered by one I loved.

So I did not pull away, but instead gazed into my king's eyes, letting myself empty into him through the touch of his hand. As I watched his eyes grow wide with wonder and close in astonishment, I felt my head become light and my forepaws slid from beneath me. Dimly I sensed my body sinking, laid down by hands beneath my ribs.

I passed into night. Not an empty darkness as I might have feared, but one alive with sensation. I knew the gift of touch, for I felt the wiry softness of my own fur against a human hand. With an acuteness that was almost painful, I touched every hair that glided beneath my fingertips and began to learn a small part of what it was to be a human creature.

My king had closed his eyes, and I was grateful for not having to accustom myself to any additional sensations. The ones pouring in on me were overwhelming enough. Folds of cloth, bound around me, entangled my legs and constricted my waist. Textured stone bit into my now tailless and tender backside. Unable to find relief by squirming, I let the body do what was natural to it, which was to leave the bench and stand upright.

My head seemed to soar. Even without opening the eyes,

153

I sensed the height. I towered, I loomed over everything in existence, and I tottered, cursing the precarious balance of this upright stance. My instinct was to drop to all fours, but before I could do so, my king stopped me and took control of the body we now shared.

Together we remained standing while I grew accustomed to the vertical position, the height and balance of my human head. He opened his eyes and I nearly fell. I recoiled from a world exploding with fierce intensity. A blossom flamed its image into my brain. Leaves burned and shimmered. Even the soil at my feet was a cave-deep shadow, and a brilliant sky seemed to press down on me with a fearful weight. For an instant I squeezed my eyelids shut and then opened them again, forcing myself to endure the onslaught. Everything was too close, too intense, too demanding. I would have fled back to my cheetah body had not my master gently held me, saying, *No. See my world as I do.*

He gave me the word to comprehend what dazzled and panicked my mind. It was color. Not color as I had previously known it, but something so intense as to be unfamiliar, needing new words to describe it. These he provided me. I saw the blossom again in crimson. The leaves became emerald and the sky turquoise. As I began to understand, my distress faded. The hues around me remained as strong, but I knew that these eyes were made to bear it. No longer did everything seem to press down and in on me. I took a deep breath and stared about the courtyard.

As I gathered the richness of the scene through human eyes, I recalled how I had seen it from the four-footed shape that now lay as if sleeping by the stone bench. In memory, colors seen through cheetah eyes seemed dingy and faded compared to what I now beheld. Blues and greens I had been able to see, but red barely existed, becoming at best a pale pink when seen at close range.

Slowly I tottered on two legs around the courtyard garden, stopping to touch blossoms and drink in their hues. As I explored I discovered other differences in how I now perceived the world. The wider range of vision and the way details were preserved right out to the edge of sight made me realize the vision of my cheetah body was limited to a narrow horizontal band acutely sensitive to detail and motion. Above and below that band, my cheetah sight blurred out.

I was beginning to feel dissatisfied with the memory of my cat vision when a hummingbird whirred over the wall and hovered among the jasmine. The jeweled sparkle of its throat fascinated me, but I wasn't too distracted to notice that I couldn't see its wing feathers. I blinked and stared again but was unable to follow the rapidly beating wings through their cycle of motion, as I had been able to in my cheetah form. Concentrate as I might, the hummingbird's wings remained an uncertain blur.

I knew then that these eyes could never follow the sprint of a gazelle across the open plain, or detect the slight shift in its stride that betrayed a sudden swerve to left or right. These eyes could never pick out the one weak animal in a herd that stretched across the horizon, nor hold their gaze on the target within that milling herd. These eyes had their own magic, but they were not hunter's eyes.

As startling and wondrous as the transfer seemed, I sensed it not to be an end in itself but instead a step on the way to something more. I could feel the change continuing,

merging the two halves of my mind which once knew themselves as man and hunting leopard. I turned back to the
sleeping feline body by the stone bench and saw its true
beauty. The rich velvet black of its fur, the slender grace of
its form, the long sweep of its tail; all these things made me
want to kneel and stroke reverently the form that had been
in part mine.

Now I, both human and cheetah in one, gathered up the
cat body and held it in my arms, as if it were a corpse I
could wish to life. Even as I held the empty shell of what
I had been, I felt my being spreading out to encompass it.
At first, I thought the cheetah part of me was returning into
its feline form, but that was not so. I was not fragmenting or
transferring, but expanding. The being I was now animated
two bodies; I stirred and woke within my own arms.

I knew instantly that this was the conjoining of which the
old papyrus had spoken; this was the royalty of man and
animal fused into something beyond either. In wild joy I
gazed up with both pairs of eyes and again caught sight of
the hummingbird. Its colors shone as vividly as before, but
now I could track the motion of its wings with ease.

Unable to contain myself, I galloped about the courtyard
on both four feet and two, clapping my hands and whisking
my tail. The happier I become, the faster I ran, leaving the
two-legged part of myself behind as I shot around the enclosed court. I realized suddenly that I was running within
that small space at a speed far greater than I would have
otherwise dared. I found I could control my muscles with
better precision, and the enhanced depth of my sight gave
me greater confidence in choosing my path. I slowed, pant-

ing exuberantly and lolling out my cheetah tongue at my grinning human face. What else might I be able to do!

It was the portion of me who walked upright that provided the answer. From my waistband I took an iron-bladed dagger with a beaded gold hilt and tossed it at the bole of a palm tree. The cheetah part of me followed the knife in its flight until its blade struck and split scaled bark. My teeth retrieved the dagger, placing it in my hands. I stood at a distance twice as far from the wounded tree and again threw the weapon. Again I doubled the distance and again the blade flew, to land exactly in the same split in the same scale.

Surprised at my skill, I retreated so far from the target I could scarcely see it. I thought then that I must fail, for even though my arm had strength enough to send the knife home, I doubted my ability to aim it. As I drew back my arm for the throw, my uncertainty lifted, for I suddenly knew how the blade must fly. I knew its exact position and speed at every instant. My hand whipped forward, launching the dagger as if it had been a hunting cat set to the chase. I seemed to ride with the blade as it left my fingers on an arched trajectory, giving it mental nudges to correct its flight against a vagrant cross breeze. Only after the *thok* of iron into pith echoed across the courtyard did I comprehend what I had done.

As I approached, the hearts of both my bodies beat hard as I saw the dagger blade buried to its full length in the tree. Even a Nubian archer would have been hard put to equal my throw with his shot, and I had done it without the added power of bent bow and taut string.

Dizzy with success and amazement, I sought the stone bench again. My two bodies leaned against each other with one thought slowly dawning. It was not only the precise control of shoulder and arm that had given the blade its perfect course. Somehow, by becoming what I now was, a blend of cheetah and human, I had gained an intuitive understanding of the hidden nature of motion. With that knowledge, I had been able to reach out and pilot the blade even as it flew.

I challenged myself by casting the knife and trying to flip it from its course with the strength of my will alone. At first the task was difficult, bringing the sweat of concentration to my brow as well as my paw pads, but soon the blade would skip in its flight as if it had glanced off an invisible wall. I also found an interesting peculiarity of my talent. Try as I would, I could not affect anything standing still relative to me. Only if it moved could I deflect it. The faster the object moved, the more amenable was it to my direction.

In puzzling over this, I suddenly felt an overwhelming weariness. Both my cheetah self and my human self retired once again to the stone bench. Sensing the imminent dissolution of my composite being, each of my bodies clung to to the other. Separation did come at last, but it was a gentle unmixing of parts and a reconstitution of each separate self, unlike the painful rending I had feared.

Once again I became cheetah and he became man. I saw then the rosy dusk of the sky, heard the evening song of crickets, and felt my king's arms about my neck as I sank into sleep.

. . .

Kichebo nodded awake, still drowsy enough to wonder if she had indeed come back to herself. The arms embracing Asu-Kheknemt were still about her, and a heavy head lay against her shoulder. She blinked and peered up between sandstone columns to a pale-pink sky, which held the colors not of sunset but sunrise. The noise had changed from cricket's chirping to Menk's snoring.

The young cheetah lay still, becoming used to the sensation of being once again alone within herself. A shaft of sunlight came through the temple, touching Menk's dusky skin and warming it to the same golden-brown as Tut's had been. She held Kheknemt's memory in her mind, unsure whether to accept or disbelieve. A part of her still wondered if the royal black was, after all, a creature shaped from her own wishes. Even as she questioned, she knew that the visions she shared with him were far too strange to be of her own creation.

She glanced down at Menk, struck again by the resemblance between her and Kheknemt's companion.

How much like you am I, my brother-in-time, she wondered. *I look as you do, but have I any of your gifts? Could I ever accomplish with Menk what you did with Tut?* There was no answer, yet she sensed a certain . . . possibility. But how? And would Menk accept such a thing or would she retreat in fear, unable to understand? Kichebo felt too uncertain yet to try. And Menk was still asleep.

Later that day, Kichebo lifted her muzzle from a clump of dry grass where her neighbor had left a scent-sign. It was too fresh, which made her uneasy. Although this time she was patroling their shared border herself instead of asking Gray Cape, she still shied away from the idea of encountering Rahepsi. She would speak to him when she was ready, she told herself. She wasn't ready yet.

An enraged squeal cut into her musings. Menk again, she thought but then realized she had left the little creature under Gray Cape's care. Snuffles and grunts made Kichebo's ears twitch forward, but they flattened again at another piercing squeal.

Her gaze swept the open ground beyond her border. At first she saw only the broken shapes of village walls amid the clumps of low scrub. Then she caught sight of several stiff, upright tails moving swiftly along the top of a low ridge of stone. In the time it took her to blink, a file of warthog piglets emerged from behind it. A cheetah broke from cover and made a dash at them, but the squealing mother intercepted Rahepsi's charge, driving him back with fierce thrusts of her tusks. His speed made it easy for him to escape her ponderous lunges, but each time he tried to duck around her to attack a piglet, she managed to be in his way again, swinging her heavy, ugly head and stabbing at him with her tusks.

One piglet broke from the trotting line and veered toward Kichebo's border. Distracting the sow with a feint to one side, Rahepsi darted around her and chased the errant piglet. Grunting with rage, the warthog pounded after him, drawing close enough to jab his hindquarters. The piglet fled toward Kichebo's territory, shrilling its terror.

Just before it reached the boundary, Kichebo saw Rahepsi grimace with annoyance. He broke off his pursuit and whirled to deal with the mother. Both were lost in the blowing dust. The young warthog ran past Kichebo, who launched herself after it. Her short sprint put her beside her prey and a swat from her paw sent it rolling. It struggled only briefly with her teeth in its throat and she hefted it, trotting back to her scent-boundary.

Yowls and squeals met her ears as Rahepsi tried to fend off the angry female warthog. He had gone for another one of the piglets, only to be driven away again. For a moment, Kichebo watched. Then she laid down her piglet, making sure it was on her side of the boundary, and charged in to assist.

The sow could harass one cheetah, but two were more than it could handle. The combined attack sent it retreating, its small tail stuck high in the air with indignation and outrage. Kichebo guessed it knew the rest of its brood was safe. When she was sure the sow wouldn't return, she turned back toward her territory, passing a panting Rahepsi.

She seized the piglet and was about to carry it off when something made her glance back. He had come to the edge of her boundary and was looking hungrily at the piglet, yet was unwilling to step onto her ground. She started to wrinkle her nose at him in a threat-grimace, then thought better of it. She could stalk off to the ruin with her prize and he wouldn't follow, but. . . .

She loosened her jaws and let the piglet drop. "Menk nearly took your prey," she said, trying to sound gruff. "Since Menk is mine, I owe you a meal."

The big male gave her a long stare, making her wonder if he intended to mention the other debt she owed him, but he didn't. Instead, Rahepsi shook himself, then entered her territory, watching her carefully. "You eat first," he offered.

"There would have been nothing for either of us if you hadn't caught the piglet."

Kichebo didn't need his urging. Her appetite had grown in the few moments she had carried the prey, tasting its flavor. She ate some and let Rahepsi have her place. Before stepping aside she hesitated and said, "Leave enough for Gray Cape."

She noticed that Rahepsi was careful to do as she asked, and more, leaving some of the choicer meats for the old cheetah. When he was finished, he gave Kichebo a questioning glance and stretched out in the shade of a palm tree.

"That sow gave me quite a chase. I wasn't sure who was after who for a while there. I appreciated your help."

Kichebo said nothing, but she let herself settle on her chest, eyeing him.

He continued, almost speaking to himself, although he shot her glances from time to time. "I forgot how tricky it is to hunt warthogs by yourself. It's much easier when you're with a hunting group. Much easier."

Kichebo found herself remembering the chases with Nasseken and Beshon. Her loss stung her again. She had only begun to feel as though she was an important member of the threesome before the courting circle fight had forced her out. She suddenly envied Rahepsi his place among his brothers and wondered if he felt as lonely away from them as she did when she left Nasseken. Remorse clawed at her and she let her head sink onto her paws.

She jerked her head up again when she realized he was studying her closely. Flustered, she looked away, cursing her impulse to share the kill. She flattened her ears, not wanting to hear the quiet voice that said, "Youngster, I can't say

I didn't resent you for attacking me. Every time I tried to run with this stiff shoulder, I wished you had become lion-prey. But the stiffness is almost gone."

Kichebo stole a glance at him as he rolled on his side, yawning and stretching until his rigid legs quivered. His wound was still a puckered, angry red, but the marks of her teeth and claws would fade and shrink in time. So too, perhaps might her shame.

"What is it like, living in a hunting group such as yours?" she asked. Rahepsi lolled his head back, grinning with happy recollection. He told her about his brothers, about hunts in which the banded males ranged afar across dry plains to bring down oryx or eland, prey too large for a single cheetah or even a pair to tackle alone, of the rough but close cama-raderie, of wild chases, sparring games, and boastful brag-ging. He also told her some things that startled her. Not all such groups were made up of siblings, nor were they uniquely male. Recently a young female had sought and been granted acceptance into Rahepsi's.

"Of course that means she won't have any of us when it comes time for her to mate," he said with a tinge of regret in his voice. "She thinks of us now as brothers, not suitors. But Bahkti is as fleet in the chase as any of us," he added hastily as Kichebo began to brittle at the mention of courting. "I don't have to tell you how much I miss my group, but the way this wound is healing, I will soon be back with them. And in the meanwhile, you're a pretty good substi-tute." He paused. "If you want to continue hunting to-gether, that is."

For a minute Kichebo stiffened again, then she made her-self relax as she thought it over.

"Well, chew on the idea, for a while," said Rahepsi, getting up and shaking dust from his flank. "Why don't you fetch Gray Cape while I keep scavengers off the kill?"

The hunt with Rahepsi had taken Kichebo's mind away from Asu-Kheknemt, but thoughts of him soon came creeping back. She sat in the shade of the temple, watching Menk tease a dung beetle with a piece of straw as it made its way sedately across a stripe of bright sunlight between two columns. At last Menk grew bored, crawled over to Kichebo, and curled against her.

At first the young cheetah thought she might join the little creature in a late afternoon nap, but she found herself instead becoming more wakeful. She was oddly aware of Menk's presence: her musky-sweet smell and the blunt angle of the small shoulder pressing against her own ribs. As the cheetah looked down on a headful of tangled black curls, Menk yawned, sat up, and gazed at her curiously, as if sensing her restlessness.

Menk's open stare was both discomfiting and inviting. Kichebo answered the stare, feeling that she should drop her gaze, yet fascinated by the intent depths of the little creature's eyes.

What do you see when you look at me, Menk? What I see in my own reflection, or something else?

She knew that another cheetah would be starting to resent such a direct and close stare, but Menk didn't seem to be bothered. Instead she sprawled on her stomach, still keeping her gaze fixed on Kichebo. Hands on chin and almost nose to nose with the cheetah, Menk began to croon softly to herself. One finger absently smoothed the fur on Kichebo's foreleg. The rhythmic stroking and humming lulled her into a tranquility that was not drowsiness. Her eyes remained open, seeking. Inwardly she trembled, feeling the strong awakening of a hunger such as Asu-Kheknemt had known, one that drew him into the eyes of his king.

My brother-in-time was bred for such a purpose and served it. I have no such place, Kichebo thought.

She knew the onset of the change as it began. She recognized the dulling of awareness. Menk's hand became still, yet she did not pull away, and the cheetah centered herself around that touch. As her vision tunneled and grayed out, she saw Menk's jaw tense. The creature's eyes flew open wide, then squeezed shut.

Kichebo woke without the sense of her body as she had always known it. Even the shared experience with Kheknemt had not prepared her for the shock of this, the sense of being stripped to a naked conscious point, drifting in darkness. And entering Menk's mind, she found, was far different from experiencing Tut's. The boy was old enough for his images and feelings to be tamed by words. Menk, however, had only the beginnings of language.

At that realization, fear struck Kichebo. She tried to back out, only to find herself strangely tethered. Fire erupted all around her. Screaming soundlessly, she writhed against the leash that bound her, drawing her toward the searing heart of the fire. The furious rush and roar threw her into mindless frenzy and she fought, almost tearing herself apart in the effort to escape.

And then something velvet black appeared against the

165

flames. Amber eyes glowed. Ivory teeth shone in the fire-light, but the teeth turned away from her bare flesh (for she had somehow lost her fur) and instead cut the tether.

She tumbled free into a swirl of fragmented memories. Burning days, the sun a white hole in the sky overhead. Relentless starry nights. Sand, weariness, and more sand, grinding her skin raw as she fought loneliness with a dogged patience born of desperation. And at the end of it all . . . a rough, wet tongue that soothed, and wiry soft fur to cling to.

Somehow the deep purr that filled her ears was blended with the husky whisper of a sound that once might have been her name. A vague image of a human visage was over-laid by the striking black-and-gold cat face of her new guardian.

Almost lost in the tumble of human memories, Kichebo fought to keep her own identity. She gathered herself, try-ing to separate from the wrappings of another conscious-ness, thinking of retreat but deciding to try once again.

Menk!

Soft fur, pretty eyes . . . takes care of Menk.

Yes, it's me.

Sunshine eyes, tickle-whiskers, in here with Menk?

Kichebo, she answered. *Yes. In here with you.*

Knowing that seemed to calm Menk. The welter of feel-ings faded, letting the sensations of a new body filter through. Like Kheknemt before her, Kichebo was glad Menk had squeezed her eyes shut, for she needed time to accustom herself to this new form. For the first time, she felt the sun's warmth directly on her skin rather than muffled by a coat of fur. Gritty, dry sand rasped her elbows where they rested on

166

the ground. Her sense of smell became dulled, b heightened sense of touch more than replaced it.

Recalling the shock Kheknemt had felt when .. looked through his king's eyes, Kichebo braced herself and cracked open an eyelid. What she saw first was a black cheetah face, chin laid on paws and breathing softly. As Kheknemt had seen his beauty through human eyes, so did she now see hers, raising a trembling hand to stroke the velvet sheen of fur. Raising an oddly shaped and heavy head, she stared up into the vaulting cross members of the temple, noticing how sun and shadow played with the colors of sandstone columns, turning them from flaming gold to beige, buff, and eye-blinding white. A flock of waterfowl winged by overhead, drawing her attention with plumage of fevered pink and orange.

She realized her jaw was hanging open when her dry tongue began to itch. Shutting her mouth, she gulped and swallowed. Recalling the next stage in the process of transition, she crawled close to the slumbering cheetah form and embraced it, seeking to expand herself into it. Even as she fumbled with her new power, she felt an overwhelming weariness overtake her. She fought against it and was able to make the cheetah legs twitch and jerk before she tumbled headlong into exhaustion.

Kichebo knew she was back in her own form before she opened her eyes again. Nearby, Menk sprawled on her front, one cheek squashed against crossed forearms. Slightly worried, Kichebo sniffed the little creature, but nothing about her looked or smelled wrong.

This . . . joining is not as easy as it seemed, the cheetah

thought ruefully, reflecting that having another's experience, however intimate, was nothing like having your own.

Menk is much younger than Kheknemt's companion. Perhaps this will be easier when she grows.

Menk emerged from the episode seemingly unaffected, but there was a certain excitement in her eyes that told Kichebo she understood and remembered what had happened.

Feeling drained by the experience, the young cheetah decided to resume her original plan; a long afternoon nap in the shade of the ruin. Although she was sleepy, she couldn't lose her awareness, and she seemed to hear Kheknemt's voice asking her to listen to more of his story.

TEN

My journey with Tutankhamen to the artisans' village of Set Maat took place shortly after the feast of Ophet, when Hapi's flood had reached its peak. We departed from the palace compound at Thebes to the quayside where a gilded high-prowed barge waited to bear us west across the river.

One might have thought this occasion to be a formal procession, judging from the number of nobles, courtiers, and priests who followed in the king's train. It had originally been planned as a simple visit to the craftsmen who earned their keep by fashioning gifts and furnishings for royal tombs. Tut had intended so, but he found to his dismay that it was impossible for a king to travel without soldiers to protect his person, priests to guard his spirit, and of course the favorites of his court, who insisted on accompanying him to enlarge their status in the eyes of lesser men.

It was not that my king expected death to come soon. Although of a frail and sometimes sickly line, Tut himself was limber and wiry, with health glowing in the bronze of his skin and the sparkle of his eyes. The new tomb being hewed in the arid valley beyond the Temple of Hatshepsut was not intended for him but for Aye, against the chance that the increasing burden of age might tumble our great granite block from its base. Ever mindful of his debt to the Divine Father, my master had commissioned the finest of the craftsmen's works.

Yet he had not ignored the fact of his own mortality and took the opportunity to request a few special items for his own tomb, even though the digging of it had not begun.

And so we went, he on the high seat of a wagon as gilded and ponderous as the barge and I at his feet, raising my nose over the sideboard to peer at the assembled crowd. Behind us sat Aye and a retinue of high priests from Amon's temple at Ipet-Sut.

"They are going to see that their gods are properly honored in the selection of burial furnishings," Tut whispered to me from the side of his mouth while lifting his hand in blessing to the crowd. "What a fuss it is. When my time comes, I wish to commend my spirit to Father Aten and have a simple grave in the desert."

Once across the river, he was carried on a litter past the huge twin statues of his father, Amenhotep, to which he made obeisance. I strode beside the sedan chair in the company of Aye until the party reached a dusty village. There, at the house of the master craftsman, the royal procession paused. Tut disembarked from the litter, motioned Aye and me after him, and walked through the cool dimness of the house to the workshop beyond.

The master craftsman preceded us, walking backward and bowing. "A great honor, Son of the Sun," he said, gulping, catching his heel on the lintel and nearly falling. "A very great honor."

"Well deserved, if you have done what was requested of you, craftsman," Tut answered and motioned Aye to bring me forward. The courtiers minced around chips and shavings, pulling up their drapes of fine linen from splashes of paint mixed with sawdust on the clay floor. I breathed the scents of pine, cedar, and sweat-dampened leather, relieved to be out of the miasma of perfumery that hung about the royal retinue.

They gathered first about a collection of objects fashioned for Aye, and I could see from the looks on their faces the priests were well satisfied. Two funeral beds had been made for the Divine Father, one done as a cow, sacred to the goddess Hathor, the other a beast with the head of a hippopotamus. Representations of jackal and hawk-headed figures adorned every item from alabaster unguent jars to bow guards. Nowhere was the forbidden image of the Aten to be seen. General Horemheb, who had come with the other nobles, made a particularly keen inspection of each work, as if he could find something traitorous hidden there.

After Tut had given his approval to the collection, he withdrew, letting the priests and courtiers circle about tables on which the items lay, admiring the inspired details of craftsmanship and praising their beauty. My king did not linger there. He took my lead from Aye and slipped away with me into a little side shed adjacent to the workshop.

I moved to his side as he approached a rude bench on which stood twin figures, side by side. Each was a lithe cat form, bearing on its back a block on which stood a gold statuette of the pharaoh. The artisan's skill had given each king figure the exact form and expression of Tut's face. Pleased, he took one and turned it over in his hands. He knelt to show me how the carver had faithfully reproduced in the cat shape the color and lines of my body. Inlaid gold traced the markings on my face and tail, delicately capturing even the amber edges of my ears.

"There are two of them," he said, placing the pieces back to back, "and this is how they will stand, facing outward like the lions of morning and evening. Your likeness shall guard me, my black sphinx, and when the time comes, you shall bear me to the horizon."

He went to another bench where there was something else, a long, low piece draped in cotton sacking. He drew the cover off slowly, taking in his breath as he did so. Even I, who have little appreciation for the art of men, felt my eyes grow large and not just because the piece depicted in full size a reclining black cheetah.

I knew at once this had come from a master hand and one who had been guided by knowledge and deep love for my kind. Tut stroked the wooden back and regally lifted head as if it could come to life and jump down beside me. Indeed, I almost believed that it could. Every part of the piece was perfect, from the extended claws of ivory to the gold-inlaid tearlines and eyes of polished amber. It crouched, resting on its chest, rear legs drawn up on either side, forelegs extended in front, head high and watchful.

As Tut picked up the cover to drape the statue once again, a voice came from behind us. "What is this, my lord?"

Two men had pushed their way through a cowhide doorflap. The taller I knew at once as Horemheb. On the back of the shorter man was a leopard skin. His bald pate was bare, marking him as a priest, but in his cackling voice and ingratiating manner he might have been a beggar off the streets. I noticed that Horemheb hung back and let the priest do all the talking.

"Is this to be part of the Divine Father's burial furnishings," the priest asked, shuffling forward to peer and poke at the statue with one bony forefinger. "If so, why has it not been presented with the other items?"

"It is not for Aye," said Tut quietly, laying down the cover. "I had it made for myself."

The old man's brow wrinkled and his eyebrows would have risen had they not been shaved off. "The hunting leopard is not a creature sacred to Amon. Nor to any of the other gods we serve." He broke off, studied me and then the statue again. "I am frankly surprised, my lord, that you would divert the skills of your best craftsmen from their rightful duty of creating works to honor the gods and instead employ them in sculpting an image of your pet!"

I could feel my king's anger in the fingers that stiffened in my fur. He stayed quiet, letting the high priest rattle on while Horemheb stood behind, his arms folded against his chest pectoral, saying nothing. As the old man eyed the wooden image once again, I could see he knew he had been mistaken in accusing Tut of frivolity. The solemn dignity of the work told him it had not been fashioned for mere amusement, and his face grew even darker with disapproval.

"Peace, old rattlebones." Horemheb placed a hand like the paw of a lion on the priest's stooped shoulder.

"Don't you see what has been done, General? This . . . cat thing . . . has been fashioned in the same manner as the traditional image of Anubis. It has been done to mock the Jackal God. Even more, it is clearly intended to usurp the Jackal's place as guardian of the dead. Son of the Sun," he said, turning angrily to Tut, "it is not within my power to interfere with your wishes, but I can tell you now, the gods do not approve."

"Surely the gods do not need to approve if this work is to grace the pharaoh's chambers or, better yet, the House of the Swift," said Horemheb heartily, yet he smiled only with his face, his eyes intent on measuring the effect of his words on Tut. "You read too much into this, old man. Our lord may be young, but not so rash as to flout the gods in the faces of their earthly representatives."

As he spoke, Aye came in and I was struck by the differences and similarities between the two men. Both were tall and powerful, showing traces of the Nubian in the darkness of their skin and texture of their hair. But while Aye gave the impression he would never use his massive strength if he could find a gentler way, Horemheb delighted in his ability to cow opponents by his sheer physical presence. Together they were two lions, the young and the old.

Horemheb continued to speak as if he hadn't been interrupted. "The quality of the work is high. You might consider this, my king. When the time comes for you to assemble provisions for the afterlife, you might salvage this statue by removing head and tail and substituting those of the Jackal. The body is of the right form and color. Why even the claws are extended like those of a dog. Once it was done, not a soul would know the difference."

I could feel Tut's fingers turning to claws at the back of my neck. With a growl rolling in my throat I stepped forward and placed myself in front of the general, fixing him with the full intensity of my gaze. Horemheb looked down at me, then at my young master, his eyes filling with a sudden contempt.

"The cat doesn't like my idea. He answers me back in a way I understand. Does he answer for you also, my lord? Have you gone mute and given your tongue to this brute animal?"

"Asu-Kheknemt is not," Tut's voice shook, "a brute animal."

Horemheb ignored him and turned instead to Aye. "Divine Father, how much longer can this go on? I have known times when the power behind the throne was a woman, or god help us, the king's male lover, but this overgrown stilt-legged cat? He is seen more often with the boy than is the princess who is supposed to be his wife!"

"General, it is not your place—" began Aye, but Horemheb interrupted him. "If it is not my place, then whose is it? The people are beginning to think the boy is soft in the head like his damned heretic brother if he can't rule without having his pet always in his lap."

My growl got deeper at the word *pet*, but Tut's sharp command cut across Horemheb's words. "Be still, *ba meht!* And you, General. I think you will find that my head is as hard as your heart and my wits as sharp as your tongue. You may address your remarks to me rather than over my head to Aye, for although he exceeds me in height he does not have the power to have you hacked apart and fed to crocodiles. Do I make myself clear?"

Horemheb was too controlled to start or blanch, but I could sense this was a reaction he hadn't quite anticipated.

I could also see in his eyes how his mind was turning, scheming to take advantage of my master's sudden show of determination. He must have found it, for his face relaxed, a sign I disliked.

"Forgive me, Son of the Sun. I often speak bluntly and without thought. I have no wish except to do your bidding."

"Let us hope that is so," said Tut, a little sourly. "Aye and I wish to speak together. Return to the other room and prepare our party for departure, for I am sure they have grown tired of gazing at statues and funeral beds and will soon take an interest in our exchange if they haven't yet."

When Horemheb and the old priest had gone and the babble in the other room faded, Tut brought his fist down on the table.

"Curse him. Curse both of them, the priest as well. The gods do not approve, says the mouthpiece of Amon, as if he speaks for all the divine beings. But there is one the priest does not speak for. Indeed he is highly offended that I continue to honor the god I was raised with. What would the priests have of me, Divine Father? I have raised up the old gods my brother cast down. I have rebuilt their temples and filled their empty coffers with gold. I have given orders that my brother and his ways are to be forgotten, even though he was as bright as the Aten disk in my eyes."

"My lord," said Aye, "it is the nature of gods to be jealous and those who have been eclipsed and restored are often most arrogant."

"Like my brother before me, I grow tired of this arrogance. I do not flaunt my belief in the priests' faces. That priest did not see an altar carved with an image of Father Aten. He saw the figure of an animal sacred to a god few people even remember. This," he laid his hand on the statue, "is no threat to them, yet Horemheb would have me desecrate it by hacking off the head and tail and replacing them with those of the dog Anubis!" He spat. "I have been surrounded by too many dogs and jackals that one should watch over me in the afterlife."

Aye was quiet a while. At last he lifted his eyes to Tut's and said, "Your temper, my lord, is the greatest weapon your opponents have against you."

Tut bent to stroke me, then looked up again with a rueful smile. "That is a lesson I can't seem to learn, Divine Father, but I will try once again."

He covered the statue and left the room. As Aye fastened a lead to my collar, he murmured softly, "Son of the Sun, if you would live to rule, you have no choice but to learn."

Kichebo woke near sunset with Aye's words still in her mind. Although Kheknemt's ears had heard the undercurrent of threat in the scene, it was she whose skin prickled with uneasiness. Sitting up, she fluffed her fur angrily. What good did it do her to witness things she could do nothing about? She had enough worries on her mind without that.

To distract her thoughts from Kheknemt and his king, she began a stalking partnership with Rahepsi. Using the ruin as a base and leaving Menk in Gray Cape's care, she ranged afield with the older male, searching for game farther downriver. At first she was careful to time her chases so that she ran in the concealment of dusk or before the faint light of dawn. Each time she began a charge, she searched the wide horizon for any signs of two-legged hunters and found nothing.

Perhaps the danger was receding, the ones who had tried to capture her having lost interest. At first she only hoped this was true, but each time she sped across the plains, the fever of pursuit making her show herself openly, she grew more convinced that she was no longer hunted. It was true that her color could still catch the attention of a prey-beast, but she learned how to use every sparse patch of scrub to conceal her approach.

Rahepsi showed her how to hunt the oryx, the drought-hardy antelope who was starting to displace other game as the high plains and hills above the river dried to desert. Oryxes traveled in small bands, making it easier for a charging hunter to target and stay with the chosen prey, but the kill was not easy. Even the yearlings were fast and vicious fighters, using their long scimitar horns to gore and jab. Kichebo came rapidly to respect these large buff-gray beasts, with humped shoulders and wide black cheek-straps that carried the line of their horns across their faces.

There were many hunts when the cheetahs' intended victim turned and chased them off or fought them to a standstill. In the kills they did make, Rahepsi and Kichebo were so exhausted that they often had to sprawl panting beside their prize, barely able to fend off the scavengers that descended on it. It was then that Rahepsi bemoaned the absence of his hunting group and Kichebo agreed, knowing the two of them alone were often inadequate against the oryxes.

As Rahepsi regained the strength he needed to wrestle prey to the ground, he spoke more often of rejoining his hunting group. Kichebo expected the sting of regret those words brought; it would not be easy to lose a hunting partner as effective and resourceful as he. What she did not expect was a feeling more subtle, yet sharper than simple regret. She realized that she had grown used to being with him not only during their hunts but whenever they carried meat to Gray Cape or lolled in the shade watching Menk play. Somehow the fire of her anger had guttered out and been replaced by a new kind of warmth, that of friendship.

It was for that reason she pushed his coming departure to the back of her mind. She had nearly forgotten it when one morning Rahepsi announced he was leaving. He was healed, he said, and ready to reclaim his place among his brothers. But he added something else that startled Kichebo out of her dismay. To take advantage of the better hunting in this area, he intended to bring the group north.

"We'll be close enough to you so that you can join us if you wish," he said. "I'm impressed with your stalking ability and your speed."

Kichebo didn't know how to reply. She stammered her gratitude, but she wasn't sure if she could accept his offer.

"Well, you don't have to decide right away," Rahepsi answered. "While I'm gone, you'll have time to think."

After he left, she spent a long time staring at his tracks. Gray Cape came and sat alongside her. "I heard what Rahepsi offered you. I think you should take it."

The young cheetah looked up at the elder's sharp blue eyes and dove-gray mantle. A shuffling noise and warm, bare hands stroking her coat told her Menk had come, too. The little creature curled close and hugged her.

"I won't leave her. Or you either," said Kichebo vehemently.

"I don't think it's a question of leaving us. Rahepsi said

the group would be close enough so that you could come and go almost as you do now. I can look after Menk."

Kichebo fell silent, watching the reflection of the moon spread along the surface of the river. She heard rather than saw the elder settle next to her. "Kichebo, I think you know what you want. Take it."

"It's not only you and Menk," she answered in a low voice. "It's everything else that's happened. The ruin. Asu-Kheknemt and Tutankhamen."

"And the question of you. What you are; what you were meant to be."

"That . . . too," said Kichebo reluctantly. "You once told me I wasn't just a normal cheetah . . . that I couldn't be."

"I think I did you wrong in saying so," Gray Cape answered. "You do have some unusual abilities; there's no doubt about that. But having them shouldn't cut you off from your own kind." She paused. "Youngster, there is one thing you should understand about me. Some people are ruled by their bellies, some by what they fear others think about them. I'm ruled by my curiosity, wanting to find out why odd things happen."

"What's wrong with that?"

"Nothing, except that what may satisfy my curiosity might not be what is best for you. I could say that if you do choose to spend time with Rahepsi and his people, you are turning your tail on an unusual chance to discover something new. But the truth is that *I'm* the one who wants to explore. What happened to you intrigues me to the ends of my whiskers, and of course I want to know more about it. But I shouldn't stand in the way of what you want. And need," she added, as the young cheetah stared back in astonishment. "Don't deny it. You do. And this is your chance."

"But what about. . . ."

"The one who visits your mind and the two-legged one who is his companion? Well, you'll have less time for them, it is true. But think about it this way, youngster. If enough footprints have been left behind on this trail you call time, then the lives of these creatures ended long ago and their bones are dust. Even if they can call on you from a time when they did exist, their needs should not override yours."

The blunt reality of Gray Cape's statement drew Kichebo a little out of her despair as the old cheetah continued, "So you see, they have no claim on you. Or even if they do, perhaps they can stand to wait until you've reclaimed enough of your life to make up for what you have missed."

Kichebo felt a tentative happiness begin to dawn in her and she let it grow steadily. Perhaps she could have what she wanted. "If I join Rahepsi's group, I'll bring you and Menk the best pieces from my share of our catches."

"Not too much, or they'll throw you out for greediness," warned Gray Cape, but Kichebo was too happy to listen.

"I'll feed you both until you're fat and sleek. You just watch me."

Gray Cape twitched a whisker. "That, you might find a challenge. I have never in my life been what you might call fat. Menk, now, well, she could get a belly on her."

"You just watch me," said Kichebo gleefully.

ELEVEN

As the time approached for Rahepsi to return with his hunting group, Kichebo grew nervous. He had said he would accept her, but what of the others? Only Rahepsi had seen her stalk. What if she made some terrible mistake that cast his praise of her into doubt? What would they think of her if, in her eagerness to show her skills, she broke from cover too early and sent the prey fleeing? The thought drew cold streaks down her back and legs.

Worse still, she must not show any of these seasoned hunters the uncertainty that gnawed at her. If she didn't trust herself, why should they? Try as she would, she couldn't argue these feelings away. Unable to admit them, she grew restless, patroling constantly or pacing the riverbank.

Once Rahepsi arrived with his hunting group, he introduced her to the others, who seemed willing to accept her. There was still the inescapable fact that her dark pelt marked her as different, not only to the cheetahs she would hunt with, but to the prey she coursed.

"You're worried about your coat, aren't you?" said Gray Cape. "From what I've seen, you more than make up for it with your speed, but I'll tell you a trick I saw a warthog use. He had skin nearly as black as your fur and he rolled in a bed of fine clay to lighten it. Maybe we can find some around here."

Cheered by this idea, Kichebo led the way up and down the riverbank until they found a suitable deposit. By rubbing herself against it, she transformed her pelt from sleek black to streaky gray.

"Here, I can even give you some spots." Gray Cape pressed her muzzle against Kichebo's powdered fur. Flakes of dry clay stuck to her damp nose leather, exposing the dark pelt beneath. After making several more fake spots, the old cheetah began to sneeze.

"That should be enough," she said, eyeing Kichebo critically. "If the wind doesn't blow it all out, you'll be fine."

When the two presented themselves to Rahepsi, he agreed that the change had decreased Kichebo's visibility, although she looked very odd for a cheetah.

The sun was halfway along her trail when the group assembled for the day's stalk. After sitting briefly in a star formation and licking each other's faces (which Kichebo couldn't do for fear of losing the camouflage on her muzzle) they set out. She expected Rahepsi to lead, and he did, but soon another male took his place, who then yielded to Bahkti, the other young female who had recently joined. The group had no need for a formal leader; they all seemed to know where they were going.

Skirting other ruins that surrounded the ancient temple, the cheetahs crossed the river floodplain and climbed out of the valley, seeking the uplands where bands of oryxes roamed. As they climbed a rise to survey the barren country beyond, a faint buzzing made Kichebo look back the way she had come and then up.

A speck on the horizon began to expand and take on a definite shape. The noise increased, becoming an irritating sound somewhere between a drone and a hiss. The object flew nearer, showing a streamlined fish form cutting through the air. It sailed close overhead, making the cheetahs flatten and raise their hackles. Then it was once again a faraway dot, diminishing against bleached sky.

The noise faded into the sound of the wind. The other cheetahs rose and shook themselves. They traded questioning looks with each other, but none of them had answers. Only Kichebo, still in her fear-crouch, thought she knew and hated the fact that she did. She searched the horizon ahead, dreading that she would see the speck appear and grow again. When it didn't, she got up stiffly and followed the others, who were moving off.

Her first impulse was to run to Rahepsi and beg him to turn the group back, but she hesitated. What would she say? He had no knowledge of two-legged hunters or strange birds with single gleaming eyes or giant beetles that crept up silently, disgorging attackers to fall on you as you slept. Neither he nor any of the others had been made prey to such things as these, nor would they, she thought.

It was she the hunters wanted. Kichebo's legs shook and her mind went too numb to think any but the simplest thoughts. Turn away. Run now. The group will be safe if you aren't with them. Even as the idea crossed her mind, she saw Rahepsi wheel and trot back to her.

"Don't be frightened," he said, "I've seen these things in the sky before. They never do anything."

"Too close," quavered Kichebo, unable to speak her real fears. Beneath the numbness, her mind was jumping around like a frantic insect. She swallowed and steadied her legs, wondering if he now doubted her courage.

"I don't blame you," he said, and the young cheetah nearly hated the understanding in his voice. "I was startled myself. I've never seen one fly so near us. But it's gone now."

Kichebo's impulse to flee still remained. She looked at Rahepsi, then beyond him to the other cheetahs. She knew if she left them now she would lose what she had longed for all her life. If she tried to explain, they would think she was mad. She could only trust that the airborne seeker would not return, or if it did, it would see an ash-gray spotted pelt instead of a black one.

She rejoined the group and they resumed their search for game. From atop a low ridge, they sighted a slow-moving cloud of dust that betrayed a group of oryx antelope traveling across the plain below. Carefully the cheetahs came down the rocky flank of the ridge, circling wide to keep downwind of the prey. The sun, now at zenith, beat down on Kichebo's back and the fitful wind teased flakes of clay from her fur.

With the others, she crept up behind the small herd. The sight of buff-gray oryx bodies and ebony horns made her pause. She remembered the battles she and Rahepsi had waged with these animals. Grinning to herself, she licked her whiskers. This time the odds would be in the hunters' favor.

So she thought, watching one of Rahepsi's brothers begin his approach. His stalk was flawlessly controled, yet before he could launch his charge, a nervous buck spotted him and honked an alarm call. As one, the herd wheeled and galloped off, leaving the hunters grimacing and twitching their tails.

Bahkti had the next try, then Rahepsi, but the oryx remained wary, never relaxing their guard.

"I don't know what's making them so skittish," complained Rahepsi as he plodded back to the others with his tongue hanging out. Kichebo studied the antelope, noting how they stamped and tossed their heads, trying to impress the enemy with their scimitar horns. But which enemy, the young cheetah found herself wondering. Us? Or something else still hidden. Something else that had perhaps flown close overhead?

"I'll try next," she said quickly, wanting to banish the uncomfortable thought with action. Wordlessly the others scattered and posted themselves nearby to be of aid if she succeeded in separating an animal from the herd.

She crept up directly behind the herd, crouching so low that her chest and belly brushed the ground. She made the scant cover hide her or froze so completely that even the sharp-eyed guards among the bucks didn't see her. This, she knew, was her best performance yet. If she kept control, focused all her attention on the stalk, she could get within sprinting range.

An animal was lagging behind the rest of the herd. Kichebo moved her head to bring a gray rump in line with the center of her nose. She lifted her muzzle, bringing her two gold sighting stripes into view at the bottom of her visual field and locking the target between them.

She burst into the charge, feeling the rhythm of her body increase with every pace. Her back arched and extended; each footfall thrust her farther and faster; she knew now she could not be turned from her prey. . . .

The air about her began to thrum and then to throb with an intensity strong enough to disrupt the cyclic rhythm of her run. Behind her, a cheetah screeched and the voice was raw with alarm. She slowed enough to pull her attention momentarily from her pursuit and then bounced to a stop.

Spotted bodies galloping away on all sides told her that her fellow hunters had suddenly become prey. It took her an instant to recognize the intruder as the sleek fish shape that had crossed the sky. Her own yowl joined the cries of the others as she poured out her dismay and rage. She had drawn it here. She had endangered the others. She had known it would come, yet had been too timid and tongue-tied to warn the hunting group.

The craft gathered speed, moving with impossible smoothness across the plain. Through a smoky translucent cover, Kichebo could see a reclining shadow with a round head and long monkeylike arms. As she watched helplessly, the craft bore down on a cheetah running far ahead of it. Despite his flashing legs and heaving sides, he lost ground steadily. Just as it was about to overtake him, it veered aside.

It cruised along the edge of the fleeing oryx antelope herd, making abortive moves toward several of the scattered cheetahs, but only chasing each a short distance. Kichebo saw Bahkti and Rahepsi trotting together. As if the craft were following her gaze, it swung toward the two and began to accelerate, leaving a swirl of dust in it wake.

She thought the invader would harass them only temporarily as it had the others, but the chase continued as first Bahkti and then Rahepsi were driven to their full speed. Baffled and horrified, Kichebo raced after them.

Rahepsi was running in wild zigzag patterns, doubling back on his path and forcing the craft to slew back and forth in tight turns. Kichebo circled wide and then angled into cut between the craft and its quarry. As she passed Bahkti, the other female somehow found breath to yell something Kichebo knew; her black coat was starting to show in streaks and patches.

Her rage left no room for fear. This was the enemy who had harassed her all her life, who had forced her to hide when she longed to be running free on the plains. Within the skin of this fish who flew over land was the enemy who had now shattered her hope of belonging among her kind. Rahepsi, Bahkti and the others would never forgive her for drawing such a thing down upon them.

The thrum from its motors beat against her, forming an almost tangible barrier of sound. Inside the smoked dome set into its carapace, Kichebo saw the figure moving. Its gestures were quick, almost frantic. The cheetah lifted her nose and brought the shadowed form between her gold sighting stripes. She kept the image there as she hurtled toward the craft, ignoring the thing's looming bulk and the eye-stabbing sunglare from its surface.

It flung grit in her eyes as it yawed away from her, blocking her attack with a stubby wing-vane that thrust out from its body. Nearly blinded, she leaped. Her bared dewclaws scored the translucent cover. Her rear pads slipped and her claws screeched across a smooth surface that sank alarmingly beneath her weight. A hand slapped against the cover from inside, darkened fingers splayed against the curved plastic—a hand the same shape as Menk's.

The vane she had landed on swept down to the ground as the craft wallowed, then rose again. The rising wing carried her up with increasing speed as the craft rolled in the opposite direction. She crouched and sprang as it catapulted her up over the canopy. For an instant she feared she would hit a wing on the opposite side and then she was beyond it, on the ground and running.

The shock of landing that resonated through the bones of her forelegs made her wince as she ran. Glancing back, she felt a quick surge of satisfaction in seeing the invader still rocking and wallowing. It dragged a wing-vane on the ground and spun around helplessly for several moments.

Kichebo turned her back on it and loped over to Rahepsi. Behind him lagged Bahkti, gasping and stumbling. Both gave her numb glances and then looked beyond her to where she had left her disabled victim. Those stares told her before she even turned around that the invader had recovered.

"It wants me," she told the other two cheetahs. "Save yourselves. I'm still fresh enough to draw it away." As if to emphasize her defiance, she whirled and faced the slowly approaching enemy. Rahepsi lurched toward her, his mouth open as if he wanted to speak, but the growing thrum swallowed his words. He lowered his head and galloped away with Bahkti.

Kichebo held her ground, lashing her tail against her flanks. She displayed her teeth in the fiercest grimace she could produce, thinking that she must be as mad as some said she was. Only a mad cheetah would stand alone against a creature like this. Pacing a few steps forward on shaking legs, she waited, expecting the thing to slow and confront her. Instead it veered around her and once again sought Rahepsi.

Her jaw dropped in astonishment and outrage. Before she could dive between Rahepsi and the enemy, a puff of smoke billowed from under the craft's nose and something whizzed through the air. The male staggered, recovered himself, and then turned dazedly to nose a dart that hung like a parasite in the skin behind his foreleg. He turned in circles trying to reach it, fell over, and did not rise again.

The craft approached until it hovered almost above him. Bahkti and the others were spots against the horizon. A mouth opened in the enemy's side behind a stubby wing-vane, disgorging two figures who dropped down and crouched beside the fallen cheetah.

Kichebo stood her ground, facing into the wind. Deliberately she fluffed the remaining clay out of her fur. She knew the hunters had seen her when they flung out their arms and pointed. Even before the hatch closed and the craft began to move once again, Kichebo broke into a choppy lope, knowing she could draw pursuit. The hunters had not been satisfied with one catch. They still wanted her.

The enemy's momentary halt had given Kichebo a fair lead, but soon that distance began to narrow. Her ribs heaved and the breath burned in her throat. The ground became uneven beneath her flying paws, forcing her to lessen her pace, and new fear beat in her throat along with growing exhaustion. When she could spare a glance over her shoulder, she saw that the enemy too had lost speed as it veered and bucked across rough terrain.

The black cheetah swung away from a path that would have led her back onto even ground. Instead she plunged down steeper gullies and scrambled up sharp rises. She could hear the invader's engines surge and whine as it fought its way after her. Ahead lay a rockfall at the foot of a low cliff. The sun's track across the sky had cast the tumbled stones into deep shadow and they might hold a crack into which she might crawl. She set her face toward it and forced more speed from her aching muscles. The terrain grew increasingly rugged until each stride risked a fall that might break one of her slender legs.

She ducked into cool shade, scrambling and floundering across the rocks until at last, bruised and shaking, she found an opening between two stones that had fallen together. She dived to the far end of a narrow cave, curled up in a huddle, and tried not to pant too heavily. Trying to restrain her breathing made her dizzy and at last she gave up and gulped air as she waited for the sound of her pursuer.

At first she heard the howl of engines and then the grating of stone against metal. Hope stirred inside her. The craft was too large to make its way through. The pulsating roar faded and she lifted her head, knowing it was backing off. A few moments later, the sound changed to a steady drone. Now it came from above and grew louder, freezing her inside her refuge.

Outside, its shadow rippled across the stones and a flash of reflected sunlight dazzled her. Again it passed low overhead, engines shrieking. The sound echoed back from the cliff, making Kichebo flinch and tremble. She fought the impulse to break from cover and flee. Instead she curled into a tighter huddle than before, closed her eyes and buried her nose in her tail.

So far did she withdraw inside herself, she did not notice when the droning noise faded away. Her terror gave way to the stupor of exhaustion and then to sleep.

A cramp in one of her hind legs woke her. Despite the pain, she kept herself still until she was sure the enemy had gone. Crawling out to stretch, she felt a deep ache in her lungs and she smarted all over from bruises and scrapes gotten from her scramble across the rocks. Worse still was the memory of the cheetahs in the hunting group scattering before the enemy's charge and the startled look in Rahepsi's eyes before he fell.

Moaning aloud, Kichebo hung her head until her whiskers brushed the ground. Why had she even run away this time? Why hadn't she stayed with Rahepsi and let the two-legged hunters take her? The hunting group was broken and scattered. Even if they managed to assemble again, they would have nothing to do with the one who brought such an evil down upon them.

Slowly and stiffly, she picked her way out of the rockfall, wondering how she had avoided tripping in her headlong race to safety. She knew now why she had run instead of letting herself be taken. The memory of that hand splayed against the canopy from the inside sparked a memory of another, smaller hand that slapped mud, threw eggs, and gently stroked the fur on Kichebo's cheek.

And she remembered the image of a black cheetah that lay before her in a sunlit pool beside the ruin. Only he could answer the questions that lay deepest in her heart. Perhaps if she returned to that place, he would come again.

She looked across the barren plain to the glow of the setting sun. There was only one path for her life now and she must take it. Wearily she lifted her head and began her journey back to the great ruin beside the river.

The young cheetah arrived before the great gateway just as the dew was drying in the first heat of the morning sun. Behind her the river sparkled and sang its constant song, but even Hapi's music couldn't drown the noise that seemed to echo inside her mind: the roar of engines and the cries of other cheetahs as they fled. In her haste, she had neither hunted nor eaten, and hunger made her legs unsteady.

There was no sign of either Menk or Gray Cape. The ruin lay as still as it was when she had first approached it. For a moment, a feeling of relief displaced the longing that had drawn her back here. For a little while, at least, she could delay having to explain what had happened. She wandered away from the gateway toward the river's shore and lay down in the shade.

The next thing she felt was a blunt claw, gently prodding her awake. Shame and a sudden, dull anger washed over her as she squinted against strong sunlight. She wasn't ready. Not yet.

But Gray Cape, as if sensing her reluctance, held her questions and instead nosed Menk toward her. The touch of the child's hands woke the pain that had been dulled by time and the journey back. Kichebo laid her head against the smooth bare chest and opened her mouth wide in a soundless cry. Menk bent her head close, letting her tumbled hair fall about the cheetah's face. For a minute Kichebo was still, letting the mute comfort soak through her. A stray Menk-hair tickled her nose and she sneezed several times, making Menk giggle with delight.

Feeling slightly better, Kichebo shook herself and sat up. A fishy smell rising from the ground near her feet told her that someone had caught another one of her namesakes. No sooner had she scented the catch than it was in her mouth and down her throat. She rubbed her head against Menk, for the scent on the grubby little palms told her who had caught it.

"I was starting to patrol this morning," said Gray Cape brusquely, yet with a certain awkwardness, as if she didn't know where to begin. "I didn't get to our southern border. If you would like to finish it yourself. . . ."

Kichebo gazed into the old face, reading the curiosity and concern that lay behind the schooled expression. Gray Cape must have worn the same detached, diplomatic look in her career as a messenger. It was an offer to delay speaking or hearing ill news. Kichebo didn't take it.

"I came back alone," she said, trying to flatten her feelings along with the tone of her voice. "Rahepsi and the others are gone."

"Were you attacked?" asked Gray Cape.

Kichebo's mouth fell open. "How did—"

"I didn't. Shortly after you left, one of those sky-creatures flew low over the ruin. Menk and I hid and it soon went away, but I could guess who it wanted."

Kichebo started and began to shake. "Then I am not safe, even here," she wailed.

194

"Hush, youngster. They didn't find you here so they will hunt you elsewhere."

"The sky-creature did find us. It came down to the ground and chased us. It threw something at Rahepsi. He fell and lay still. The rest of us scattered and I ran and hid where it couldn't get at me, but when I came out, I had to travel by night and even then I heard sounds. It might have tracked me here. It might be crawling toward me now, coming to swallow me as it did Rahepsi. . . ." Kichebo's tongue was too dry for further words.

The mane rose along Gray Cape's back, but all she said was, "Don't scare yourself more than you have to, youngster. None of the birds or animals I saw this morning seemed disturbed, and they certainly would be if any creature like that was close. All the same, maybe you'd better stay out of sight."

After glancing suspiciously over her shoulder, Gray Cape led Kichebo around the gate into the ruin. They both agreed that the shady niches it offered would make the best hiding places. And, although Kichebo did not mention this to Gray Cape, she thought that her return to the place where her brother-in-time had once walked might bring him again. She fell asleep holding that thought close in her mind.

TWELVE

Although Tut tried to ignore Horemheb's words and listened instead to the counseling of Aye, I could see that the general had aimed and struck true. The accusation that my king could not reign without me by his side rankled deeply. I was no mere animal; both Aye and the king knew that well; but who else would believe it? And so, for the first time, Aye kept me away from the king for the journey back to Thebes and I did not see my master again until we were again within our palace quarters.

He was as affectionate and respectful to me as ever, but I sensed something had changed. Our trips to the House of the Swift became fewer and finally ceased. He stopped reading and studying the papyrus that had so intrigued him at first. It was difficult for me to believe that he could turn his back on all we had done, especially that final joining of spirits that fused both of us into an entity with powers beyond either. It was then that I learned of the human ability to convince itself that what had happened was not so, to

196

deny the real truth of wonder for the false truth of drab existence.

He managed to persuade himself that the creature he and I had become in the shaded courtyard on that day was a mere dream, a figment of an over-wishful imagination. I noticed that he avoided that courtyard and even gave orders that the knife-scarred palm tree be cut down and burned. And, most of all, he never looked me full in the eyes, fearing to see the possibility he had now turned away from.

I was often left in the care of an attendant while he went about his duties of state, and there was even talk in the household of returning me to the House of the Swift. When I first heard the news that a royal gazelle hunt was being planned for the month of the lioness, Sekhmet, I grew hopeful I might regain my partnership with him in the intensity of the chase. But as I watched the preparations being made, the chariot horses being groomed, provisions being loaded on wagons, and the best of the coursers chosen, I slowly realized I was to be left behind.

At first I grew angry, but my rage soon gave way to trepidation. I remembered well those hunts, the noise, the shouting, the milling confusion as chariots rumbled and weapons flew. I remembered the smells of the men around my king and how there were a few whose palms might itch to loose an arrow through his neck. In the wild confusion it would be easy to claim that a shot went wide and that the killing was an accident.

The more I thought about it, the more I grew certain that this was Horemheb's gambit. Again I wished bitterly that I had a human voice to warn Tut, for in his outraged pride he had cast away the other means by which I might have reached him. All I could do was paw and grimace. He would push me away, gently but insistently, refusing to look in my eyes.

On the morning of the hunt, I woke early in a chamber near his apartments and paced restlessly. The previous evening I had tried to hide to emerge later and follow my king in secret. But before I could escape, I was caught by a house servant and shut in. My only hope was that the room I was confined in lay on the hall through which my king would pass on his way from his quarters to the great courtyard.

I lay crouched, my head against the heavy door. When I heard footsteps, I drew back and hurled myself against the barrier, putting all my rage and anguish into yowls. The thought that he would ignore me and pass on was too much to bear. I battered the door in my fury.

The footsteps stopped. I heard a low babble of voices, Tut's among them. The bronze bolt eased back and I forced my muzzle into the crack that opened. With his knee firmly against my chest, he forced me back inside and then knelt beside me, stroking me gently. The quivers of arrows he had hung about him bumped against me and the broad twin sashes of his outer-kilt twined around my legs as I sidestepped with mingled joy and panic.

His eyes were soft, but the planes of his face were set beneath the gold band of the khepresh-war-helmet as he spoke to me. "Asu-Kheknemt, I know you have been my guard and companion since I first came to the throne. I remember the day you stood with me as we faced the snake-goddess. I was a child then, but I am a man now. And I must rule as a man."

I opened my mouth wide as if I could somehow beseech him not to go. "*Ba meht*, I think Aye has spoken to me the words you cannot say. I know Horemheb would goad me into recklessness. I have determined I will not fall into his trap. But in his goading there is some truth. If I have not the strength to face my enemies, I have no right to rule. *Ba meht*, I will not always have you. The years creep faster over your kind than mine."

His hand slid from my head and he stood gazing down at me from beneath the uraeus-snake on his brow. I stared back at my pharaoh, magnificent in his hunting regalia, and I felt helpless and foolish. Yes, there would have to be a time when he would rule without my companionship, for as much as I hated the idea that I was growing old, I had to accept it. But did it have to come on this day? I am far from feeble, my king, I longed to cry. The gouged and wounded door shows that.

He would not heed me. There is a moment when the half-grown cub must try for his own prey without help from anyone else. That moment had come for me, and I knew then it had come for him. Nothing I could do would stay his attempt and perhaps I was wrong even to try. I could only hope that he had judged the quarry's strength as he had judged his own.

I did not try to force my way past him as he left the chamber. Instead I crouched, lying with my chin on my paws as his foosteps died away. A short time later a keeper from the House of the Swift came and clipped a lead to my collar. Perhaps it would be better if I spent the day on the training field instead of lying here in the palace. I heaved myself up and went willingly, although I could not help the heaviness of my step and wondered if I was after all beginning to feel the aches of age.

We were just leaving by the servant's way when I caught a well-known scent and heard the slap of familiar sandals. Aye's big hand took my lead. With the other he gently shoved aside the keeper, over the young man's protests that he would be punished for not obeying the pharaoh's instructions to take me to the House of the Swift.

"Asu-Kheknemt has other work this day," said Aye and told the trainer to take us to the wagons carrying the royal coursers to the chase. They were still in the stableyard, not having been brought up to the courtyard to join the main party of light chariots.

"Good," said Aye and led me past a wagon full of yelping greyhounds to the one holding cheetahs. Behind the wicker bars I saw my son, Neba Resu. Quickly, the Divine Father took me aside into a corner and smeared my gold markings with charcoal mixed with tallow from a little pot in his sash. At his order, the young keeper opened the cage-wagon and took Neba Resu out. My son's collar and leash were transferred to me.

The smell of the beef tallow made me want to lick my muzzle, but I knew I must keep my disguise. Even as the wagons started to roll, Aye handed my leash to the now-confused keeper and sent him running after the train, calling, "Halt, one has been forgotten."

The wagon rumbled to a stop amid complaints of mules and driver alike. When the cage door opened, I sprang to Neba Resu's place and crouched, taking care not to disturb the black ointment that covered my markings. When the cart halted again and the huntmaster came to inspect us, he sniffed at the odor of tallow but saw nothing amiss. So, playing the part of Neba Resu, I rode the wagon in the train of the king's hunt.

Our party had to travel far into the rocky desert of the Gebel before scouts found signs of game. Sunset came and we made camp in the shadow of the Theban hills.

Tired and cramped from a bumpy ride in a wicker cage, I longed to jump out when our grizzled huntmaster opened the cage door, intending to let me stretch my legs before feeding me. Fearful he might recognize me despite my disguise, I hung back, ducking his attempts to stroke me. He gave up and tossed the meat into my cage, muttering that Neba Resu was not his usual self tonight. He might have examined me more closely for signs of sickness had he not been preoccupied with feeding and exercising the other cheetahs.

Enviously I watched as he tended to them. Before he shut them once again in their cages, he played briefly with each one, dispensing the rough affection that to him was as important as diet and exercise.

Relieved that he had not been prompted by my behavior to take a closer look at me, I settled down in my cage at the back of the wagon. Being confined did not annoy me greatly. On other hunts, I had been tied on a long chain or, as the king's favorite, had slept in his tent. This time, with a pack of greyhounds picketed close by, I was just as glad to have what protection the traveling-cage offered me.

Insects began to saw and chirp. Cooking fires flickered in the dusk and I heard the voices of men, muted by the heavy heat that still lingered from the day. I listened to other cheetahs turn restlessly in their cages before falling asleep. I yawned widely and laid my chin on the floor between my forepaws, wondering what the following day would bring.

Just as I started to drift, I heard two sets of footsteps approaching the wagon. Above the murmur of talk in the camp, I caught mingled voices, one deep and boisterous, the other lighter and more nasal.

"I am looking forward to seeing our hunting leopards course gazelles tomorrow, General," said the second voice. "I have long been an admirer of these fierce hunters, their beauty and speed."

"Agreed, they are pretty to watch," the first voice answered in a pleasant but bored tone, "but I wouldn't call them fierce. From what I've seen, they're a cowardly bunch. They'll spit and snarl, but they won't hold their ground against an enemy. Give me a good hunting dog, one who'll dig in and fight. Our boy-king can keep his long-legged pets."

"What game have the scouts found?" asked the other voice timidly after a brief silence.

"What we expected," Horemheb answered, for by now I recognized his voice. "Oryx, gazelle, ostrich. They crossed the trail of a panther, but the wily bastard is probably far into the hills by now."

"His Majesty must be disappointed that they have found no trace of a lion. I hear he hoped to shoot his first one."

"No doubt he would. Perhaps then the gold panels he has made to portray his heroic deeds would approach the truth."

As the two men came near, I lifted my head and drew my feet beneath me. My companions, in adjacent cages, stirred and woke. I caught the odor of contempt in Horemheb's smell and, under that, a whiff of vicious intent. The general's companion peered in at me. His smell reminded me of a fawning jackal and I could not help growling deep in my throat. The man blanched and stepped back.

Horemheb's face immediately replaced his in front of the bars. I cursed myself for drawing his attention as he crouched, his hands on his knees, studying me. "Well, what do we have here? One of those inky sons of bitches that used to be temple cats under the reign of the Heretic."

"General," said the other man nervously, "maybe we should refrain from disturbing the creature."

"Afraid? Let me just show you what cowards these animals are." A malicious grin came onto his face and he leaped up, flinging his arms wide. He was of a formidable height, and I had to fight an overwhelming instinct to scramble to the rear of the cage.

I faced his bulk through the bars of the cage. For the first time I felt the impotent rage of the trapped animal. I wanted to rip the wood and rattan apart with my dewclaws and hurl myself at this tormentor. He was goading me, just as he had goaded my king, into wild and reckless anger. And the knowledge that he would strike Tut down as coldly as he would slay me lashed my rage to a frenzy.

The butt of a heavy staff thrust against my chest. My claws splintered rattan as I was shoved to the rear of the cage. "Curse you," he breathed, shoving his bloated stubbled face close to the bars. Shouts were starting up behind us as the keepers realized someone was molesting one of their charges, but I barely heard them. My attention was focused on the hand that held the pole against my chest, the hand slipping with the pole into my cage, between the bars, coming within my reach. . . .

With a wrench, I freed one of my forepaws and lashed out. My forearm slammed against a bar. My dewclaw caught and held human skin. The stick slipped. I lunged, trying to bite, and struck the side of my head against the cage. With a curse, the hand was snatched back and the staff fell with a rattle to the floor.

I hoped to see Horemheb bent double over his wounded hand, but instead the man stared at me, seeming almost oblivious to the blood painting his palm. "Look," he hissed, pointing at me and then at the smear of black ointment on the bar where I had struck my head. "Look at that gold edge on his ear. That's the damned king's cat!"

With a brief look over his shoulder toward the keepers' tent Horemheb paused, staring at me as if my image was burning itself on the back of his brain. There was a scuffle as his unnerved companion took flight, but I barely noticed him. I knew that in giving way to rage, I had ruined the disguise Aye had so carefully put on me. What chance now would I have to protect my king from those set against him? And what was the chance I would even live to see the dawn after betraying myself so?

"So you would hunt the lion, Son of the Sun." Horemheb spoke, but not to me, even though he kept his eyes fixed on me. "So you shall."

Then he was gone, leaving me with a dull pain where the pole had thrust against my chest and the sharper one of knowing I had been an utter fool.

Our keeper arrived, circling the wagon and muttering imprecations on the scoundrel who had upset his animals. I huddled miserably at the rear of the cage trying to hide the gold edge of my ear from sight. If they found I was not Neba Resu, there would be no end of a commotion and I would probably be sent back to the palace.

They posted a guard over our wagon, but as I watched the man grow sleepy and lean heavily on his spear, I became more nervous. Each noise, whether it was the sudden chirp of a nearby insect or the rattle of pebbles under a sandal made me start and sweat from my paw pads. I fought sleep, often jerking back from an incipient slide into oblivion to imagine the shadow of an archer with drawn bow aiming his arrow through the bars of my cage.

It was not I who was struck down that night, despite my fears. Toward the end of the first watch I heard moans coming from the keepers' tent. One man after another emerged at a shaky run to fall to his knees in the moonlit desert scrub and empty his stomach. A few other men in others tents sickened and the word began to be passed around the camp that tainted food was the cause.

Hearing this only convinced me that there was more mischief afoot. From what I could gather from the conversations outside my cage, the sickness seemed only to have struck a few, although all had eaten the same fare. To my relief, there was no sound of tumult from the royal pavilion. Whatever was attacking the men had chosen to spare their king, at least for the night.

One other thing became clear as I strained my ears to catch hurriedly exchanged words of men scurrying back and forth past my wagon. The sickness had struck selectively. Many of the victim's names were men I had seen at various times with Aye when he had visited the palace. I knew then that the Divine Father must have secreted those loyal to himself and the King within this expedition with orders to emerge and defend him if an assassination attempt was made. Aye had not sent me alone, wise man that he was.

I grew cold with the thought that I had undone that wisdom. A man such as Horemheb would know the motives of everyone in the camp. He would have managed to locate Aye's men and track them with agents of his own. But unless he knew that his plan was betrayed, that there were worms in the meat of his kill, he dared not draw attention by striking them down. Now he knew. By revealing myself in my careless rage, I had warned him. Those who might have aided me could only writhe helplessly with their hands pressed to their bellies, poison drenching their guts.

How he had done it, I don't know. That he had, I was certain. The thought kept me circling within the small confines of my cage, wondering if I should try to claw my way out of the wood and wicker and escape before dawn. I tested my strength against the cage and discovered it was stronger than it looked. I might be able to break out before sunrise, but the noise might well bring guards and keeps down on me.

I gave up and sat rigidly, listening to the night. Just after the guard changed for the third watch, I heard the slap of the reins and the rattle of harness as a chariot sped away. None of the men around me heard it, for by now the entire camp had fallen into a heavy slumber and exhaustion had dulled the guards' attention.

In my mind, I kept hearing Horemheb's last words before he left. "You would hunt the lion, Son of the Sun. So you shall." Those words had seemed a prideful boast when he spoke them, but now as they echoed inside my head, they began to take on a sinister sound. No doubt he meant himself, for even I had to admit he had the right to claim himself a lion among men. Yet a voice whispered to me that he meant something more.

Despite my struggle to stay wakeful, I fell into a doze and dreamed of great tawny shapes pacing back and forth in front of me, filling the air with thunderous roars. Under the paw of the greatest lay a young bull, wounded and dying. He bled not the thick, heavy blood of cattle, but the bright blood of men, and his eyes, when they turned to me, were human.

Shivering with fright and the cold dew of early morning, I woke. The sun topped the Theban hills, sending shafts of sharp light between ancient peaks like spears thrown down into the camp. A light breeze blew between the bars of my cage, ruffling my fur and pulling at my whiskers. It bore the odors of food on the cook-fires, the oils used to rub leather and bowstrings, and the sweaty scent of men rolling out of their cots after a hot, restless night. There was one more odor, so faint I could not identify it at first and so tenuous I was not sure. Perhaps it was just the remnant of my dream.

I faced into the wind and shut my eyes, trying to concentrate on what my nose was telling me. For an instant the smell became distinct, bringing an image into my mind. A lion yes, but one starved and cage-galled, maddened by ill-treatment. The fleeting image was gone instantly and the shifting breeze brought me only the smells of horses, dogs and men.

A little later, scouts came back into camp, bearing news of a large herd of oryx antelope further ahead. Quickly we were made ready and our wagon rolled out of camp in the wake of the two-horse chariots. Soon my nostrils filled with the pungent scent of the prey, for the hunters were careful to approach downwind. The wagon creaked to a stop in a little hollow. A man I didn't recognize came to fetch me. He must, I thought, be a replacement for my handler, who had been taken sick. I thought of hanging back in the cage, then springing out to attack him and make my escape, but his words to the huntmaster made me think again.

"I have word that our lord wishes Neba Resu, son of Asu-Kheknemt, be the first to course." The old man eyed him for a minute and then gave assent. Unfamiliar as this new handler was to me, he clearly knew his business. With a reassuring pat, he leashed me and jumped me down off the wagon. He seemed friendly as well as attentive and some of my apprehension faded as I followed him.

On our way to the line of chariots, he paused and straddled me, pinning my ribcage between his legs. I thought then that he was going to hood me for the chase, for I smelt no malicious intent in his odor. Suddenly my vision was blocked as an oil-soaked linen cloth made hard swipes along my muzzle and over my head, removing the black paste covering my face and ear markings. Startled, I shot up, hitting him in the crotch with my back, but he clamped his knees about my loins and wrestled the hood onto me. Unable to see, I could only follow the pull of the lead as he led me past the line of chariots.

Blinded and totally baffled, I was made to sit, wondering

what part I was to play in this. Why had this new trainer, if such he was, cleaned the concealing ointment from my face and then covered it again with the hood? To the king and all watching, I was still Neba Resu.

Across the plain I heard the milling and bawling of antelope. Their smell filled my nostrils, distracting me from other thoughts. Suddenly all that had happened seemed ridiculous and irrelevant. I was a hunter set to stalk prey. That's what I had been bred for through thousands of years. My instincts surged to the fore, shouting that it did not matter whether one man lived or died this day. What were the monkey games of men compared to the clean, swift beauty of the chase?

I felt the ties loosening on my hood. A hand grasped my head, turning it swiftly, pointing me to the prey. I knew I would run alone, for this man lacked any means to guide me once I left him behind. In my anger and defiance I was glad. The hood was snatched away and my target was there between my sighting stripes, a young male antelope, standing slightly apart from the rest of the herd, nervously stamping a rear hoof.

My claws tore the ground as I dove at the beast. My back arched and bowed. My speed filled my nostrils and mouth with wind and I drank it, feeling the stretch and power of my limbs. How could I ever have thought myself old, I wondered.

Brown-and-buff bodies thundered beside me as I cleaved a path through, holding the image of my victim steady in my eyes. I drew closer, gathering myself for the final lunge and downstrike with bared dewclaws. Suddenly dust spurted, covering the antelope's legs as he skidded to a halt and reared. As if they had met the edge of a cliff, the entire herd turned as one and wheeled back toward me. It was then I smelled the lion.

I caught only a glimpse of him through the welter of hurtling forms and billowing dust. His mouth opened, but the roar I heard came from hundreds of pounding hooves. His charge, more fearful than mine, had turned the herd back on me. I wrenched myself around, shocked out of the intoxication brought on by the chase. I had no chance of a kill within this mass of crazed animals. I launched myself into a run, but my charge had spent me. With cold terror streaking down my back as I ran, I knew I would soon fall beneath those lashing hooves.

Through the rumbling around me, I heard the sharp crack of a whip and the shrill whinny of horses. Lifting my head, I saw a chariot separate from the line and plunge into the melee. A voice cried out, first in a deep shout and then cracking into a scream. "To me, Asu-Kheknemt! To me!"

The young king's keen eyes had seen that the coursing cheetah was not Neba Resu. Men ran to seize the reins of his royal chariot but they were left behind. The blue khepresh on his head and ribbons of gold flying from his shoulder cape left me no doubt. As I veered my course toward his chariot, I saw him bind the reins about his waist and yank his bow from its case, loosing an arrow toward the lion. The shot went wild and nearly cost him his footing in the flimsy vehicle.

I was cut off from him by a river of antelope and fled madly in the opposite direction. Again I tried to reach him, but he was now far on the other side of the herd, throwing up dust from the wildly spinning wheels and churning legs of his horses. Again he drew and shot. The arrow quivered in the lion's flank, turning it from a fresh kill. I heard the bellow of rage as it lunged and clawed at the streaking chariot.

The contraption lurched up on one wheel and I thought it would tip, but somehow it righted itself and my king still clung to the leather-and-wood frame. Now the horses were running free, the reins flopping loosely on their backs. I leaped and dodged as never before, fighting my way through the milling herd, ignoring the burning in my lungs and the leaden ache dragging at my legs.

Without control the chariot horses slowed and ran in confused circles, making them a tempting target for the wounded lion. Tut knew this, for I could see him leaning far over the rail trying to grab the flying reins. I saw a gap in the herd and flung myself through it, racing in the wake of his chariot. Spent as I was, I managed to overtake the cantering horses. I saw the leather straps trailing on the ground to the side of the horses' feet. As the chariot swung wide in another panicked turn, I seized the reins in my mouth and put the last of my strength into a desperate leap.

I landed badly, hitting the front rail and nearly knocking Tut from the swaying platform. He had the presence of mind to seize the reins from my jaws and haul my dangling hindquarters inside. I sprawled on the woven leather floor between his legs, thinking my heart would burst. A knifing pain in my chest told me I had splintered a rib. I could only lie limply, trying to get my breath as Tut fought to control the horses.

I thought then I could do no more, but a deep roar close by brought my head up over the side. A tawny form loped alongside us, angling in. By some miracle Tut had kept his bow and quiver. Taking the reins in his teeth, he shot, striking the beast high on the shoulder. I thought that would discourage it, but it kept chasing us. I could see its drawn belly and the stretch of skin over its ribs. The hunger-mad glint in its eyes was not the look of a wild lion, and the dry sores on its legs were evidence of its previous captivity.

Each bound brought it closer to us. I knew one swipe of those heavy paws could throw the chariot over. Tut fumbled for an arrow, but an abrupt lurch spilled his quiver. I clung, watching the lion through the open weave of the side panel. When the beast drew close for a vengeful blow, I sprang up.

Tut saved me from falling under the wheels as I brought my dewclaws down on the lion's muzzle, laying his face open and blinding him with blood. As the beast reeled away, an arrow shot from behind us thudded deep into his chest.

My king's shout of surprise was cut off by another shaft that bounced with a crack off the spinning chariot wheel. I looked back to see several vehicles coming after us, their drivers yelling and bowmen firing at the wounded lion. Their shots toppled the beast, but still the hail continued, some of the shafts coming uncomfortably close to us.

An arrow smacked into the quilted pad on the back of one of our horses, making it scream and rear. Another whistled close over my head, tearing a rip in the side-panel. My suspicions flared into anger. Whether this was in Horemheb's plan or not, he was taking advantage of it. Tut's death in a hunting accident would be easy to explain. As my king glanced at me, I saw the same idea dawning in his eyes.

Quickly Tut lashed the reins to the wooden rail, letting the horses do what they wished. As the chariot bucked and turned, he flung his arm about me. "Asu-Kheknemt," he whispered raggedly, "forgive me for trying to push you aside. If that moment in the courtyard wasn't just a dream, let us be once again what we were then."

I knew instantly what he wanted. I remembered how, as a joined being, we had deflected a thrown knife from its path. Too relieved and grateful to resent his previous treatment of me, I welcomed this new partnership, but I had no time to rejoice; the arrows were striking close about and only the chariot's wild rocking saved us. Driven by panic, we threw ourselves together into the contact, merging man and cheetah into the one who had power to save us both.

Unlike the previous time, I experienced no intermediate transitions. I came to full life in my two bodies, feeling my abilities wake with me. The sharp tossing of the chariot became to me a gentle rocking and the hail of arrows a soft fall, like the down-drift of leaves. My feet, both sandaled and clawed, balanced on the swaying leather weave with ease. I looked up to the first descending shaft with its fletched end fluttering from the wind of its flight. With the hand of my will, I knocked it aside and sought the next. Some I took pleasure in sending back in the direction they had come, although not with sufficient force to cleave flesh, for I felt myself beyond that need.

Setting part of myself the task of deflecting arrows, I grasped the reins and tried to control the maddened horses. By extending my shield over them, I managed to regain command and as I brought the chariot around, the rain of arrows faltered.

From the drivers of other vehicles approaching through

swirling dust, I sensed disbelief and awe. Both my cheetah and human jaws stretched wide in a howl of triumph. Soon they would know what their king had become. Soon all who tried to kill me would prostrate themselves before me, begging forgiveness. I would grant them pardon, even Horemheb, for I would not need their deaths, knowing I was immune to their petty and pitiful efforts to strike me down.

A small but sharp voice from the depths of myself sounded a warning. I could not count on remaining indefinitely in this state. Taking some heed, I examined myself and found no sense of weariness or impending dissolution as had terminated my first experience. Encouraged, I whipped up my horses and drove in triumph toward the first approaching chariot.

Its driver's grit-and-sweat-stained face broke into a grin of welcome, but with my new acuity of sight, I saw the corners of his mouth tremble. As the warning came, so did the attack. The driver ducked aside as a husky form in dust-covered leather armor reared up behind him, hefting a javelin.

I focused my defense on the glittering spearhead, thinking to turn it easily aside but quickly learned that the brutal thrust behind it would not yield as readily as a speeding arrow. The bronze point reddened and deformed with my effort against it, but as it slowed, my power faltered. When I drew on further reserves, I felt with dismay the first twinge of weariness that would herald my separation back into two separate selves. In the first surge of desperation, I flew at the assassin's eyes in my four-legged form, but my cheetah-body had barely launched itself when the two chariots collided.

To the human I had been, it would have happened in an instant. To the being I had become, it seemed to take an eternity for the coal-red glow of the spearpoint to find my left cheek. I both saw and felt how the impact of the crash forced open my jaw as the searing bronze tip pressed and then pierced the flesh of my face, slicing my tongue, shattering my palate, and driving through my sinuses to the center of mind itself.

In the last startling instants at the close of my life, the eyes of both my selves found each other in a fleeting horror-filled glance. From cheetah eyes I saw my human body arch back, screaming and clawing at the spear hilt, sticking like a grotesque tusk from the tear in its face. Then I saw, as death faded human sight, my cheetah body convulse in midair, pitching over and dropping as if struck through with the same shaft. My being was wrenched apart in a blood-red flash, sending its two pieces spinning into oblivion.

THIRTEEN

Kichebo woke just before dawn, her mouth dry, her heart racing. It took her a few moments to understand that she was back in her own self again. She shuddered, remembering Tut's end and Kheknemt's plunge into unconsciousness. Had he died too? If so. . . .

She shook her head until her ears flapped. It was too confusing to think of such things. Kheknemt and Tut were both long dead, their bones now dust blowing across the desert. Yet she wanted to fling herself down and cry aloud to mourn them. How could their lives have ended so abruptly and brutally? What purpose was there in forcing her to share their pain when she had enough of her own?

Kichebo rose from where she had slept, curled up in a recess deep within the ruined temple. Nearby, Menk and Gray Cape mingled snores. She didn't wake them. It was still too early to get up. Besides, all she could look forward to was a day of hiding amid the tumbled stones, trying not to think of what had happened to Rahepsi or what might be lying in wait for her.

She lifted her head, watching pale light creep between the great pillars. This place was as much a home as the world had ever offered her, but even here, she didn't feel entirely safe. And what of Menk and Gray Cape? If she stayed, she would draw danger to them as well. She knew the attack would eventually come. The only question was when.

She shivered and flattened her ears. The morning was curiously quiet. There were no birds peeping or insects droning by. She seemed to hear her own breath echoing between the pillars. Even Menk and Gray Cape sighed once and quieted their snoring.

At first she thought she was listening for the approach of the enemy. Even when silence told her it was not there, she continued to listen, though not so much with her ears as with her mind. She thought she heard a voice, so quiet that it was lost in the stillness. Nervously she paced between the columns, as if by moving she could bring herself closer to the one who would speak to her. Even as she did so, she chided herself for foolishness, knowing that the voice came from within.

Are you there, my brother-in-time? Kichebo stood with her eyes closed, focusing all her attention inward. All was quiet both within and without, telling her that even if Asu-Kheknemt still lived, he lacked the strength to reach her.

Disgruntled, she shook her head and resumed her pacing. As the shadow stripes of the columns fell across her back, they felt cold. The vaulting roof beams, which had once seemed as lofty as the sky, seemed to press down upon her with menacing weight. She found herself wondering how long this structure had stood and if it might choose this moment to collapse.

"Don't blame you for worrying about those sky-creatures," said Gray Cape, misinterpreting Kichebo's upward gaze. The old cheetah had wakened and was trying to rouse Menk. "I got the shivers when hunters flew over here yesterday. This place is no longer safe. I say we go north."

"Downriver?"

"Where else? We haven't much choice if we're going to escape those pesky hunters. If we keep to the brush near the shoreline, we won't be seen."

Kichebo only half heard the old cheetah's reply. An odd impulse made her gaze through the worn pillars to the river and its far bank. It was on that side that Kheknemt had lived and hunted. Beneath those cliffs rising up from the dry floor of the western valley, Tut had met his death in the crash of a chariot and the thrust of a javelin. The young pharaoh's story was finished and surely Kheknemt's must also be. Why then did Kichebo feel drawn to the far side of the river, as if there lay a trail she might find and follow?

Not footprints, she thought to herself. Another kind of trail.

The longer she stared at the distant cliffs the more certain she became that her journey must take her to that shore and beyond. She sighed unhappily. To go across instead of downriver flew in the face of common sense and survival. She heard the old cheetah come up behind her. "Kichebo?"

"Gray Cape," she said without turning her eyes from the river. "Do you remember how you told me to trust my feelings about Asu-Kheknemt? He called me to him again last night. Something happened . . . I don't know how to tell you about it yet, but . . . I can't go downriver. I have to go across."

There was a long silence before the other asked in a low voice, "Are you sure?"

"Yes."

"Well, if this crossing is Kheknemt's idea, he's not making your life any easier. Not to mention mine. Tell him it's a scatting foolish idea."

Kichebo stared at the ground between her paws. "I can't. Is there even a way to get over the river?"

"Well, I suppose I could save myself a lot of trouble by lying, but the scatting truth is that yes, there is a way. I used it when I was young and stupid."

"There is? Can you show me?"

"All right," Gray Cape said gruffly, "but let's get a few things straight. First is that if you go, Menk and I go with you. I can't hunt enough for myself let alone her. Second is that if you're dead set on making it across, you risk losing one or the other of us, most likely me. I don't have any illusions about how easy this will be. The last time I did it, I sprained a shoulder and nearly drowned. I was in much better shape then than I am now."

The young cheetah's whiskers had been bristling with excitement. Now they drooped.

"Don't think I'm trying to talk you out of it, youngster. If you have to go, you have to. I'm just trying to tell you what the choices really are." Gray Cape padded away, leaving Kichebo alone.

She sat, flexing her dewclaws in annoyance and trying to ignore the impulse that kept plucking at her to gaze across the river. The idea that she would be willing to take chances with the lives of her companions in order to satisfy this strange compulsion horrified her.

Go away, she thought at Kheknemt, as if he were still trying to reach her. *I don't owe you anything. You're dead.*

Even as she tried to push him out of her mind, she felt her throat tighten. He and only he held what she so desperately sought: the truth about herself and her life. If somehow she could follow him through the rest of his story, for she sensed there was more, she might gain the answers. She knew that if she gave in and followed Gray Cape, she might save herself, but something in her innermost being would die and rot.

When the old cheetah returned, Kichebo couldn't look her in the face. "I'm sorry. I have to go," she said, letting her head droop along with her whiskers.

"Hold your head up, youngster. No need to be ashamed to do what you must. In my life I've run many a strange trail, but the one you're leading me on promises to be the queerest yet. I'll stick with you to the end, if just out of curiosity."

Kichebo guessed that more than curiosity was involved, but Gray Cape would never admit it. She lifted her chin, then started as Menk tugged on her tail, demanding attention.

The little creature sat with her knees drawn up, her head cocked and her eyebrows raised. With a toss of her head, Kichebo bade Menk follow, but before the creature obeyed, she took one long look around the temple and ran her hand along one of the rough broken stones, as if saying farewell.

"She knows this isn't just another hunting expedition.

There's more going on in that little head than you might think," said Gray Cape.

Together they paced out of the ruined temple, keeping near the riverbank. Kichebo willingly gave up her position as leader, letting the old cheetah guide her. She was puzzled when Gray Cape took the same route she had used many times for her own journeys to and from the temple. She didn't remember seeing anything that might help her cross the river.

Menk seemed to have forgotten her sadness over leaving, for she cheerfully trotted along between the cheetahs. A freshly tied-on vine tail trailed in the grass behind her. Kichebo noticed that the little creature's feelings seemed to be much more transient than her own. Menk could be contentedly slapping together mud-pies at one instant and in a tearful rage the next. Yet, underlying her volatile emotions, the young cheetah sensed in her companion a growing loyalty whose strength surprised her. She hoped that bond would hold through the trials of the journey to come.

Kichebo jogged along behind Gray Cape on the strange wide trail and past piles of rubble that now seemed insignificant compared with the great ruin that had been her home. They passed ground where Rahepsi had hunted. Kichebo tried not to see his fading footprints in the powdered earth and pushed away the memories of his capture. After seeing him fall to the hunters, she had no hope that he was alive.

Soon the old cheetah halted on a rise, allowing them to look over a forest of papyrus onto the river's expanse. Squinting against sunglare in the direction Gray Cape showed her, she made out a curious black-and-silver line in the water. The structure was bowed out in the center, as if it had long resisted the current's drag.

"It's exposed when the river's down," said Gray Cape. "Only reaches halfway, but far enough to let us swim to the sandbar. I used it once myself, back in my more foolish days."

Before Kichebo could ask what the thing was, Gray Cape was off again, striding stiffly but purposefully toward the riverbank. Sharing a puzzled glance with Menk, Kichebo followed.

After making their way through brush and reeds, the two cheetahs and Menk found themselves on the shore, looking at a strange structure rising from the water like the partial skeleton of some great drowned beast. It was tethered to shore by what appeared to be heavy twisted vines hung with tatters of dried waterweed. Touching them, Kichebo found they were much stiffer and stronger than she expected.

Between these cables hung platforms with an openwork grid that reminded Kichebo of the leather weave of Tutankhamen's chariot. Still clinging in pieces to the hanging grid were slabs of material that looked like gray basalt but that gave beneath her feet. The substance was also oddly impervious to her claws. She found she could dent it, but even a hard swat with a dewclaw failed to penetrate.

"What is this?" she asked.

"Nothing living and nothing dead," was Gray Cape's reply. "My guess is that it comes from the same source as the ruins we passed. Some long-dead creature made it. Hurry up, youngster," she added sharply as Kichebo tried once more to puncture the strange substratum underfoot. "The longer we dally here, the more likely that the hunters will spot us before we make it across."

Kichebo gave a nervous glance back to where two squat stone pillars anchored the cables. She didn't like the way the whole thing creaked and swung when Gray Cape walked along it. Menk didn't either, and only a firm nudge from Kichebo got her started across.

Neither cheetah liked the feel of the meshwork grid beneath her feet. Kichebo tried to walk only on the gray slabs, but soon these became fewer. Some of the grid sections were nearly horizontal; others hung at crazy angles. By threading her fingers and tough callused toes through the grid, Menk made her way across. Having no fingers and unwilling to risk blunting her dewclaws, Kichebo used speed and momentum, launching herself up each tilting platform and scrambling madly across it as she began to slide down. Gray Cape crossed more sedately, fastening her teeth in upcurled edges of the gray slabs and forcing her worn claws through the mesh.

As the three worked their way along, the platforms and suspension lines hung closer to the water. This was fortunate, for the span grew increasingly dilapidated, and several times frayed and corroded cables holding a section broke beneath the impact of Kichebo's crossing. The first time she managed to scramble free of the platform as it sheared away, but the second time, she rode it down as it plunged into the river, her nape and tail bristling with terror. Luckily the drop was short and the only damage done was to her confidence. Shaking and dripping, she managed to scramble back up while Gray Cape kept a wary eye out for hunters who might have been drawn by the noise.

Soon the way became so rough that only little Menk could find a path through the maze of twisted struts and tangled cables. Both cheetahs gave up and dropped into the water to swim as far as they could, stopping to rest on beams that had sagged beneath the surface. They found they could walk along these girders for short distances, watching catfish swim between their legs and waterweed drift in the current. One large impudent fish, who tried to nibble on Gray Cape's tail, ended up in her jaws and became shared refreshment. As the cheetahs finished their meal, passing tidbits to Menk, who sat up above in the crotch of two joined beams, Gray Cape lifted her slick head and peered out from beneath the shadow of the span. "I thought I heard a droning sound."

"Dragonfly," said Kichebo, squinting against the sun.

"Too loud. Listen, there it is again."

This time, she heard it, a low ominous hum that gradually grew louder. A glittering point in the sky. She felt a sudden dread sink her courage. Hunters!

"Duck down," said Gray Cape. "In this murky water, not even a kite could see us. Just keep your nose above the surface."

But Kichebo wasn't ready to hide herself. "Menk's still scrambling around up there," she said, rearing up and hissing at the little creature. Menk took no notice. The intertwined struts and beams formed a wonderful playground for her to climb and swing on and she had long since gotten over her fear of the height. "Come down, you little mud-ape!" Kichebo growled, trying to stretch up with a paw, but Menk was beyond her reach. Beside her a submerged Gray Cape bubbled through her whiskers, "Youngster, by the scats of the sun, will you get down?"

Just as Kichebo was about to abandon Menk to her own devices, she caught sight of the creature's fake vine tail hanging down between two girders. With a desperate lunge she grabbed it and yanked hard.

Menk gave a dismayed screech, toppled backward off her perch, and plummeted down on top of Kichebo, knocking her off the beam into deeper water. For a panicked moment, they both thrashed, tangled up with each other, buffeted by the current. The cheetah felt little hands and feet clamber up her chest and face, pushing her down further and threatening to drown her. Then Menk was pulled away, letting her fight her way back to the surface, gasping hugely.

Gray Cape held one wet brown arm between her teeth, forcing Menk under in a welter of bubbles and froth. Only the creature's nose and mouth showed above water amid a tangled raft of black hair. The drone of the hunting craft grew in Kichebo's ears until it matched the sound of the river and then became louder. Then, almost unbelievably, it faded.

Gray Cape kept Menk down until the hunting craft was a distant speck in the sky. Then, with a grunt of relief and disgust, she shoved Menk at Kichebo. "Why they didn't spot us, I don't know," she said as the young cheetah tried to soothe the outraged little creature. "You two couldn't have made it any more obvious than if you'd left a fresh scent mark on a trail. Come on, both of you. I'm fed up with being soggy."

She swam away. With Menk clinging around her neck, Kichebo followed. Since the way above was now impassable, even for Menk, the three kept to the water, using sunken girders as rest stops. Gradually, as more of the strange structure became submerged, the cheetahs had to swim longer distances.

Kichebo paddled determinedly, grateful to her foster-mother Nasseken for making her learn to swim. Legs that were made for sprinting on land made slow headway in water, and swimming, unlike running, demanded steady endurance. When they pulled out on the last rest stop, Gray Cape said between pants, "This is it, you two. Open water until we reach the sandbar on the other side."

The three waited until they had regained their breath and plunged in again, Menk clasping her arms about Kichebo's neck. The young cheetah set to stroking, ignoring the molten burning in her chest and legs.

Halfway to the sandbar, they halted, switching Menk to Gray Cape. Kichebo could quickly see that the load was too much, but the old cheetah refused to trade back even though she was nearly floundering. Kichebo could only set a landing place on the sandbar between her sighting stripes and beat her way toward it, hoping her companion would hold up.

Gray Cape began faltering badly, barely keeping her nose above water. Kichebo swam close, grabbing Menk's arm and pulling her away. Swift, gritty water threatened to tear Menk from her. She felt the creature lock her hands together and kick fiercely. Kichebo rolled, nearly went under, and righted herself again. She bucked the current, driving her legs until they cramped.

Not until she had fought free of the river's grip and splashed into shallow water with Menk did she think to look back for Gray Cape. The empty expanse of the river gave her a sudden jolt of panic. Had the old one gone under or been swept away? Kichebo suddenly hated herself for the thoughtless impulse that made her neglect her own kind in favor of Menk.

Then, far downstream, she glimpsed a slick, wet head bobbing in gray-green water. With a gulp of relief, she sprinted along the shore, flinging mud from her pads. She took a flying leap into the water, sending up a plume of spray and nearly upsetting the old cheetah, who was thrashing her way weakly to shore. Gray Cape's legs buckled before she could haul her dripping frame out. She went down in the shallow marshy water, and lay gasping, her head on a tussock.

"At least . . . I got . . . you . . . across," she panted while her bony ribs heaved under wet fur. Kichebo stared down at her, immobilized by fright. Had the old one made it only to die of exhaustion on the shore? Again she cursed the misguided loyalty that bound her to Menk.

Gray Cape took a long shuddering breath and let it go with a sigh. The next one was so long in coming that Kichebo feared her companion had gone, but one rheumy old eye cracked open and the voice croaked, "Not crocodile meat yet. Give me time. Just like you young ones—always in such a hurry."

"Gray Cape, forgive me. I thought of Menk instead of you."

A corner of the grizzled mouth twitched. "Youngster, I expected that. Menk's more important to you . . . even than me. That's the way you are. I don't think you've even had a choice."

Menk waded in, her thumb stuck in her mouth. Tears

trembled in her eyes as she reached out to stroke the mud-streaked silver fur on the old cheetah's nape.

When her breath came easier, Gray Cape was able to slither on her belly up the bank where she lay with chin on paws. "Last time I was here," she said, eyes closed, "I found a place to rest, a sort of above-ground den, like your old temple, but much smaller and cruder. Mostly filled up with mud by the floods, but it'll offer some shelter."

"I'll go look," offered Kichebo. On the black-soil plain beyond the shore, she found the refuge. It was small, blocky, and half-buried in hardened silt, but there remained enough space at the top of the doorway to squeeze through. She found it musty but dry and free of snakes. Its clay walls radiated heat gathered from the sultry day.

By the time she returned, evening had begun to settle over the river, sunset painting its surface with gold and lavender. Leading the wobbly Gray Cape to shelter, Kichebo could hear her shivering violently, but once curled up in a warm corner, the old cheetah ceased shaking and fell into a doze. Menk soon followed.

Kichebo felt exhausted enough to sleep, but something whispered at the back of her mind, troubling her. Turning her awareness inward, she listened. The voice seemed to come from a great distance and was so weak she scarcely understood it.

"Asu-Kheknemt?" she breathed, hardly daring to hope he was still alive. The faint reply came.

I lie between life and death. Help me.

With her mind, she reached, caught his faltering touch and held, letting herself be drawn from her time back into his.

FOURTEEN

For eons I seemed to drift in a thick, dark sea, sometimes rising to the wan light above, sometimes sinking into the cold below. I trailed blood into the water from a gaping wound, such as would be left had one of my limbs been hacked off, yet I could feel all of my body. What bled slowly into the ocean was a severed umbilical, the ragged remains of a cord that had bound my life to that of the human boy when we were one creature, strong and prideful in its power. The bronze spearhead had cut far more than human flesh.

Was it Horemheb whose hand had guided the javelin and whose strike had been given additional violence by the chariot crash? I will never know, for at the time I couldn't spare the instant to glance aside from the weapon's point to the face of its wielder. At last, I decided that it didn't really matter. Whether he had delivered the blow or trusted the task to another, his desire sent the point to its mark, bringing a brutal end to a united being scarcely created, casting half aside into death and half into an endless sea of insensibility.

Yet relentless as Horemheb was, he might have been turned aside had I played my assigned part. It was I whose temper had flared at a stupid insult, bringing his attention to my presence and thereby warning him of plans to protect the king. It was I, seduced and intoxicated by the sight of a bull antelope between my sighting stripes, who ignored the danger threatening my pharaoh. And it was I who served as bait, drawing him into the trap that had been set amid the milling oryxes and the charging lion. Had I been one of the plotters myself, I could not have served them better. My instincts had betrayed me. I was, as Horemheb had said, nothing but a brute beast. I let the bitterness weigh me down and began to spiral slowly into the waiting depths, drawn by the current.

I felt a hand grip the fur at my throat. Vaguely annoyed, I pawed back blindly, wondering who was in this water with me. My paw struck a hard, gnarled forearm. The hand clenched and shook me. At first I rolled slowly, impeded by the water, but it seemed to thin, and I jerked with each shake. The blackness turned first to mud, then to mist, which slowly dispersed as I shook my head and opened my eyes.

I stared blearily into a leathery face whose strong features were marked by rage and grief. For an instant I did not know Aye; then the familiar lines of his countenance rose from my memory. His cheeks were thinner than I had seen them last, riven with cracks, as if the granite we had thought him made of was turning to clay and starting to fracture beneath the burden of age.

My chin lay atop his hand as he gripped my ruff. I tried to make some sound of recognition, but I was too weak and the effort almost plunged me once again into that dark sea that lay beneath awareness.

My head wobbled as he shook me again with the fierceness of one who would not be abandoned. "I will not lose you yet, Asu-Kheknemt. You are the last link I have to him."

Such was the strength of his will and the pain in his eyes that I fought my way back. When my eyes fluttered open once again I saw a tentative smile touch his lips. "Father Aten be praised. He has preserved his last sacred beast. Perhaps there is some use in faith after all," he said softly, leaning on the couch where I lay and stroking my head with the tip of his forefinger.

Something gleamed on his brow in the dancing lamplight, drawing my gaze. It was the gold uraeus-snake, rearing out from the band of his khepresh-helmet, whose leather was freshly dyed and tooled, recently made to fit the head of a new ruler. I stared numbly as he answered my gaze, then self-consciously removed the headpiece and held it in his hands. I did not need to hear the words he spoke.

"You know, don't you, *ba meht*. I am pharaoh now."

Much as I had loved Aye, hearing him use Tut's name for me nearly threw me into a rage. I knew my king was dead. I had known it from the pain of that seeping wound of the spirit as I had rocked in the depths of unconsciousness. Somehow the feeling had remained deadened and distanced, as if perhaps I clung to the hope that it wasn't true after all, that my experience was just a nightmare and that I would see Tut appear over Aye's shoulder in the shadowed doorway.

The doorway remained empty. The image of the royal

cobra on the old man's brow told me it would always be. There was an instant when I teetered on the edge of madness, wanting to kill him for forcing the truth on me. Despair sent a ghostly stab of pain from the left side of my face, through the roof of my mouth, deep into my head, making me shudder as if I had taken that spear-thrust once again.

I opened my mouth in an agonized howl, but my breath was too shallow to give any strength to my voice. I felt his hands on me, soothing, stroking, holding. I felt the strength that was still in them. With patience and kindness, he stayed beside me and then, when the paroxysm had spent itself, he drew my racked body onto his knees, feeding me gently with a cloth dipped in goat's milk. When I had taken what I could, he laid me down again and darkened the room so I might sleep.

Whenever I woke, he was always there to feed me or stroke me. I suppose I should have wondered how an old man bearing the burden of kingship could have spared the time and care to look after me himself instead of turning the task over to servants. I imagine there were many whispers behind his back as to why their pharaoh was so devoted to a sick animal. Yet whispers or no, throughout the days of my illness, it was his hands that ministered to me.

I was beginning to wonder if I would be an invalid forever, when I began to regain my strength. I was able to eat meat again. Walking was more difficult, for my limbs were stiff and often slow to obey. Slowly I recovered under Aye's care, but I knew the shock that accompanied Tut's death had pushed me over the threshold of age. Now I truly felt my years. I began to take walks with Aye to get some limberness back into my body. Together we shuffled through the great halls of the palace, a pair of creatures grown old too abruptly.

Sometimes Aye would sit with me and stare deep into my eyes, as if he wished he could merge with me as the boy had done. I let him look; I did not turn my head away; but he found only the amber depths of my eyes. The wound of my spirit had healed, but the remaining scar had sealed away my ability to commune with any creature other than my own kind. Had I been able, I would have tried, if only to ease the old man's loneliness with memories of the young boy he had guarded and led to kingship. But the power had fled from me and to him I was as mute as any other animal.

I hoped that on our walks about the palace grounds we would go to the House of the Swift, for I longed to be among my own kind after the pain of living among men. But although our slow and faltering steps took us to many parts of the palace grounds, we did not venture there. At last I grew impatient with him and when we passed the way that led to the House, I pulled against my lead.

He said nothing, only stood looking down at me with deep sadness in his shadowed face. I knew then that something terrible had happened and that the House as I knew it was no longer there. For the first and only time I jerked my lead from my master's fingers and made off down the path.

My attempt at a sprint soon degenerated into a shaky trot, but I kept going. I startled several stablehands who were cleaning mud from chariot wheels as I passed the stables. I set the whole kennel full of greyhounds yelping but spared them only a quick hiss. These things had not changed, I thought, as I tried to coax some speed from my wobbly legs. Perhaps I was mistaken and I would soon see the coursing fields and hear the cries of the trainers.

The only sounds were those echoing in my memory. Everything else was quiet. Weeds had taken over the training fields and the netting over the enclosures was loose and rotting. The building itself still stood, shrouded by the stink of ash. Slowly I paced around it, seeing how the roof had fallen in a mass of charcoaled timbers. The building's fire-gutted interior lay open to the noon sun. I entered through the soot-stained doorway, remembering how it had once been. The soothing coolness of the shade within those thick walls had been so welcome after working hard in the sweltering heat. Now all that had gone. The drinking-troughs lay dry and cracked. Rubble and charred timbers covered the flag-stones of the floor. There was no trace of the Aten's altar, nor of the many scrolls once kept in the library. I saw shriveled and crumpled things that might have been burned remains of man or cheetah.

Shaken and sickened, I backed away. Where were they all now? My son Neba Resu? The many other children I had sired and the females I had once taken as mates? Where was the grizzled old trainer and his apprentices? Did their bones also lie amid these ruins?

"Some lived," said Aye's voice behind me. "I sent them north to Heliopolis on the Delta where worship of the Disk still survives. I will send you there, too, Asu-Kheknemt, if such is your wish."

I whirled around to face him, and he must have seen the agony in my eyes. He knelt and I buried my head in the folds of his linen robe, wishing I had human tears to weep.

"It was burned the evening before your master died," he

234

told me. "Late that night, Horemheb's men brought in oil-soaked bales and set fire to them. Most of the keepers were away on the hunt and the House left with only a light guard. My palace regiment tried to fight the fire with buckets, but the flames spread too fast. All we could do was to rescue those who could be reached and abandon those who couldn't."

There was nothing to do but walk with him back to his quarters. At least I had a choice. I could stay with him in Thebes, serving my last days as companion and friend, or I could make the journey to Heliopolis to live out my life among the remnants of my kind who had survived the fire. Since it was clear that nothing would be done about me until my dead master had been laid safely in his tomb, I decided to stay with Aye, at least until after the burial.

Tutankhamen's death transformed not only the members of his household but the palace of Malkata itself. In the main gallery, now named "the golden hall," a canopy was raised to cover my master's body while it was carefully prepared for the afterlife. The golden hall they might have called it, but to me it was an evil place, reeking with nose-stinging scents and fetid odors. Somber yellow hangings draped the palace walls, symbolic of that place of dryness and death to man—the desert.

What was done to the dead king behind the walls of the senefer tent I did not know and did not want to. The priests called the process "restoration of life," but I was sure even they did not expect the corpse to rise and walk again. No. These preparations were for a different sort of life, one I barely understood and one, I suspected, that lay only in the hope and dreams of these men.

There was a constant yet subdued stream of people in and out of the golden hall. Slaves lugging lengths of linen and baskets of mineral salts, potters carrying glazed clay jars with lids shaped like animal heads, craftsmen with amulets and jewelry, all these went into the senefer tent to contribute to the fallen king's rebirth.

The wearying task seemed to drag on forever, filling the palace with vile smells that penetrated everywhere, making my eyes water and my belly clench. I thought again of going to Heliopolis. To me, Tut was dead. No amount of fiddling with his remains would bring him back. More than once, I wished his kind had given him to the desert, to be taken back into the soil like the dead animal he was. But these men seemed to have forgotten, or worse yet, grown to fear their mortal part that would rot and crumble once they had left it.

I listened to the endless chants and rituals, desperately trying to understand what solace they gave to those who grieved. Perhaps it was I who lacked essential insight. Perhaps my animal nature did limit me after all to a blind skepticism that denied what men called faith. What were their gods to me but carved and painted images? I worshipped only the sun-cheetah, the mother of my kind, and she knew better than to interfere with earthly life or death.

In my grief I might have fled to seek for myself the end I had wished for him. Or perhaps to find my own way along Hapi's shore to Heliopolis. It was Aye's need that kept me. Each day the burden seemed to lie heavier on him, its weight increasing with the gray length of his beard, for during the time of mourning he was forbidden to shave. Other people tried to comfort him. Ankhesen-Amon, the pharaoh's young widow whom he had married to legitimize his kingship, grew close to Aye, yet sometimes even she couldn't reach him. He sat alone with me and wetted my fur with old man's tears, knowing I would neither judge nor shame him for weeping. Then he could gather up his strength, mold his features into the face of a king, and shoulder his duties once again.

The river had risen to full flood and begun to ebb again, and cornflowers were blooming. It was then, in the month of Rennutet, that our vigil ended. At last came the day when slaves hauled away the remaining bundles of linen and baskets of natron salt. Priests and courtiers gathered as the senefer-tent curtain was drawn back, revealing what Tutankhamen had become.

Aye, freshly shaven and clad in the leopard-skin dress of a setem priest, took my collar to let me lead him to the bier. As the assemblage of white-robed nobles parted for us, fans waved to banish lingering odors. I reached the funeral bed and looked up in disbelief at the swathed and resined body. This massive rigid thing that lay like a slab of stone upon the bier—was this what they had made of him? Yes, he had grown in size and majesty, but it only seemed to emphasize the leaden stillness that now claimed his limbs.

Aye helped me place my paws on the edge of the bier so I might gaze down on the gold mask covering Tut's head and chest. The likeness was so accurate that it stunned me. So skillfully made was the mask that I had the fleeting impression that his tranquil features might soften into a smile or the eyes light with recognition. I regreted bitterly that moment of weakness, for when the realization rushed back over me that this was only an image in cold metal, I felt as though he had died again before my eyes.

The eternal beauty of the work was marred, for I knew how much it lied. The golden face bore a serenity my master had never known in life. The smooth surface of the left cheek showed no trace of the mortal wound that had felled him. For me the mask was too beautiful, too perfect, and I felt a mingled surge of awe and hatred for those who had fashioned it.

I could not stifle the cry that welled up in my throat. Shaven heads turned. Outraged eyes glared at me, telling me I had no right to be among the mourners, much less to sound my grief. What was I, the king's closest companion? To them only an unfeeling animal. Only Aye's touch on my head kept me from tearing loose and running wild in the crowd, staining their linen robes with blood.

Horemheb and his friends were among those who cast disapproving stares. I thought how easy and right it would be to avenge Tutankhamen's murder by sinking my fangs in the man's throat. How it would astonish and dismay them to see the pharaoh's harmless pet go mad!

Without the voice to accuse Horemheb of the murder, my attack would mean little. I was not sure I could kill him before his powerful hands choked away my life. And I would not be the only one to pay a high price, I thought, glancing at Aye's worn face. I dropped down on all four feet, stilling myself and letting the moment pass. Aye took his place beside the bier and the funeral ceremony began.

I listened to the words of ritual that rolled from his tongue. They moved me despite my bitterness.

"Hail to these, Nebkheprure-Tutankhamen. Alive is thy face. Thy right eye is the boat of day, thy left eye the boat of night. . . ."

238

It was so that they chanted, sang, and gestured. Despite the somber beauty of the ceremony, I soon grew weary and wished for it to end.

Once the parting rites were complete, the shrouded body with its golden death mask was carried out of the palace into the brilliant morning sunlight. In the forecourt stood a brace of red oxen, harnessed to a massive wooden sledge. On it lay another bier in the shape of a boat, high at prow and stern and shaded with an immense canopy. My pharaoh was solemnly placed on it.

Aye and I took our places amid a group of chosen favorites, misnamed—since it included Horemheb—the Nine Friends of the King. We assembled in front of the ox-drawn sled, which was given into the charge of a portly individual with the title of "The Mouth of God," although I could hardly see why. Even the oxen failed to give this man the respect to which he was entitled; they kept swinging their heads and trying to poke their horns into his pompous backside.

The procession was readied, a second smaller sled being drawn up behind the one holding the king's body. Onto this were loaded the animal-headed jars, linen wrappings and materials used in preparation, statues, and other grave goods.

Surrounded by a wailing crowd, we set off from the palace. The oxen groaned and their harnesses creaked. Women of the household wept, rent their mourning tunics, and covered themselves with the dust from the road and their tears. Ahead of us, the high priests trod, chanting dirges and pouring out libations of milk.

Feeling overwhelmed and bewildered, I pressed close to Aye, trying to close my ears against the throbbing funeral drum and the monotonous chanting. I could not help flinching each time a fresh outburst of lamentation broke from the throats of mourners near me. The royal princesses, who always seemed so cool and distant in their sculpted Nubian beauty, now threw themselves onto the road, writhing and ripping their robes with such frenzy that they scratched and bruised their skin.

As wave after wave of human grief broke over me, I wondered how much more I could endure. Much relieved was I when we came in sight of the funerary temple by the banks of a canal leading in from the river. Bearers carried Tutankhamen's body not into the temple but onto one of several canopied high-prowed craft moored in the canal. Painted eyes beneath each back-curved prowpiece seemed to follow us as Aye led me up the boarding ramp and along a narrow deck, where we stood apart from the retinue accompanying the dead pharaoh.

He bade me recline and I did so, feeling slightly better. Freed from the oppressive crush of bodies around me and the jarring noise, I lifted my whiskers to the breeze blowing down the canal to the river, watching as the rest of the procession boarded similar ships. At last the lines were cast free, the sails set, and we slid down the canal to Hapi's open waters.

As soon as our craft met the river current, its bow began to dip and surge in a regular motion. Fascinated by sunlight dancing on the curling bow wave, I sat up and peered overboard. The ship's shadow glided with it across the milk-green flow, carrying the outlined shapes of men and one slender four-legged animal.

Aye, his cloak drawn about him against the freshening wind, knelt to stroke me. I bumped the top of my head gently against his chin and managed to coax a purr from my throat.

When we neared the eastern bank, the ship did not come to land but swung downriver, following the shoreline. I admit I never fully understood the purpose of this journey. It seemed too random and wandering. Every so often our craft nosed into the bank and a party of white-robed priests disembarked. They bore shrouded objects and statues that they unveiled with much ceremony and left on the muddy bank. I watched them flounder ashore and back, their ivory-colored sandals caked with muck, their linen robes stained with pond scum. What use their gods would have for the ornaments and images I had no idea. The sun-cheetah would only be baffled if her people offered her such things.

At last, with the sun sinking low above the western cliffs, we made our last stop and turned about to row our way slowly back upriver. I remember being fed dried meat and being allowed to relieve myself onto a pile of straw, then falling asleep once more.

In the morning our ship came to a mooring once again at the quay near Tutankhamen's funerary temple. His body was carried into the still incomplete building while Aye and I followed, treading a path through chips of stone and plaster that littered the floor. My head was swimming with dirges and chants by the time we set off on the last stage of our journey—from the funerary temple to the tomb itself.

This time the red oxen were left behind. The sledge bearing the young pharaoh's remains was moved by the power of men. More than once Aye took his place among those who pulled, adding his remaining strength to theirs.

For me the journey was a trying one. I had to slow my

241

usual walk to the dismal pace of the procession. Progress became even slower once we passed the twin statues of Amenophis, the temple of Hatshepsut, and began ascending into the dry western hills. I almost wished at times that I could slip my own shoulders into the traces and add the strength born of impatience to move the ponderous sledge even a little faster along its way.

To either side of us, hills and bluffs rose, each more bleak and barren than the last. The road became a dusty heat-trap. Sweat ran from mens' brows and backs while I walked in the sledge's dwindling shadow, panting. The mourners, who had been weeping energetically and flailing stalks of papyrus, now faltered, and their cries became harsher as thirst dried their throats.

At last the road descended and we made our way into a narrow graveled valley. At the head of it, a pile of fresh rock chips and turned clay marked the new tomb. I saw Aye's lips twitch, for he knew this work had originally been in-tended for him. So sudden was Tutankhamen's death that there had not been time to complete the larger excavation nearby that would have been more suitable for the burial of a king.

Here our procession halted. At the tomb's mouth, cut into a rock-strewn slope, priests spread a layer of fine white sand. Carefully the Nine Friends of the King removed Tut's shrouded body from its canopied sledge and set it upright as if their king had once again risen to stand among them. The setem priest poured libations of river water over the golden death mask. I could not help remembering a nine-year-old boy who had blinked and grimaced beneath a similar sacred deluge, but the face I had loved was now serene, open-eyed, and eternally still.

Aye came forward to drape a garland woven of olive leaves, blue lotus, and cornflowers over the forehead of the mask. With trembling fingers he hung it over the royal symbols that reared from the king's brow—the paired vulture and cobra.

As he made obeisance and retreated, I heard a hoarse shriek break from the throats of the women. My king's young wife and other princesses of the royal household threw themselves at the feet of the corpse and flung their arms about it, as if by the fierceness of their grief they could drag Tutankhamen back from death. I had to suppress my own wish to cast myself down among them and howl my loss. I knew, from the hands that shook slightly on my collar and the downcast eyes, reddened with unshed tears, that Aye envied the women their freedom to grieve openly.

Amid wails and cries, the dead pharaoh was carried down a set of steps into the tomb. The mourning reached a peak as the body disappeared from view and then faded into sobs and moans. From other sledges, priests and servants unloaded everything the pharaoh would need for the afterlife. I saw his ivory-inlaid ebony throne being passed from hand to hand. His sennet-game table, his sandals, his storage chests, and even his folding camp bed were entombed with him. His chariots had been dismantled into wheels and frames to pass through the tomb's entrance. With renewed bitterness, I noticed the absence of the vehicle in which he had met his death.

One of the last items to be taken down was a large piece

covered with a shroud. I recalled the life-size statue of a
black cheetah Tut had shown me in the workshops of Set
Maat. I was sure this work must be it and waited impatiently for the wrap to be undone. Instead the priests
carried it, still enshrouded, beyond my view. I sought Aye's
glance as it passed by, but he did not look down.

Sunset drew close before the last grave goods were placed.
Some slaves carried a table and benches into the tomb while
others began cooking the funeral feast. Once all was ready,
the priests bid us enter.

Aye paused on the threshold, allowing me to accustom my
nose to the cavelike odor and the ruddy flicker of firebrands
on the rock walls. The first chamber was so packed with
things that we could hardly make our way through. I caught
the shimmer of gold, the gleam of ivory, and the scents of
precious oils as we passed them by and went directly into
the burial chamber. There Tutankhamen's body stood upright at the head of a long feast table, as if bidding us to his
last meal. Firelight reflected from his faience-glass eyes and
gently curving gold lips.

Despite the tempting smells and the morsels offered me,
I could not eat. Somehow the presence of the masked corpse
unnerved me, as if I sensed the fake metal image was trying
to replace the master I had known. Instead I turned my eyes
from it and wandered about, squeezing behind the guests as
they ate, for there was not much space left in the chamber.
I stared at the paintings on the wall, being careful not to
brush against them, for they were still wet. Even to my eyes,
muted in the perception of color, these images seemed intense and alive in the torchlight. Their hues were those of
the earth, rich oranges, deep browns, sunny yellows, and

solid blacks. I recognized Tut's face amid the images of gods and symbols. It was here he was truly resurrected, not within that inert column of resin and brass that stood at the table's head, gazing at us with dead eyes.

When the last bowl of beer was drunk and the last bone gnawed, servants cleared away the remains of the feast, removing table and benches. The one remaining item was now brought in on the backs of straining slaves, a massive stone outer coffin of rose granite.

Before the young king could be laid to his final sleep, ritual figurines had to be set up and consecrated. One of these was the shrouded work that must, I thought, be the reclining black cheetah. Eagerly I watched, but as the wrapping came free, revealing a pair of upright jackal ears, my heart sank in dismay. The statue had indeed been altered to fit the wishes of the priests. What had been an image of Aten's black hunting leopard was now the God of Death, Anubis. Little cries of wonder at the size and beauty of the work came from the throats of the assembled nobles, but I saw Aye's stare grow cold and his veined hand clench into a fist. A linen scarf had been tied around the statue's neck, possibly to conceal the joining of a new head to the original body. The old pharaoh's look told me he had been helpless to prevent this. I flattened my ears and turned away, not caring if anyone noticed my anger.

Aye took a strangely shaped ceremonial adze from a nearby priest and performed the last ritual of parting. Touching the eyes and lips of the golden death mask, he intoned, "With this I open your eyes and your mouth. Wake, Tutankhamen. You live again, you live again forever, you are young, you are young again . . . forever."

After the ceremony, everyone left the tomb, but Aye stayed inside with me, watching as workmen carefully encased the body into a series of coffins made of wood, bronze, and solid gold before lowering it into its stone sarcophagus. Despite myself, I could not help staring in amazement as the massive weight of nested coffins was slung on ropes and maneuvered above the hollow granite block. Muscles strained and joints cracked as, bit by bit, Tutankhamen sank into his death-cradle of stone.

Together Aye and I gave him one long look before the heavy lid slid into place. I was ready then to leave, but the old man stooped beside me, saying, "Wait, Asu-Kheknemt. I have something else to show you."

Taking a torch from its bracket, he led the way. In an adjoining room, he knelt beside a small upright cabinet. Glancing back over his shoulder to see if anyone had returned to chide him for lingering, he took out one of two cloth-wrapped statuettes. My breath caught as he showed it to me. I remembered well the figurines Tut had showed me in the workshop in Set Maat. His gilded image still strode proudly atop the back of his black cheetah guardian.

Aye stroked the statuette with a fingertip and said to me, "I could do nothing about the large work, *ba meht*, but I made sure no one tampered with these. Part of the truth at least will be saved. Who shall learn it, I don't know, but I have done what I can."

The knot of anger in my breast loosened. I bumped my head against the old man's chest, wishing again that I had the gift of human speech. He had done all within his power and for me that was enough. I tried to tell him so with the soft flutter in my throat. I saw him smile beneath his weariness. "Asu-Kheknemt, it seems ages since I heard that purr." He scratched me behind the ears.

We both gazed at the statuette one last time before he wrapped it, placed it beside its twin, and sealed the box shut. I left the tomb with him, lighter in heart than when I had entered. Behind us, I could hear workmen completing the final steps of Tutankhamen's burial. Soon, I knew, the tomb would be closed, sealing him away from all eyes but those of memory.

When Kichebo woke, she could only stare ahead into the darkness, still feeling the keen edge of Kheknemt's grief. Trembling, she remembered the slow sorrowful journey to the tomb. She mourned for someone she had never known, hearing the stone lid grate as it slid across a beloved face. As she shared Kheknemt's loss, so did she share his comfort, the touch of Aye's hands and the promise that the truth about his kind would survive, hidden with the little statues placed in the tomb.

Perhaps the statuettes are still there, she thought.

She had not known, when she crossed the river, where she intended to go. Her only thoughts had been vague ones; she would follow the path of Kheknemt's memories and perhaps hide from hunters in the western hills. Now her purpose lay clear. She must journey to Tutankhamen's tomb. Perhaps amid the treasures heaped within she would find answers to the mystery of her life and her strange bond with the past.

Nearby, Gray Cape stirred and coughed. "Can you travel?" Kichebo asked, nosing her.

"My voice has gone to the crocodiles and I can run about as well as a newborn antelope," the elder rasped, "but that's nothing new."

As best she could, the young cheetah tried to explain where they were going and why.

"I'm still not sure I understand," said Gray Cape at last, "but I'll go anyway. Lead on."

Kichebo roused a grouchy Menk and they were off. As much as she disliked the idea of traveling in open daylight, she had no choice if she was to rely on Asu-Kheknemt's memories for guidance. Carefully watching for signs of pursuit she led the way straight across a long spit of land cut by a canal. By the time they reached it, the sun's edge was just showing over the horizon, streaking the cheetahs' shadows out ahead of them and laying silver threads between ripples on the water.

Once again Kichebo felt Asu-Kheknemt's memories stir. She knew it was here that the funeral barge had landed, after turning from the main channel of the river into this canal. It was here that the high-prowed vessel had bumped against its quay, now long since crumbled into sand. As if in a faraway echo, she could hear the sails flapping, the ropes creaking, and boatmen shouting hoarsely as they made the ship fast and threw down massive planks to form a gangway for the king's bier.

A splash nearby distracted her. She glanced aside to see Menk prancing in the sluggish canal, brandishing a flopping catfish. Kichebo became suddenly aware of the hunger gnawing at her insides. Pushing ancient impressions aside, she sloshed in to catch breakfast.

Later that morning as she jogged atop a wide embankment,

listening to her belly gurgle, she decided her next meal had better be meat. Fish could sustain her for a short time, but she was never meant to live on it. A dyspeptic belch from Gray Cape, behind her, confirmed that thought.

As she topped a slight rise, she forgot her belly's complaints. In the distance, where the black soil of the river's flood zone gave way to the arid desert, stood two squat spears of yellow-gold rock. Approaching the twin towers, she saw that they had shape. From this distance, their outlines reminded her of huge seated cheetahs, their heads turned aloofly away from the travelers. She knew instantly that they were not, and the certainty of that knowledge sent a stab of mingled excitement and awe through her.

Despite her need to believe wholly in Asu-Kheknemt, she had lingering doubts, which she had kept secret even from Gray Cape. It was still possible, said a faint but nasty voice deep inside her, that the royal black cheetah and all his experiences had been a product of her self-deluded imagination. There was no other like her, so she had made him up and somehow invented his life. She could, the voice argued, be completely mad and this journey only a further plunge into insanity. Even the fact that the ancient temple where she had lived matched the one in which Kheknemt had seen his boy-king crowned was no proof. It was difficult but not impossible for her to have reconstructed the temple as it might have looked from her own knowledge of the ruins. Even the eerie familiarity of this landscape could somehow be a trick of imagination.

But these two spires of rock she had never seen before, but Kheknemt had. Eagerly she broke into a reckless sprint, leaving Menk and Gray Cape behind in her rush to discover whether the black cheetah's recollections matched what she would see.

She reached the twin statues and stood open-mouthed before them, overwhelmed by their size. They were not great cats, as they had seemed from a distance, but images of a king. She stared, seeing the statues as Kheknemt had, at a time when sculptor's cuts were still fresh in stone and the serene faces gazed out toward the river, undamaged by time or weather. Even though chunks had fallen and their feet were sunk deep in dried silt, Kichebo recognized them.

Her doubts fled. She dashed back to Menk and Gray Cape, flinging herself high into the air with exhilarated leaps.

"Sun-scats! What's got into you," snapped Gray Cape querulously as Kichebo bounced in circles around her, crowing, "It's true. It's true. Kheknemt's not just something I made up. He's real and he can guide us. Gray Cape, he's real!"

"Just you settle down a minute before you bring the entire countryside down on us. Now, chase that past me again."

Trying to contain herself, she told Gray Cape about the twin colossi. "Of course Kheknemt is real," said the old cheetah with a sniff. "Anyone who drags you off into his world without a thought for what's happening in yours has to be."

Kichebo remembered the danger of being on open land and pulled herself together. Drawing on the royal black's memories, she squinted down the path. "Beyond these statues lie more ruins. The old road we want runs northeast from there along the foot of these hills."

She trotted ahead, letting Gray Cape follow. The elderly cheetah glanced dourly at the twin colossi as she passed them. "Is that supposed to be your friend's companion? It doesn't look anything like the spindly two-legged creature you described."

"These ones, called kings, made their images much larger and stronger than they really were. The lion's mane makes him look huge and terrifying to anyone who tries to attack him. I suppose it was something like that."

"Oh," said Gray Cape, refusing to be impressed. They went on.

As the three traveled the remains of a dusty road that skirted the foothills, Kichebo saw ruins that matched many of Asu-Kheknemt's memories. From a distance, she caught sight of a terraced monument, hewn into the golden rock of the cliff face. Again, the royal black's impressions overlaid hers and for an instant she was gifted with a vision of the temple as it had been in his day, complete and unscarred. Even he, an animal with little appreciation for human creations, had been impressed by the quiet and simple strength of its design.

There were other remains of which he had no memories. Some appeared to be of the same type as the ones he knew, but others were different. Crumbling domes stood atop clusters of clay walls, incised with sinuous carvings, that, unlike the inscriptions in the old temple, held no meaning for either Kichebo or Asu-Kheknemt.

At last, after leaving all the ruins far behind, they took a sharp jog westward as the old road led them up into the low Theban mountains. Soon, over the tops of worn hills, a cone-shaped peak appeared, beckoning them to the valley that lay in its shadow.

The way grew more difficult. Slides of boulders and gravel blocked the travelers' path. Menk could often scramble over with a boost from Kichebo, but the two cheetahs had to find another way around. They fought their way up the contrary road, feeling the day's heat grow steadily.

Incised cliff faces rose beside the road on one side, fracturing and flaking off in layers. On the other lay torn and graveled slopes. Bright midmorning sunlight shone mercilessly, blinding them with glare from quartz and cream sandstone.

The further they went, the more lifeless and forbidding the ravine became. Kichebo had traveled across a great deal of desert terrain, but never had she known anything like this. Here it seemed that the earth itself was dying, falling into dust and rubble. Under full sun, the rocks glowed with molten color, making the cheetahs' eyes ache and their heads swim. They moved warily in this sterile, silent place, often starting at the distant bay of a jackal or the sound of rocks dislodged by their own footsteps.

The stifling heat soon became too much for Gray Cape after her near-drowning in the river. Menk, too, grew tired and cranky. Kichebo began to wonder what sort of hell she was leading her companions into. She knew she wouldn't need water for at least a day, and Gray Cape had probably swallowed enough to bloat her, but Menk needed to drink more often than the cheetahs.

At last they gave up and retreated to such sparse shade as they could find, waiting for afternoon to lengthen and deepen the shadows cast by the cliffs. Kichebo licked Menk to cool her, enjoying the salty sting of dried sweat.

"Unlikely as it may seem," said Gray Cape, studying a dusty trench that cut into the side of the old road, "there may be a spring higher up. This looks like an old stream bed to me."

Kichebo stared at it doubtfully, but when they renewed their journey, she noticed that what she thought was just a rut became deeper and wider, winding across the old road and eating away at it. Soon they were walking on the rim of a small but steep gorge. Kichebo began to wonder if she had somehow gone astray, for Asu-Kheknemt had traveled an unbroken path. Yet everything else—the cliffs, the flattened, cone-shaped peak ahead—looked right.

She walked dispiritedly, head down. If they were lost, she would be responsible. Maybe Gray Cape was right when she said that the land might have changed too much for the memories of someone in a far time to be a reliable guide. Suppose the tomb had been covered by a slide or washed out by a flash flood? Suppose that the entire thing was, as she had feared, a product of her own fevered imagination?

She suddenly staggered back, her skull ringing from an unexpected impact. She blinked away sparks from her vision, staring at the twisted iron uprights she had blundered into. The old structure swayed, and a rusty crossbar dropped off. She had no trouble in making her way around, for the barrier only stood in isolated sections.

She gazed up the arid valley, her heart starting to hammer with hope. Yes, this was the place. The valley floor looked higher than Kheknemt had known it, and it was cut by the channel of a seasonal stream unknown in his time, but it was the same.

Beyond the crumbling entrance gate, the valley spread between graveled slopes. To Kichebo's left as she came down the road lay blocks of stone, once laid in a rectangular arrangement, now jumbled by gullying and rockslides.

Her pace slowed as she passed these remains. She saw Gray Cape hang back, keeping Menk with her, as if the old cheetah sensed Kichebo needed to enter alone. Except for the sound of her own footsteps, all about her was utterly quiet, yet she seemed to hear the faint march of sandaled feet and the chanted dirges for a dead pharaoh. As Asu-Kheknemt had walked this ground in his master's funeral procession, so now did she cross it, seeing as he had the solemn splendor of the king's last journey.

And then all faded. Kichebo was alone within herself again, trying to swallow through the surge of emotion. Other tomb mouths gaped in the hillside, but she passed them all, heading directly for a square pit in the ground, surrounded on all sides by an old lattice of iron. Corrosion had gnawed at the bars, but not enough to eat through them. Angered at being shut out when she was so close to her goal, the young cheetah slammed her shoulder against the barrier, raising a gritty cloud and streaking her coat with rust. She hit it again, ignoring the protest of her bruised shoulder. One embrittled bar fractured. Another bent. Menk ran up, seized a heavy rock with two hands and flung it against the bars, sending ringing echoes up the valley.

Kichebo's impatience grew almost unbearable. When at last the barrier yielded enough of an opening, she had to suppress an impulse to shove Menk aside and dive through.

She raced down the stone steps and then stopped to test stale air drifting from the underground shaft. Feeling her neck fur slowly rise, she lifted a forepaw.

"Wait," said Gray Cape behind her. "Let me go in ahead and check for snakes. Better I get bitten than you."

The young cheetah started to protest at the idea of Gray Cape being the most expendable member of the party, but her own memories of what happened at the river kept her silent. Gray Cape gave her a shrewd glance and said, "Youngster, if you get bit and die, I'll never know the answer to all this. Unsatisfied curiosity is a worse poison to me than cobra venom." With that, she disappeared into the tomb.

Kichebo waited tensely while Gray Cape shuffled around inside. "No snakes in here." Her voice echoed hollowly from within the nearest rock chamber. She paused. "I thought you said that the creatures who dug this burrow crammed it full."

"They did," answered Kichebo, thinking of the multiplicity of large and small treasures that Kheknemt had seen carried into the tomb.

"Well, someone's gone and cleared it all out. Place is as empty as an eggshell. Come see for yourself."

Kichebo needed no further invitation. Quivering, she went inside. Once within the first chamber, the outside daylight faded rapidly, giving way to the most absolute blackness she had ever experienced. She knew it was no use waiting for her eyes to adjust; her poor night sight would never penetrate the close darkness. Feeling her way with her whiskers, she followed the scrape of Gray Cape's pads against the bare rock floor.

In the chamber beyond, she heard a muffled thump and

a squall of annoyance. "Spoke too soon, youngster. There *is* something here. It's a big block of stone that nearly fills up the place I'm in. Almost broke my nose against it, so be careful."

Even though Kichebo could see nothing with her eyes, her mind filled the room with details. Once torchlight had shone on newly hewn stone and drawn ruddy fingers over the treasures piled within, giving textured gold a warm glow and gleaming on inlaid ivory. Memory guided her left until she came into another chamber adjoining the first. Halting at the threshold, she wondered whether the walls still held their ancient murals. The paintings were there in her mind, their rich ocher and yellow pigments still shining wetly in flickering torchlight, as Asu-Kheknemt had last seen them.

She wished for light in order to see with her own eyes the hypnotic beauty of stylized pictures made by the ancients. She wanted to gaze for herself at the portrait of the young monarch whose life had been so strongly bound to Asu-Kheknemt and through him to her. But she had no way of illuminating the chamber and, strain her eyes as she might, she could make out nothing in the solid wall of black.

Her sigh of regret was interrupted by a little hand seizing her tail and giving it a petulant yank. Mortified at having left Menk behind, Kichebo turned and nuzzled the indignant little creature. "Come here, Kichebo," said Gray Cape's voice nearby. "I thought this piece of stone was solid, but it isn't."

The young cheetah found her way to the old one's side, brushing against the oblong block. Its curiously smooth surface tempted her to nose it, and she felt the tepid silkiness of polished granite.

Again images floated through her mind. Ropes stretched taut beneath the metal coffin as it swayed above the rose-granite sarcophagus. Muscles bunched and skin beaded with sweat as the coffin was slowly lowered to rest within the hollowed heart of the stone.

Finding the top edge with her nose, she pawed a stone lip, rearing to get her chest and forepaws onto it. With one foreleg lying along the narrow ledge, she used the other to feel about inside the hollowed block. Her claws scraped something that sounded with a hollow brassy ring, amplified by the stone trough in which it lay.

She shivered at the thought that the young pharaoh's remains might lie within the container she had touched. Again she wished fervently for a way to bring daylight into the tomb so her eyes could confirm what her mind insisted was true. But there was no way and she dropped back to the floor in disappointment.

"What's Menk found?" asked Gray Cape abruptly. "She seems to be playing with something."

Kichebo heard inquisitive murmurs and the sound of some object being turned over between two callused little palms. As she went to share Menk's discovery, she made one of her own. Something slender and flat-sided rotated against the pad of her left forepaw, making a grinding sound against the floor.

She snatched her foot back, thinking she had stepped on a snake. She drew breath through wide nostrils, searching for traces of snaky musk before again sweeping her paw across the floor. Snagging the object, she drew it to her and got her jaws around it. A slight nick at the corner of her mouth warned her to use more care. She mouthed it gingerly, taking the unsharpened cylindrical end between her teeth. Her tongue touched an oddly pebbled surface, making her hasten to examine her find outside in the sun.

Menk reached the slanting afternoon light at the tomb's entrance before she did. When she saw what the little creature held, she dropped her own find without thought. What lay between those grubby little hands was more than a statuette. To Kichebo it was proof that an ancient life and friendship had existed. Her eyes were riveted not on the striding figure of the boy-king, but on the black animal underneath.

In sunlight the pacing cat figure had a tarry gleam, making it difficult for Kichebo to see subtle tracings of gold on its face and ears. Sinewy legs with long fetlocks and a deep-chested lean body were the definite marks of her own kind. Menk too stared at the black cheetah figure. She frowned, touching one grimy finger to it, then to Kichebo, making her tremble even more. This, even more than the remote twin colossi was evidence that the past was more than an uncertain image in a borrowed memory. Worn, perhaps, and pitted by the time, the statuette was complete, solid and, most of all, real.

Menk ran torn and dirty fingernails curiously over the miniature face and then along Kichebo's muzzle, following the gold markings on both. She felt the amber edging on the figure's ears, then gently stroked Kichebo's.

But Menk's fascination with the statuette wasn't confined to the figure of the black cheetah. With wide eyes, she studied the raised arm of the little king and made a fist to imitate the way he gripped his staff. Then she stared long and hard at her own arm.

258

Kichebo was too overwhelmed to notice Menk's discovery. Trembling with excitement, she called Gray Cape out of the tomb.

"Supposed to be your friend, is it?" The old cheetah peered at the statuette. "Hmph. Could have done a better job. Head's a bit too large and the legs should be longer. And if that's Kheknemt, he should know better than to let some spindly two-legged critter walk on top of him."

"The king didn't really," protested Kichebo, wondering how to explain the idea of human symbolism to Gray Cape when she barely understood it herself. She decided not to and finished lamely, "It's just the way the two-legged ones made it."

"Not the way I'd have done it," was Gray Cape's caustic retort, making Kichebo grin at the idea of the two figures being reversed, with the cheetah on top. She gazed again at the statuette, a little frightened by her attraction to it. At last, she forced her gaze aside and sat down to wash.

She had a paw halfway down her face when she heard a metallic clink and Gray Cape's exclamation of surprise. "Oh, that was something else I picked up from the floor in there," Kichebo replied, taking a casual glance over her shoulder. Her voice trailed off as she caught sight of the object being pawed by the old cheetah. She got up quickly, her bath forgotten. Something about that plum-colored haft, set with pebbled gold, as well as that rust-streaked iron blade. . . .

Once human fingers had closed about that handle and a will that was human and cheetah combined had sent the knife unerringly to its target. Her neck fur prickled. I don't believe it.

That the statuette remained after everything else was gone

was startling enough. That Tutankhamen's dagger would be here too. . . .

Someone knows about me. What these things mean to me, she thought with a shiver. Again she took the hilt of the knife in her jaws. It felt oddly familiar in her mouth, reminding her of how Asu-Kheknemt had retrieved the blade from where Tut had cast it. She carried the dagger to where Menk was playing with the black cheetah figurine.

Why these two objects out of all the treasures once crammed into the tomb? These two things most symbolic of the partnership that had joined man and hunting leopard . . . could it be that someone, perhaps the hunters, had placed them here deliberately for her to find?

Menk, attracted by the glittering sunlight on the beaded gold of the dagger's hilt, made a grab for it. Kichebo's first thought was to stop her, fearful she might hurt herself. The second was stranger; she wanted to see the dagger once again between human hands.

Menk turned the blade over, examining it closely with her tongue clamped between her teeth. At first she was careless and earned a nick on her hand, but the ancient knife had lost most of its edge to rust. It barely drew blood. Too fascinated by the dagger to be distracted by pain, Menk only grimaced and sucked the wounded finger.

Kichebo nudged Menk, making her look up. With the intensity of her stare, she told Menk what was wanted. Recognition shone in the brown eyes. The knife forgotten, Menk leaned toward the cheetah, arms out.

Kichebo barely felt the small hands cup her face. At the first touch, her being seemed to melt out of her body. The transition was much easier than before. Yet, unlike what had happened in previous attempts, she did not have to abandon her own awareness to join Menk's. She remembered Kheknemt's sensation of expanding to encompass both cheetah and human form. She knew the feeling now as her own, for she was now neither Menk nor herself, but something new.

A joy so strong that it was almost terror swept through her. Sobs caught in a human throat and gasps filled a cheetah's deep chest. Yes, this was the true joining of selves that Tut and Kheknemt had known. It was not something that could be given a word, for neither the language of humankind nor hunting leopard could describe it. Thoughts of the royal black and his boy pharaoh made two sets of eyes seek the dagger. Jaws picked it up and passed it to hands.

And then the being who was both Menk and Kichebo together became aware she was being watched. She had forgotten Gray Cape, who stood eyeing her with a mixture of annoyance and trepidation. She saw the old cheetah first as a double image, the silver and fawn of her coat taking on more subtle and beautiful shades as the two images blended.

"Kichebo?"

She turned both of her heads at once, making Gray Cape start visibly and mutter, "Sun-scats! What's gotten into those two now?"

Kichebo's human part gave out a peal of laughter. A cheetah tongue lolled. "Gray Cape, don't be afraid," she said as the old one's eyes narrowed. "I'm still Kichebo, but I'm Menk, too. Don't you remember what I told you about the partnership between Tutankhamen and Asu-Kheknemt?"

Gray Cape found her voice. "I thought you were exaggerating."

"No! Everything is true. Everything. Do you remember how they threw this knife? Let me show you."

Her arm sent the dagger spinning out over the graveled floor of the valley. Her will reached out and deflected the blade from its flight.

"A shift in the wind," said Gray Cape.

Kichebo gritted her teeth. The knife flew again and bounced back as if it had struck an invisible wall.

"All right, all right. I'm convinced. Now put that scatting thing away. It looks dangerous."

But Kichebo was too excited to halt her experiments. At last, when she felt the first pangs of exhaustion that warned of the coming dissolution into separate selves, she decided to try one more thing. Tut and Kheknemt were never able to move the knife when it was sitting at rest. She decided to try that task, throwing all her energy into a burst of will that must surely lift the dagger from the gravel where it lay. It didn't move. Not even the slightest tremble.

Her elation drained away. There were apparently limits to her power. Fierce in her frustration, she bent her will again to the trial. This time, perhaps, the knife gave a slight twitch, but her vision suddenly blurred out as exhaustion swept over her. The last thing she saw then was the sight of both her selves staggering toward each other as the light faded from their eyes.

Kichebo woke later, slightly chastened, to find herself back in her own body with Gray Cape standing over her. "Is . . . is Menk all right?" she asked.

The reply was gruff. "I took her into the tomb. She stumbled down the steps without even opening her eyes. I see you're in similar condition."

She didn't argue. Leaning against the old one's bony ribs, she descended the stone stairs and barely made it across the tomb's threshold before sleep claimed her.

FIFTEEN

Kichebo woke, bothered by thirst. She peered out at the dawn light and wished she hadn't slept beyond sunrise. Even though the hills around this narrow valley hid her from enemies, she still feared showing herself in daylight. Yesterday she had no choice, for her inward guide knew the landscape only by day. Only luck had saved her from being sighted.

She swallowed. The scratchiness in her throat warned her she couldn't stay here long without water. She glanced at Menk, still sleeping with the statuette clutched against her chest. Sand powdered the little creature's dry lips.

We may be able to do without food today, but not water, thought Kichebo. If there's none here, we'll have to return to the riverbank, despite the danger of being hunted.

Gently she pawed Gray Cape awake, though the old cheetah's evident exhaustion made her hate to do it.

"We have to find water," Kichebo said. "You thought there might be a spring in these hills."

The old cheetah pushed herself up on her rickety forelegs and, with a grimace of pain, raised her hindquarters. Watching her, Kichebo felt the sting of guilt. The river crossing and the parching heat had nearly worn her out. And what had the demanding journey brought either of them? Answers that were still incomplete and a mystery that had only deepened. Was that worth exhausting the dwindling resources of the old one's life?

She came with me by choice, Kichebo argued back at her conscience, but somehow the thought brought her no comfort. Turning to Menk, she found the young one sulky. "You too," she said. Kichebo had to take the black cheetah statuette from her and give her a nip to get her going. With Menk carrying Tut's dagger, they padded out of the tomb, up the stone stairway and squeezed through the opening in the iron fence. Kichebo paused, thinking of the statuette left behind in the tomb. Much as she wanted to take it, she knew it would only hamper her search for food and water. The valley was still, empty even of the far-off howls of jackals or the dry scuttling of scarab beetles.

"Better find that old stream bed and see if we can trace it to its source," said Gray Cape, but Kichebo wasn't listening. She stiffened, suddenly alert, thinking she had heard a soft crunch, made by a paw on gravel. Ears pricked, she waited, but caught only the fitful hiss of the wind.

"Hunters?" asked the old cheetah.

"No." Kichebo remained wary.

"Don't blame you for being skittish. We haven't seen those two-legged things since leaving the river, but they're still around. Every so often my nape prickles."

Kichebo lowered her head and was about to go on when she heard a clatter of pebbles and a harsh yowl. She whirled about to see a spotted form charging up the valley, ears flat and teeth bared. Amazement and disbelief slowed her response as she recognized the large male. How could Rahepsi be here?

She stared again. It *was* Rahepsi, but not as she remembered him. Wild-eyed, fur rumpled and bristling, he seemed about to charge right over her when he slid to a stop.

"You," he growled, fixing her with his gaze. Head lowered, he began to stalk her as if she were prey. His tail lashed against his flanks. "You, black leopard. You brought those hunters down on my kin-group. I came to my senses on *this* scatting side of the river and today I stumbled across your track. I should have killed you in the courting circle, black leopard. Now. . . ."

Kichebo was tensing to run when she caught sight of the yellow band about his neck. "Where did you get that?" she asked.

Rahepsi halted, as if caught off-balance by the abrupt question. "This?" He pawed the collar. "I would think you'd know more about it than I do. Those two-legged animals put it on me before they let me go."

"Let you go? Why—"

"What does it matter to you, black leopard?" he snarled, his dark jowls emphasizing gleaming fangs. "What does it matter that I was taken from my brothers, poked and pawed at, then dumped here with nothing to hunt?"

His gaze shifted to Menk. His eyes narrowed hungrily. Kichebo stepped in front of Menk. "Find other prey, Rahepsi," she growled as Gray Cape came to her side.

266

"Why should I, when I can fill my belly and take revenge on those hunters with one kill?" He grinned, his head swaying back and forth like a snake's, his eyes devouring Menk. "You don't know what she is, do you? Let me tell you. A hunter-cub."

"Stop it, Rahepsi," Gray Cape said sharply, drawing his glittering gaze to her.

"I think you know what I'm saying, old one." Rahepsi's voice went silky and soft. "Isn't it strange, black leopard," he said, turning again to Kichebo. "Here you've been running from those creatures all of your life and you take one as a companion. You let it live off you like a tapeworm in your gut, not thinking about what will happen when it grows."

Kichebo laid her eyes back and switched her tail. "Liar."

His eyes hardened. "You would call me untruthful? Even when you saw me being swallowed by that sky-creature? I did not spend all my time asleep. I had plenty of chances to see my captors at close range. I'll never forget those ugly, hairless, flat-faced monsters." He grimaced with loathing. "You know I'm not lying. Your Menk-thing is one of them."

Half-crazed as he seemed, Kichebo knew Rahepsi's words were true. She felt hot anger welling up in her, she wanted to scream denial at him, but when she finished raging, the truth would still be there, staring back at her from Rahepsi's eyes. The boy-king Tutankhamen, the hunters, and little Menk. All were, as she suspected and feared, the same. All were human in everything it meant. Everything—from the gentle and reverent touch of fingertips to the brutal thrust of a pole against the chest of a caged animal, or a spear through the skull of a royal child.

But she was no part of this. She was a cheetah, born to the chase and the clean, swift kill. Only her coat marked her as different and that was something on the outside . . . it had to be.

Again she heard in her mind Kheknemt's voice, soft, yet strong. "Whether I accept or reject it, I am as much a creation of man. . . ."

Kichebo trembled as her own memories flooded in on top of Kheknemt's: the hard-eyed metal bird that had followed her when she was with Nasseken and Beshon . . . the panicked scatter of Rahepsi's hunting group by the pursuit craft and the chase that brought the big male down . . . the heart-tearing run as it sought to take her as well. . . .

She found herself shuddering, ears flattened in terror. Every beat of her racing heart screamed in her ears.

No, no, no, no . . . I am not, I am not, I will not be what Kheknemt was. I want nothing more to do with man.

"Now that you know what she is, let me have her," came Rahepsi's voice again. "Or better yet, you kill her."

Menk, as if sensing the threat, began to whimper and clutch at Kichebo. Deliberately, the young cheetah slapped the groping hands aside. Menk's eyes went wide with dismay. She retreated a step, then reached again for comfort. Kichebo lowered her head, lifted her nape. A growl started in her throat as she remembered all the times during her cubhood when she had longed to run, yet had been forced by fear of pursuit to stay hidden.

She raised one foreleg and flexed the dewclaw. One quick blow with all her strength would end the creature's life. She stood almost nose to nose with Menk, seeing the reflection of her own emotion in the rapid rise and fall of the creature's scrawny chest. What did she owe this animal anyway? What had it brought her except a life filled with running, hiding, and terrible mistakes that hurt others of her own kind?

"Kill her," Rahepsi whispered, but Kichebo flinched as though he had shrieked it in her ear. Even as she sagged back, uttering a soft "no," the maddened male flung himself past her. Knocking over a startled Gray Cape, he lashed out at Menk. In a blur of motion, Kichebo saw Tutankhamen's dagger appear in Menk's fist and fly toward the attacking cheetah. It missed and clattered into the gravel.

Rahepsi cut the air with vicious slashes as Menk scrambled away from his attack. Then he was on her, pinning her down with powerful forelegs. A dart slammed into Rahepsi's shoulder, startling Kichebo. Glancing up she saw two-legged forms running toward her. A hunter fired again and missed. This startled Rahepsi but did not stop him from baring his teeth and diving for the choking throat-bite.

A vision snapped up in front of Kichebo: Menk flailing like a dying gazelle, mouth open but mute from the crushing pressure of the jaws about her throat, head falling grotesquely to one side as her limbs quivered in the last throes of life. . . .

Even as the young cheetah threw herself at Rahepsi, she knew she couldn't reach Menk before those teeth penetrated. A part of her seemed to detach and go hurtling ahead of her body toward Menk. For an instant she saw through the creature's eyes, felt the heavy paws on her chest, saw the contorted cheetah face with its snarling mouth and blazing eyes. Through human nostrils she smelled the rage-stink of the crazed male and felt the racing of a terrified heart.

Menk!

The image of the dagger flared in her mind, its urgency

casting aside any thoughts that it had been flung beyond reach. No longer did she cry out her creature's name, for now it was her own. The hands grappling at Rahepsi's forelegs were hers as well as the paw pads that ripped the earth in an effort to reach this one who was now her other self.

The dagger's image burned in white flames in her mind and she who was now cheetah and human together knew only one thought—strike back.

The image of the knife encompassed her awareness. Not even Tut and Kheknemt had been able to move it from rest, yet she had no choice but to try. She reached out for the iron dagger, willing it to obey. It trembled, lifted . . . and flew.

Rahepsi catapulted backward, limbs cartwheeling. Gray Cape's startled screech rang in human and cheetah ears. The two bodies that now belonged to the same mind met each other and tumbled in a helpless tangle. Both clung together, shaking with relief, then both remembered and looked toward Rahepsi.

Two pairs of eyes saw the dagger's hilt lying as if cradled between his chest and foreleg. With a shuddering convulsion, Rahepsi ripped the blade from his flesh with his jaws. It sailed through the air to land at Menk's feet. The wounded cheetah sank down and lay still.

A bolt of cold shock hit Kichebo. She seemed to snap back into herself with a fierce recoil that sent her reeling. The fiery loyalty that bound her to Menk as one being was gone, leaving only a rising sense of horror.

She knew that she had committed the final act that severed her from the rest of her species; she had slain another. Not only had she killed, she had done so not in the manner of her own kind, but that of the human creatures she despised.

Kichebo wanted only one thing now and she knew where to seek it. Fastening her gaze on Menk, she began to stalk, letting all the rage, guilt, and terror blend into a maddened keening that spilled from her open jaws. She ignored the hunter's dart that spat over her back. As if from far away, she saw Menk's fingers grope nervously for the knife. The iron tooth rose in the creature's hands until it shimmered above her head. Kichebo crouched to spring.

She looked up into the terror-filled face, with lips curled back in a snarl over ape-teeth; eyes full of bewildered tears. She tried to hate it and couldn't.

The clenched fists holding the dagger aloft sank and opened, letting it drop. Menk fell to her knees, her wet face telling Kichebo that both of them shared the same trap; neither could kill or desert the other.

Defeat turned bittersweet as Menk held out her arms to the cheetah. No longer caring that the approaching hunters watched, she came gratefully into Menk's embrace. They did not join again, for both were too exhausted. For a little while, they clung, knowing and feeling only each other. Then, slowly Menk's arms slid from around Kichebo's neck and they turned to face their captors.

Gray Cape came to stand flank to flank with her, looking shaky but determined. Kichebo willed herself to stare at the hunters, keeping a steady gaze despite the merciless hammering of her heart in her throat. The creatures stood, fixing her with the insect stare of their eye-covers.

She had sensed that these two-legged ones were similar to the creatures of Asu-Kheknemt's time. Now the resemblance was undeniable. Their bodies, hands, limbs—all the same, except for the upper halves of their faces, which seemed to have metamorphosed into something alien and insectlike. Their forms were covered in tight gray cloth, something else Kheknemt's people never wore. Their feet were neither bare nor sandaled but enclosed completely by coverings that distorted their shape.

Yet the morning sunlight sparkled on pectorals and armbands such as Tutankhamen had worn. Gold necklaces, inlaid with faience glass, short shoulder capes, belts, rings, all were known to her through Kheknemt's eyes. The confusing blend of elements, both threatening and familiar, combined with the shock of her attack on Rahepsi to numb her mind.

Slender hands pushed aside masks, letting Kichebo see beneath. The cheetah looked at more human faces, remembering the stony gentleness of Aye's weathered features and Tutankhamen's brilliant smile. It was Kheknemt's shared memory that allowed her to see the beginnings of understanding and perhaps even compassion in the human eyes that studied her.

Even so, she felt a surge of panic when two figures came and knelt by Rahepsi. Carefully they lifted him up and carried him away. Kichebo followed him with her eyes until his limp form was out of sight, then turned to the hunterwoman who had placed a pan of water on the gravel. Kichebo let Menk and Gray Cape drink before crouching to ease her own thirst. As she lapped, she kept watch on the woman who knelt and drew something from a pouch.

Before the object came free of its cloth wrapping, Kichebo sensed a familiarity in its outline. When it was visible, she recognized the ebony gleam of the black cheetah figure and the shimmering gold of the striding king. Menk sucked in her breath and involuntarily reached for the statuette.

It was not the same one as she had found in Tut's tomb. This figurine bore none of the dust or scrapes made by clumsy paws and teeth. Yet in every other way it was identical. Then Kichebo remembered seeing through another's eyes the twin figures set back to back on a workshop table. Her mouth sagged open. The other statue! How had they gotten it?

The hunter-woman crouched. Sunlight played over the textured gold of her pectoral and arm-rings as she held out the statuette by its base. A dusky finger stroked the wooden cheetah's head and then pointed at Kichebo. Menk, who had been watching with growing fascination, then snatched the statue away from the huntress and scuttled out of the woman's reach. Kichebo tensed, expecting retaliation, but nothing happened. The huntress waited, watching Menk.

It quickly became apparent to Kichebo that Menk's intention wasn't plain thievery. The little creature studied the figure of the boy-king, touched it, and then put the same finger to her chest. Hesitantly, yet boldly, she pointed at the woman.

Kichebo saw the huntress' lips move in words that sounded soft and comforting. Menk stayed still, eyeing the woman. The little one, looking more confused and suspicious than angry, allowed the huntress a few steps closer. The woman slipped a covering from the end of her arm and extended a slender brown hand. Menk stared at it, then at her own. She began to tremble.

The huntress moved closer. Menk retreated, pouting and seizing Kichebo's ruff, yet the open hand drew her to look back with longing. She took a step toward the woman, pulling Kichebo with her.

Startled, the cheetah resisted, planting her rear paws. She wasn't ready. She might now be able to watch at a distance without being overwhelmed by fear, but she dreaded getting any closer. Quickly she wrenched free of Menk's hold, scuttling to one side. The hunters nearest her moved to cut her off, but a sharp cry from the woman froze them in their places.

In an instant, Gray Cape was beside her, ready to join her in her flight. Only Menk did not come scampering to her side. The creature looked at Kichebo with agonized eyes, but the stubborn set of her jaw and the way her hand crept toward the woman's told of a need even deeper than that which bound her to the cheetah.

Kichebo tensed her hind legs beneath her. It was right, she told herself. Menk was with her own kind and she would stay. Kichebo promised herself she would live with the loss somehow, but even as the thought crossed her mind, she knew it for the lie it was. She might tear herself away from Menk, but the wound it left in her would never heal.

Again Kheknemt's voice spoke softly in her mind. *Whether or not I accept or deny it, I am as much a creation of man. . . .*

A creation of these fragile yet terrible beings who could slaughter each other with no more regret than a lion would feel when taking prey. Yet they could thrill to the sight of a cheetah on the chase or the touch of wiry fur against fingertips.

Like Kheknemt, I need them, she thought, now able to accept the words she had once fiercely denied. She spun around so abruptly she nearly knocked Gray Cape over. Trembling with defiance and joy, she crossed the ground back to Menk and bowed her head in front of the huntress.

Her fur prickled at the touch. It was not Menk's hand. The woman stroked her again, lightly. All her instincts screamed at her to flee, but she fought them down, knowing this was her choice.

A gentle finger raised her chin. Dusky hands cupped her face. She remembered again how Tut had cradled Asu-Kheknemt's head and drawn their faces together. Wondering how long her chest could contain her thrashing heart, she gazed up into the woman's eyes, not knowing what she sought. Words came through to her, a new voice speaking inside her mind.

You are also our lost child, come home at last.

The eyes were deep and kind, bearing a touch of regret, as if their owner hadn't meant things to be so painful. Kichebo understood not so much the meaning of her words but their tone.

The huntress' hands fell to her sides and she stood up, beckoning. Behind her, Kichebo heard a bewildered Gray Cape ask, "Are you going to follow?"

"Yes," Kichebo answered softly. "I don't think she'll hurt us."

Feeling Menk clutching her, Kichebo padded after the woman, with Gray Cape close behind. She was too exhausted now to feel more than a vague curiosity . . . and the beginning of a strange new hope.

SIXTEEN

Muted gray-green light tinted the ground in front of Kich-ebo's paws. She woke, momentarily bewildered by sagging cloth drapings about her. It was like being in an odd, soft little cave. For an instant she couldn't imagine where she was or how she had come. Then she remembered that the huntress had led her and her companions to a low, angular shape and pulled aside a flap for them to enter. Inside lay food, water, and places to sleep. Seeing that, she had thought of nothing else.

She glanced over to a low cot where Menk was a slumbering lump beneath covers. It was slightly unsettling to see her small companion sleeping in the manner of men rather than curled up on straw that had been given to the two cheetahs. She rose and pawed the cloth wall. It gave easily, telling her this wasn't a cage, such as those Asu-Kheknemt had suffered. Once again she settled beside Gray Cape and tried to collect her thoughts.

She wondered why she wasn't racked by despair and guilt

after striking down Rahepsi. By that act she knew she had severed any bonds to her own kind and it deeply revolted her. Yet out of the horror and revulsion had come something unexpected. There was the thread of promise in those words that still spoke in her mind.

You are also our lost child, come home at last.

Perhaps soon she would discover the reasons for her life and her strange gift. The woman's words also confirmed what she had learned from Asu-Kheknemt and finally accepted that she was in some way as much a part of these creatures as the child Menk.

Child. She had never thought of Menk as a child, even though she understood what the word meant since Kheknemt had used it to describe his young king. Menk was just . . . well, Menk.

Beside her Gray Cape stirred. She woke and eyed Kichebo. "How do you feel?"

"I don't know. Every time I think about Rahepsi, I feel terrible, but then it goes away. Perhaps having you and Menk here makes a difference."

"Are you sure Rahepsi's dead?"

"Gray Cape, you saw what Menk and I did with the dagger. . . ." Kichebo couldn't go on.

"Don't accuse yourself until you know one way or the other. I understand; you can't undo what happened. But you don't have to make it worse."

Sorrow rose so strongly that Kichebo couldn't keep it down. "I didn't want to hurt him. It's just that . . . Menk means more." She lifted her head. "Why am I like this? Why do I always choose Menk over my own kind? Some-

277

times I hate myself for it. I wanted to die after I struck Rahepsi and I wanted Menk to die, too, but I couldn't . . . I couldn't."

Gray Cape sent a quick glance toward the cot where the child slept. "Softly, youngster, or you'll wake her. You are the way you are and there's nothing to hate in that. Perhaps soon we'll get some answers." She pricked her ears at the sound of approaching footsteps.

They knew the huntress by her pectoral necklace and the armbands she wore over her cloth covering. Moving carefully, she ducked inside the tent and knelt at the cot beside the sleeping child. With one hand, she gently ruffled Menk's hair.

The child yawned and stretched, opening her eyes and rolling onto her back. There was still some wariness in her face, but she was too fascinated to flee and there was a certain gentleness in the woman's expression that drew her.

The woman smiled. Kichebo watched her, using Kheknemt's memory to recall how Tutankhamen's lips had stretched in that odd grimace of pleasure and delight.

Kichebo did not expect to understand any of the huntress' spoken words, but she found that the language was similar to what Kheknemt had heard from Tut's lips. It differed in tone and cadence, as if altered by the passage of time, but the cheetah found to her surprise that she could comprehend it.

The woman laid a slender hand on her own breast. "My name is Tiye Aasit," she said to Menk. "Yours, if you've forgotten, is Menkataten."

The child's lips formed the word slowly as if tasting it. She spoke hoarsely in a voice not accustomed to being used in such a way. Tiye pointed to Kichebo and Gray Cape, saying, "Hunting leopards. Your friends."

Kichebo pushed her muzzle under Menk's outstretched hand, wishing she could tell the woman that she and Gray Cape also had names. With a sudden thrill, she saw Tiye catch the intentness of her gaze, for the woman studied her carefully, and then Gray Cape.

"No," Tiye said in a husky voice, as if speaking to herself. "I will not make the same mistake I made before. You are not just animals. I should have known that when I saw you companioned with the child. Yet I was so afraid for her, I did not think until afterward." A weary sadness crossed her face. "Swift one, you had good reason to fear us. Even when we do not mean harm, we cause it. But I speak to you as if you could understand . . . and even forgive."

As if seized by a sudden thought, she put out two hands to the cheetah, then checked as Menk, with a possessive grunt, flung her own arms about Kichebo's neck.

"Well enough," said Tiye, drawing back with a soft laugh. She turned, making a chirping sound at Gray Cape. "Come here if you will, grizzled warrior. Let me see how you are faring."

Once Tiye had finished examining Gray Cape, she turned her attention again to Menk. Watching the woman croon and play with the child, Kichebo thought how quickly Menk was reentering the life she had once known. Her initial suspicious and sullen demeanor had vanished rapidly. It appeared, too, that Tiye could reach Menk by means other than voice, and the cheetah wondered if the woman could share thoughts with the child as she herself had done. Surely that was the only way Tiye could have gotten Menk to endure a puzzling immersion in a tub filled with foamy water and then to submit to a two-bladed instrument that removed the matted and tangled length of her hair. As Kichebo watched, she realized Tiye's wisdom in allowing the child to remain near her two companions to ease the transition from one existence to another.

Yet, Kichebo reminded herself, this was not a change from an old life to a new one, but instead a return to what Menk had previously known. She could see the child's face brighten as old memories woke to life. How long, after all, had Menk stayed with her? Barely two turns of the seasons, not long at all. But in that time so much had changed for both. As she watched Menk starting to reclaim what had been lost to her, the cheetah felt a twinge of jealous dismay. Would Menk forget or deny their time together in favor of the human life she was being prepared to reenter?

When Tiye finished, an entirely new Menk stood before the two cheetahs. Her freshly shorn and washed hair stood up in curly spikelets. Her skin glowed with a golden tone previously hidden by layers of dirt. About her waist was a pleated linen kilt, and draped about her neck and shoulders a small pectoral in links of gold and faience glass. The child stroked it, looking at once awed and pleased by her new finery.

The huntress departed briefly. Making several trips, she brought food for herself and Menk as well as for the two cheetahs. Everyone ate together in a shy solemnity that seemed to symbolize the beginning of an understanding between them. Tiye collected empty bowls, then sat Menk on her knee, placing both palms flat on the side of the child's head. Kichebo saw Menk close her eyes and lift her chin, her face stiffening with concentration.

For a little while, Menk stayed still. Then, with a gasp of surprise, she jumped down, seeking Kichebo. Fingers grasping the cheetah's ruff, she pulled her to the low cot where Tiye sat. Menk scrambled into the woman's lap, still holding onto Kichebo. With a purposeful wriggle she settled herself and impatiently slapped the side of her head, indicating that Tiye was to continue what she had started.

Leaning forward, Menk cupped Kichebo's face and drew her close. Kichebo sat, facing the woman and child, shut her eyes, cleared her mind, and waited.

At first she thought the voice that spoke in her head was Menk's, but she recognized an order and clarity of thought that could belong only to Tiye. Through Menk, Tiye could enter and explore her mind. She felt a sparkle of surprise as the voice said, "Yes, you are far more than just an animal."

Unsure of how to speak to Tiye, Kichebo could only gather all of her questions and shape them into one, casting it at the woman almost as a challenge.

"What am I?"

"A child both of man and the wild, who has grown to be more than we ever hoped. But still I speak in riddles. Now that I know you can understand, swift one, I will give you the answers you seek.

"What I show you now neither I nor any of my people have truly seen. I have reconstructed it on the basis of writings once thought lost. That is a part of the story I will tell you later. For now, look on the past as we believe it to be . . . the past of your kind and mine."

Images came to Kichebo, opening and closing like doors,

or fleeting swiftly across her mind. She sensed in their sequence the idea of years passing into decades and then into centuries. Again and again, she saw the sacred animals with those who kept and cared for them. Man and animal together raised their faces to the sun's disk, worshipping it under many names: Ra, Amon-Ra, Horus-of-the-Horizon, and the one Kheknemt had known, the name of the Aten. She saw her kind in hunts, ceremonies, crownings, and even in war, fighting side by side with their human brothers.

Tiye's words spoke in her mind once again. "The bond between man and hunting leopard in the land of Egypt is old beyond knowing. Even in the most ancient times, the sacred black had been bred for generations from the spotted ones of your kind."

As Kichebo sped down the strange mind-trail of time, she sensed a dwindling in the number of these animals and the strength of their following. Waves of invaders swept across the Two Lands, bearing weapons made of new metal that would not bend or blunt. They ebbed at last, but in the confusion and destruction, much knowledge was lost, which seriously weakened the cult of the sacred hunting leopards.

Kichebo did not need Tiye to take her along the part of the road that led through Tutankhamen's time. She experienced again the murder of the boy-king and the burning of the House of the Swift as Tiye said, "It was the pharaoh Horemheb who dealt the final blow. In rooting out the worship of the Aten disk, he also destroyed those who kept and honored your kind. The keepers and priests became scattered. The black hunting leopards themselves were not killed, but as bloodlines mixed with animals taken from the wild, matings no longer bred true. Since no one retained the skill to recreate the ancient stock, the black variant died out. The only evidence we have of them are in the grave goods taken from tombs and the writings of which I have spoken."

Kichebo listened, growing more puzzled. If all the sacred black cheetahs had vanished in a time far distant from this, why then was she. . . ?

Tiye answered her. "A variant type may die out as individual animals, but traces of it remain within the ordinary ones of its species. It was the chosen task of my ancestors to recreate the ancient hunting cats by gathering the scattered pieces together. You, swift one, are the long-delayed result."

Kichebo still didn't understand. How could one bring back to life a creature long dead? And what were Tiye and her people that they needed or wished to do such a thing? She sensed a wry sadness in the woman's reply.

"If I could avoid telling you the history of humankind in the time of my ancestors, I would. It is neither great nor honorable. But I cannot, for to do so would be to deny you the story of how you came to be.

"My people now call themselves the Heriu-Sha. It is a word in the ancient language we have resurrected. Once it meant "dwellers in the sands beyond the world," for the world to men of pharaonic times ended at the edge of the Nile Valley. We have claimed the name in sadness, for we too live beyond the edge of the world, in a desert whose sands are the stars."

"Why?" the cheetah asked.

"We were exiled there by the acts of our kind," Tiye said and told her the story.

283

To Kichebo, the time in which it began was a strange and baffling one. Ages distant from the Egypt of Kheknemt and Tutankhamen, it lay startlingly close to her own. She understood little of it save that it was a period when men and their works crowded the world. Forests and jungles dwindled and the animals with them, as humankind increased in numbers. Most people thought only of survival or, for the lucky, gaining riches. They gave little thought to the past or future of their own kind, nor to the fate of the creatures that shared their world. With the increasing burden of man on the earth came tensions that flared into war. There was a sense of impending catastrophe that lay heavily on them, yet none could say in what form it would come.

Despite threat and crisis, a small band of people labored in the Egyptian deserts, scratching up relics of a nearly forgotten past. And in a sealed clay jar, found in the depths of a simple pit grave, they found a complete and undamaged copy of a work thought lost since long before Tutankhamen's time. It was the papyrus describing the cult of the black hunting leopard and the power that arose from pairing man and beast.

"To most people, it was only symbolic, such as many texts that had previously been found," Tiye said at a pause in her tale. "To a few, who themselves were descended from the old kings of Egypt and Nubia, the writings echoed traces of legend in their own traditions. These men and women, convinced of the text's literal truth, set out to recover the old power. To do that, they had to recreate the beast in which it lay."

Tiye continued, telling of how the few remaining wild cheetahs were gathered and bred. Of how her ancestors, for that is what those early workers were to become, used their knowledge of life's ways to remake the black variant from traces that still lay buried in the wild population. The project took years, but gradually the work began to yield fruit in the form of animals whose pelts darkened with every generation and whose minds took a startling turn toward complexity and self-awareness.

"Then, just as they were on the threshold of creating the Egyptian black, everything collapsed," said the woman. "Our records from that time are still confused and incomplete. We only know that we unleashed on the world an event that killed much of humankind and forced the rest to flee.

"My ancestors were among the few who prepared, for with their knowledge of history, they had seen such a thing coming. They readied flying-craft that could take them beyond the sky and everything needed to build new homes there. With them went the old texts and artifacts from the royal past of our land and from them developed our present culture."

"And your animals?" asked Kichebo softly.

"To our bitter grief, we found we couldn't take them. I remember reading how the woman who later became the mother of my line helped set them free, hoping their new intelligence would allow them to survive in a blighted world. Now that we have returned, we find that our hope came true. They did survive. You and your kind are their descendants."

Kichebo tumbled this about in her mind. It all fitted together . . . except for one thing. "Tiye," she said, "you said that your ancestors never completed their work. They never did reproduce what you call the Egyptian black."

"True, but what we left undone, generations of breeding in the wild completed for us. Your birth was an unlikely accident, but you are here. And you apparently have all the abilities the ancients described in addition to some we don't yet understand."

"And that is what you meant when you called me . . . a lost child?"

"Yes," said Tiye softly.

"And that is why I can't be satisfied with the company of my own kind alone? That is why I was drawn to Menk?"

The woman must have felt the hidden pain in her question, for there was a sense of apology in the answer. "The black variant was originally bred to be an aid to my kind. In doing so we changed its nature and induced in it a need for human company."

At first Kichebo felt a rekindling of anger at the arrogance of these human creatures for meddling with the fierce and independent character of her species. It felt like a violation, an alien compulsion pressed on her from without. She would have been much better suited to life in the wild without this strange inborn need that tied her to these creatures. Then she remembered Asu-Kheknemt. His devotion to his royal master only increased instead of diminishing him, for he had been given a gift of intimacy unknown among others of his kind.

Even if the need that made her adopt Menk was a product of human creation, the love that now bound her to the child was entirely her own. With that realization, her anger faded.

"You said that you left this land to live elsewhere," she said and added boldly, "Why have you returned?"

"To see what had become of the animals my forebears left behind. We hoped that if they survived, we could begin again the work my people left uncompleted. But our plans have had to change."

"Why?"

"Because we found you, swift one. Not only are you the royal black, but you are far more intelligent than the animals my ancestors bred. They had only limited flickerings of self-aware thought, but your mind burns as steadily and brightly as that of any human. Is it lonely being one such among the rest of your kind?"

Kichebo's astonishment made her blink, momentarily disrupting the channel of thought from her through Menk to Tiye. "I'm not the only one!" she spluttered. "We all have minds like this. Gray Cape, the old one over there, is probably cleverer than I am."

"So . . . then you all have speech and names. I should know yours then."

Quickly Kichebo told her.

"This does change things," said Tiye thoughtfully. "In truth, we had hoped to recover you to make you once again adjuncts to ourselves. We did not expect to find creatures whose independence of mind equaled our own. This is at once a hindrance and a blessing." She paused. "Perhaps I should speak less of our needs and ask you of yours."

"I want only to stay with Menk."

"That is all? You don't wish for freedom, for a return to your people and your life? Menkataten will be well cared for, and you may come and see her as long as we are here."

"I am not fitted for life on the hunting trails. If for no

other reason, my color betrays me in daylight. You have told me why. I can't fight what I am. I killed Rahepsi because of it. To my own kind I am a renegade."

"If you are, it is we who have helped bring it about," said Tiye soberly. "But the one you speak of—Rahepsi, is it?— lies wounded in our ship nearby. We are trying our healing craft to save him and we think we can. If his mind is like yours, the task becomes even more urgent."

The young cheetah sat silently, stunned by the thought that Rahepsi still fought for his life. If he survived, then she might be able to redeem herself, although the hope was so faint that she could not hold it for long.

"Kichebo," Tiye began, using her name for the first time. "What happened is as much our responsibility as it is yours. The ancients woke this talent in your kind and my people deliberately revived it. As you know, it is both a gift and a danger. If you stay with Menk, both of you must learn to develop it in a way that will not harm anyone around you, or each other."

"Can you . . . teach us?"

"I have some knowledge. Better to say that I can share in your learning." Tiye's response had a touch of wryness. "If you will trust me—after all that has happened. It isn't an easy choice, swift one. I'm sorry."

Kichebo trembled as she felt her decision taking shape. Was it indeed hers or instead a forced choice, dictated by traits bred into her lineage by these humans? For her the traditional hunting life had never been easy, handicapped as she was by her color and markings. Yet she had proven that she could survive. Parting from Menk would leave a painful wound in her spirit, slow to heal, but she could exist. Did she not now have what she wanted, she argued with herself. At last, she knew what she was and how she came to be. Could she not take that and return to her old life with some contentment?

What kind of life would that be, another part of her whispered. Set apart from her people as a renegade, half-crippled by coat color as well as temperament? She would be only one among others who were much better suited than she to wrest a living from the dying land.

Surely the alternative offered by the humans must be better. At least she would still have Menk and, through her, access to the strange gift of joined minds that might lead both of them down unknown trails.

"One thing I must tell you, Kichebo," Tiye interrupted gently. "We have not come to reclaim this world but will be returning to our homes when our work here is done."

"Your work?"

"The study of your kind, swift one. You and Rahepsi were not the only individuals we were able to study. There was another, a female who had broken her foreleg and would have died had we not captured her. We could have learned much had we been able to communicate with her as we have with you. From watching her and other individuals, we had begun to understand your lives. It has become clear to us that the land and climate are changing in ways unfavorable to your people. After knowing that you have survived all this time, we would be saddened to see you dwindle and die, yet we fear this is what will happen if we do nothing."

Tiye paused as if another idea had occurred to her. "If, as you say, the others of your kind have equal intelligence, do you think they could understand our purpose and accept our help? In our ignorance of your true natures, we have begun wrongly, but if you could speak to your people for us. . . ."

With wry bitterness, Kichebo answered, "None would listen to me. But Gray Cape was once a messenger, even though she is now old."

"We can heal injury and even restore part of the strength taken by age. Would you ask her later if she would be willing to aid our task in return?"

Kichebo agreed, knowing that the elder would be eager to carry such a new and startling message to the rest of the cheetah community. Those she spoke to might be skeptical at first, but if the news brought hope that their lives could be something other than a wearing struggle against a land growing more hostile with each season, they would listen.

Despite her concern for her people, the young cheetah's mind leaped ahead, focusing on her own future. "After your work is done and you are ready to return, what will become of me?"

The reply was long in coming and she sensed how the woman was measuring her answer. She also felt the desire of more than one mind speaking through the words that said, "We want you to come with us."

Mingled relief and dread gripped the cheetah. She knew only that to agree meant leaving the plains of the harsh but familiar world she had known since cubhood, in the company of creatures still more than half-alien to her. In her confusion, her mind retreated to the basic needs of existence: food, water, safety. All these she felt sure the humans could provide in a form that would be acceptable . . . except one. She might be able to give up the chase, but there still remained the purpose for which her form was so well-adapted. She knew she could not deny that need without risking sickness in both mind and body.

Almost panicking with the threat of that thought, she asked Tiye, "Will I be able to run?"

She sensed bewilderment, hesitation, and then, as understanding dawned, a burst of joy. "Yes, swift one. Farther and faster than ever before. The sands of the stars will fly beneath your feet and the space before you will be vaster than the plains. Yes, you will be able to run as none of your kind has run before."

And it must have been Menk who added, "You won't ever have to run alone."

I have woken from what I know is not a dream. I, Asu-Kheknemt, dream often these days, perhaps in retreat from the increasing confusion around me. I know that I may soon lose Aye, my second companion, to age as I lost the first to treachery. I know, too, that I will companion no more kings, for it is Horemheb who will rise soon to the throne. Aye has promised he will see me sent safely to Heliopolis before the paw of the lion lies heavily on this land. There I will pass the rest of my life among the remnants of my kind— the last of the black hunting leopards once sacred to the sun.

No, I am not the last. Even before I woke with Kichebo's voice fading from my mind, I knew that one of my line still existed far down the trail of time.

I understand her story now. The talent that I thought had died with my king lives again in her and in her young companion. I know that whatever Horemheb may do to obliterate the memory of Tutankhamen and me will not be successful. Those little statues, so carefully entombed, have carried part of the truth, while she has borne the rest.

After Tutankhamen's burial, I thought I had lost the ability to reach out across ages as I had once done. Perhaps I have indeed lost it, for this time, she has reached to me. I have seen through her eyes faces that echo those I knew. Somehow the proud yet delicate beauty my pharaoh inherited from his Nubian forebears has risen again in humankind. Bitter as their struggle has been, now the world opens wide to them and to her, as well, for she has accepted her heritage.

The promise of her life is the gift she has given. It is that which makes me able to face the years ahead. What Horemheb may do will not last. It will blow away like the sand that flies from beneath her feet along the trail into tomorrow.

AUTHOR'S NOTE:

An excellent source of information about Tutankhamen, Akhenaten, Aye, Horemheb and other pharaohs of the 18th Dynasty is Christiane Desroches-Noblecourt's *Tutankhamen: Life and Death of a Pharaoh*. She has made some fascinating speculations about the role of the cheetah as protector and guardian to the pharaoh in the afterlife.

Another invaluable resource in the writing of this book was E. Wallis Budge's *An Egyptian Hieroglyphic Dictionary*.

Anyone who shares my admiration for the cheetah (a creature who can out-accelerate a sportscar from a standing start!) should read these two references:

Randall L. Eaton, *The Cheetah: Biology, Ecology and Behavior of an Endangered Species.*

Nan Wrogeman, *Cheetah Under the Sun.*